Counterpart

Quentin Black

ISBN-13: 978-1-9996006-7-9

ISBN: 1-9996006-7-3

CONTENTS

DEDICATION

To Auntie Julie.

AUTHOR'S NOTE

Any specific terms and phrases have been highlighted in italics and can be found in the glossary.

RYDER FAMILY TREE

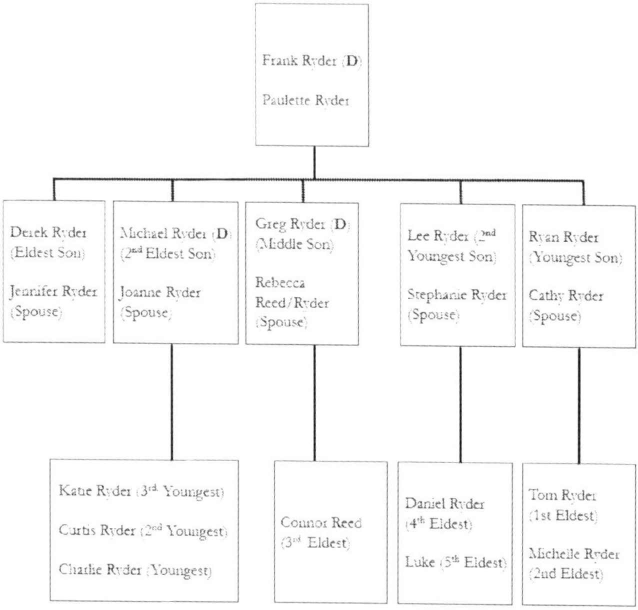

PROLOGUE

"War, not peace, produces virtue. War, not peace, purges vice. War, and preparation for war, call forth all that is noble and honourable in a man. It unites him with his brothers and binds them in selfless love, eradicating in the crucible of necessity all which is base and ignoble. There in the holy mill of murder the meanest of men may seek and find that part of himself, concealed beneath the corrupt, which shines forth brilliant and virtuous, worthy of honour before the gods. Do not despise war, my young friend, nor delude yourself that mercy and compassion are virtues superior to andreia, to manly valour."

Polynikes, Spartan warrior, in Steven Pressfield's *Gates of Fire*.

ACKNOWLEDGEMENTS

Golden-Rivet for the cover design and promotional video.

Evolution of Combat MMA promotions and Blur Tattoo.

And Chris Searle for his in-depth and polishing critiques.

1

The spectacle transfixed Eralda Mancuso. In the tiny amphitheatre beneath the mansion of Albania's most influential crime lord sat demurely dressed women and sharply suited men, all seemingly possessed at what they had just witnessed—as had she.

Her black wool dress parted to reveal her cleavage, and her jet-black hair swept around her head in a ponytail to reveal the shaven side section. Despite her looks, no one's eyes were on her at this moment.

Within the seamless octagonal cage of glass stood the massive and magnificent tiger, its front paws resting on the almost equally large Barbary lion breathing his last.

The collective murmurings rose into a cloud of gasped excitement at the appearance of a pair of African lions.

What had at first been fascinating to the Albanian-Italian assassin, now took on a distasteful tone—the tiger's reward for overcoming such a predator was the task of taking on two others.

That Oso—perhaps the most powerful man within the Albanian Mafia—had allowed the British journalist to watch such a scene in his residence surprised her. Earlier in the week, he had ordered Eralda to track and observe Ciara Robson. Given her own sexuality and the short-haired blonde's attractiveness Eralda wondered if the old man knew she would end up bedding her.

Indeed, the way the taller, stronger woman had dominated her had been refreshingly sexy. Being one of the most sought-after assassins for both the Mafia Shqiptare and Italy's 'Ndrangheta, she often sensed the intimidation that even the men from their ranks felt of her.

It dawned on her the Englishwoman—gone to use the ladies' room—may be lost in this labyrinth of a mansion.

She stood up amid the insane roars of the big cats and baying crowd.

Slipping out the door, she danced up the stairs. Reaching the first floor, her acute hearing picked up two voices speaking English from beyond the main kitchen doors, one belonging to Ciara.

They sounded…conspiratorial.

She slid through to find Ciara rooting underneath one of the cupboards. The chief caterer froze into a white, wide-eyed, open-mouthed statue.

The Englishwoman turned to look at Eralda with anger. She walked over, her face softening into a smile, and said, "I wanted to thank the chef personally."

"Then what are you doing knelt underneath the kitchen surface?"

"Excuse me?" Ciara replied with an acid edge. "She was showing me the ingredients she uses."

"Show me."

"Look yourself; we're not starting off with you following me around and demanding I jump through hoops."

Eralda paused for a moment before walking over.

When they were close, the journalist said, "Why did you follow me?"

As Eralda's brain engaged to answer, she barely saw the lightning punch aimed for her jaw.

Despite her whipping her chin around to ride the blow, the knuckles made sound contact, and she fell, skidding on the floor.

She made out the hiss of, "Lock the doors."

Who was she? What's she here for? She…she fucking used me to get in here.

Eralda shot her right foot up underneath the thin steel table and pulled it over, raining the stainless-steel utensils of chopping boards, pans, spoons—and knives.

Ciara's negotiation of them to get at her allowed the assassin time to get back to her feet.

They swapped swift, hard blows. The skill, speed and force of the Englishwoman's fists struck fear into Eralda who, though seemingly the faster, couldn't make the oppressive force take a step back.

She spotted her opportunity and dashed her forehead into her attacker's face. The taller woman skittered back a pace and Eralda leapt to press her advantage.

Already mid-air before realising she had been caught by a shoulder-throw, her bracing did little to mitigate the pain of a crushing landing.

Catching sight of the kitchen blade, she shot her hand out while tucking her head against the strikes.

The chief caterer's shout in English of "Knife!" triggered Ciara's releasing of Eralda's head in order for her to gain control of the Italian-Albanian's stabbing hand now gripping the blade.

The hitwoman switched the blade from one hand to the other before scoring it down the Englishwoman's ribs.

She cut several times, though only managing slices not stabs.

Finally, her antagonist snatched and secured her knife hand by the wrist and straightened it. The blonde's cranium smashed her vision double with bone-cracking force. Helplessly pinned, her opponent's head cannoned into her face with a sickening might.

Her consciousness ebbed away.

Eralda's left eye peeled open to the smell of petrol. Her face felt twice its size, hot and pounding. The perfect clarity of her double vision concerned her more than if it was simply blurred.

To her left, lay the dead body of one of Oso's security team named Klajdi.

On the far side of the kitchen, Ciara dropped the green plastic fuel can on the floor. The Italian-Albanian could see Ciara struggling from the knife slashes received in their earlier fight.

Eralda focused on the blade two metres away—in her state, it might as well have been a kilometre. Still, she began to shift her body, but after only a few seconds her nemesis walked over and snatched the blade.

With an effort, Eralda croaked, "You won't get out alive. And even if you do, Oso will hunt you to the ends of the earth."

"Oso is dead. So are all his guests," came the voice above her. "And no one will be hunting me when they find out you're responsible."

Obvious now that the tall, muscular, green-eyed Ciara was some kind of agent or rival organised crime member.

"Why?" she hissed. "You're English, you have no reason to be here."

"I work for a man who doesn't care what nationality evil comprises."

"No one will believe your lies."

She heard a laugh before being told, "You know they will. You're the sister of the 'Ndrangheta underboss in Calabria. People don't fight very hard to disprove their own bias—as a journalist I know that better than most. The man lying next to you will be hailed as a hero for being the one who sacrificed his life to stop you. If I wished, I have enough time to manipulate the evidence to make it look like you were responsible for 9/11."

Eralda spat with rage, "My brother will see through this. He will track you down and whoever you're working for. And he will kill you, your families and your friends. There is nowhere on this planet where you can hide. That is, if you even make it beyond the next hour alive, look at you."

The Englishwoman slowly descended into a squat. She tenderly stroked Eralda's blood-matted hair away from her eyes. Eralda jerked her head away in fury.

Ciara's voice came forth strong and confident, "Your brother, and the rest of your parasitic organisations won't have to search for us."

With that, she clamped a hand over Eralda's mouth, pinching her nose between her thumb and index finger.

The smaller woman's brain sent signals to her hands to fight for her life, only to find them pinned under the weight of Ciara's knees.

She opened her mouth wide, pulling back her lower jaw in an effort to draw in more air. This afforded her seconds only, as her futile heaves amounted to the burning of more oxygen.

Her chest began to bang to leach life force from within itself. An assortment of memories from her life—some she could never remember recalling before—flicked through her head before melding into a dream.

She fell into a pool of nothingness.

2

Six months later

The laughter and conversation of the hundred or so people packed into The Buxton Arms function room swirled warmth into Connor Reed's diaphragm. He sat at the edge of the bar on a revolving stool amongst the smells of alcoholic drinks and buffet food. He saw the guests of his Grandma Paulette's seventy-sixth birthday party thawing her usually stern demeanour—he had not seen her laugh this much since his dad and grandad were alive.

Connor Reed, a dark-blond a little over medium height, and his dark-haired elder and shorter thickset cousin, Tom Ryder, had decided the affair was to be closed to anyone other than family and their grandmother's friends.

Luke, his bright-blond, younger and taller cousin, and his expensive aftershave, appeared at his side and took a seat next to him.

"Good, isn't it?" said Luke, surveying the crowd. "Could have opened up the guest list a bit. There's a shortage of *birds* here."

Connor's strong face frowned. "Why are you bothered? You've been allowed to bring a lass, and she's a bit of a *two-looker*."

"Am on about you. I haven't seen you with a lass since that Ciara. What happened to her, anyway? She was a 'Worldie'."

"She lives down south. I still see her on occasion."

"Didn't you say she was a Thai boxer?"

"She's done a bit, yeah."

"Check this out," said Luke, whipping out his phone. The YouTube highlights of a stocky, muscular Thai lit the screen with his all-action style.

"I recognise him," said Connor. "He's the one who beat Haggerty twice?"

"Yep," said Luke. "Rodtang…can't pronounce his last name. Fuckin' animal, isn't he."

Tom approached, putting away what Connor recognised to be his 'work' phone, with his eyes narrowed.

All three cousins wore collar-shirts—which would have been their grandad's preference—with the sleeves rolled up—which wouldn't have been. Connor's denim, Luke's white and Tom's beige under a dark grey jumper.

Tom and the barmaid converged on opposite sides of the bar. Tom just shook his head at Connor, before addressing the barmaid with, "A pint of that German beer we've just got in. You drinking, Luke?"

Luke shot a glance at Connor—they'd had a conversation a while back regarding Luke's drinking habits—but Connor said, "I suspect we're all drinking, being that it's Thatcher's birthday."

Connor used the nickname he, Luke and Tom called their gran behind her back.

"I'll have what you're having, Tom," said Luke. "And my girlfriend here will have another G&T."

Connor smiled at the barb regarding his alcoholic beverage preference—he guessed the family might get bored of it in a few years' time…maybe.

When they had their drinks, Connor raised his and said, "Cheers."

They clinked glasses and sipped.

"Great, this German beer," said Luke, before asking Tom, "What did you look so het up about when you came up?"

"Aziz called. Said it's due to spark off big time in Bradford over the YouTube video that went viral."

Zain Aziz ruled much of the Bradford underworld and was an ally of the Ryder family.

"What's happened?" asked Connor.

"Keep forgetting you're not on social media," said Tom. "Jehan Zafar had paint thrown all over her yesterday. She's a Bradford City councillor and wears a multicoloured hijab so her constituents can recognise her and come up and speak to her whenever she's out."

Connor said, "I've seen her. At first, I thought it was Darth Sidious at an LBGT march."

Luke laughed, and Tom grinned before saying, "That's her. Nice lady, too."

"Who did it then?"

"Hoodies off the estates. They aren't the problem. It's that Nazi, Harold Sargent, trying to reignite *Combat 18*, who's behind it all. He's seen an opportunity with some of the Polish communities dotted around here in Leeds and over in Bradford—there're a handful of hardcore right-wingers in 'em."

"Yeah," Luke said. "Some of them can be proper Klan."

"Harold Sargent?" exclaimed Connor. "The obese fucker with a balcony of belly fat, who spouts off rhetoric in working men's clubs?"

Tom answered, "That's him. Aziz doesn't want this exploding—if his lads are at war then they are not earning. And the militants will begin to raise their heads, causing havoc. He's asking if there're any moves we can make."

Connor stroked his jaw. "Aziz wants it to be a white-on-white scenario to protect himself from any backlash."

"We've got the meeting over the sale of the Skipton hotel. Could do without drawing attention to ourselves."

"I'll handle this Adolf Titler. If he's the coordinator then maybe we can sort this out without a full-scale war. We've had enough of that for one year."

"Adolf Titler," guffawed Luke. "Does your plan involve rats?"

A protracted conflict between the Ryder family and a Liverpudlian criminal element had ended with the feeding of their nemesis to starving rats.

"There's always more than one way to skin a cat," replied Connor. "Though we're international, it's as important as ever to extinguish any flare-ups at home."

"Because we are international, shouldn't you be putting a bit of distance between yourself and a thing like this?" asked Luke. "We have developed some decent enforcers now."

Connor felt a hint of pride at his younger cousin's input. Luke seemed to have lost some of his blasé nonchalance towards life and the family business. Connor welcomed this, and he knew Tom did too, as they had struggled to find reliable people with the rapid expansion of their outfit. Tom had also told him he had put Luke in charge of a few of the businesses and he'd shown some real competence in guiding them.

"You have a good point, and one day that'll be how it should be. But this could go off like a box of fireworks if not handled right, and I don't think we're ready to rule from ivory towers just yet," said Connor, straightening his back to click the vertebrae. "Besides, I'd like to meet the man who thinks it's OK to have a lady dedicated to public service covered in paint. But it's up to the big man here."

Connor always made sure he displayed the fact he saw Tom, and not himself, as head of the family—though Tom never put himself above Connor.

"I'll leave it with you, Connor," said Tom, sipping his beer. "What's going on with you? Thought you'd be bringing a bird since you can't pull here."

"That's what I said," agreed Luke.

"I am not seeing anyone regularly, and I don't need to drag a casual to a family event only for her to get the wrong idea. You bringing that lass is a bit cruel, to be honest, Luke, because you aren't going long-term with her."

"What you talking about?" said Luke. "She's dirtier than a Charlie Sheen nosebleed."

Connor smiled. He liked that the men in his family could switch between serious business to banter when appropriate. That was another thing Luke had improved on.

"That's my point. She was in the year below me at school, and I know for a fact she's been fingered more than David Attenborough's passport."

A beer-spraying laugh burst from Tom's lips, followed by a wide grin from Luke.

As Connor looked around the room and saw how his gran, uncles, aunties and other cousins were interacting, he realised how much he loved his family—especially the two men he was now stood with. And he knew how close they came to being destroyed not so long back.

Calls of "Speech, speech, speech" grew from the crowd gathered around their gran. They collected their drinks and closed in. The gathering turned to look at Connor when his gran said, "Connor, speeches aren't really my thing. Come up here and say a few words."

He felt the air of expectation. Passing his G&T to Luke, he walked around to his gran's side, before putting an arm around her shoulders. He felt her press against him, which wasn't usual.

"I think what my gran is trying to say is she's a little out of practice with social occasions like this, since at her age her back goes out more than she does."

Sounds of amusement filled the air—*thanks, Phyllis Diller.*

"But enough about Leroy."

Gasps and groans mixed with the laughter.

"In all seriousness, it would be remiss of me not to remark on the character of the lady we all look up to. Despite the tragedy she has had to bear in losing a loving husband and sons, never once has my gran played the victim. She has always been a stalwart of this family. What I am trying to say is, if she wasn't my gran, I would wish she was."

A collective 'Ahhh' came back from the guests, and Connor could see the approval of his words in the eyes of his family.

"We had a rough year last year—preceded by several dark years—but we're all together now. And we're going to remain that way. Ladies and gentlemen, I want you to wish Paulette a happy birthday."

As the chorus came back at his gran, he looked at his family and resolved to protect them, no matter what came their way, or what mission the old man might assign to him.

Bruce McQuillan drove slowly down the long winding pathway for two reasons. First, to admire the way the sun's rays carved through the leaves and branches of the overhanging trees.

The second was to allow Jaime's security apparatus to identify him through the Range Rover's windscreen. Jaime—pronounced 'Hai-me'—was McQuillan's go-to man regarding all logistical and technology-based intelligence.

Not that the wireless cameras were visible to the naked eye; they were tiny and embedded not only into the trees on entry to his estate, but all around it.

Jaime now had a professional relationship with Darren O'Reilly, owner of Verbatim Cyber Securities, who, amongst others, had the CIA as a client. A relationship Bruce had engineered after he had helped avenge the death of O'Reilly's daughter.

Jaime would send O'Reilly his designs who, in turn, would use a few select engineers to manufacture the equipment to ensure its secrecy.

And Bruce fully understood how much money O'Reilly left on the table in not mass-producing them for the benefit of his company, and was grateful to the man.

Bruce looked in the rear-view and noticed despite the flecks of grey appearing in his black hair over five years ago, they hadn't increased significantly—*It's coming though*, he thought.

As he steered closer to the red stone country house with a steeply pitched thatched roof, he smiled, knowing the vast array of security measures now invisibly monitored him.

He parked on the wide circle of smooth stones and Jaime greeted him at the door before he had a chance to chime the bell.

The Peruvian wore a dark denim shirt, unbuttoned to reveal a white T-shirt. It pleased the tall Scotsman to see the once emaciated university student had begun to broaden across the chest and shoulders.

Bruce himself was dressed in a suit. "Hello, Jaime."

"Hello, Bruce. Have you eaten?"

"Aye," said Bruce. "I'll have my usual coffee though."

Within a few minutes, they were sitting across from one another with the aroma of fine coffee emanating from their cups. The kitchen's polished black marble and oak blended with the chrome and glass to mirror the efficiency of the owner's personality.

"How did you find the new *Star Wars* movie?"

Surprise lit Jaime's face. "How did you know I saw it? And it is a spin-off."

"I've known you for too long, my friend."

Jaime pulled a face. "It was adequate."

Bruce knew that translated into praise for the pedantic sci-fi fanatic.

"How are you in general?"

"I am good, Bruce," he answered in his now perfect English. "Less…anxious but still careful."

"Glad to hear it," said Bruce. And the Scotsman was. Jaime could not go on in the state of fear he was in when Bruce found him. The hyper-awareness did not begin to dissipate for several years, not until Jaime realised the dread would kill him before any real or imagined enemies would. However, this insight started a period of indulgent excess while sailing around the Mediterranean in a superyacht. Thankfully, this only lasted for the time it took for Bruce to remind him he had a gift that would be tragic to waste.

"So," said Jaime, "you are here to prepare our plan."

"Our council of war, my friend."

"I have made three generic dossiers: one on the 'Ndrangheta, one on the Mafia Shqiptare, and one on the relationships between the two. There is a package I have made for the travel and residence arrangements there. Standard safe houses have been difficult to secure due to the various mafia infiltrations of law enforcement and government agencies. I have purchased a multitude of Airbnbs up and down the entire country."

"Good," said Bruce. "This will be our only focus for the duration. If we can engineer and maintain a perpetual war between the two, we will have succeeded in undermining two of the more dangerous dragons in the world."

As he sipped his coffee, he noticed the expression on Jaime's face and asked, "What is it?"

The cybermaster shrugged and said, "Something has come up on my radar. I did not want to bother you with it as I fear it may be an internet rumour."

"Well, I am here and we are talking."

Jaime got up and came around to Bruce's side. He clapped his hands in some sort of a pattern, and the shelf cupboards facing them drew back to reveal a screen.

Jaime lifted a coaster to uncover a circular, shiny black surface. His finger skimmed over it, controlling the cursor on the screen.

Three separate articles appeared, with a section in each highlighted.

"These are the testimonies of three individuals. This one is a gentleman in Canada, Douglas Erickson, an architect. Read this," said Jaime, magnifying the article for Bruce to read.

It was like being a monkey in a cage. After a time, I would be taken out...I would wake with electrodes attached to my head, get asked questions, get shocked when I answered some but not others. The worst was the no-air chamber. Air, then no air, then air, then longer with no air. I begged for forgiveness, and then came the hypnosis sessions.

Bruce read the rest. The man went on to describe how, at the end, he was transferred to China as an advisor on airport construction. Details of his escape or rescue were not in the article.

Jaime repeated the magnification for the next one.

"This is a Swedish software designer, Benny Forsberg. Disappears for two months. Reappears in Tel Aviv three years ago. He has not spoken of why or how he got there but this is an account by one of his colleagues."

Bruce's eyes speed-read it.

One night I asked Benny why he would leave his native Sweden to come here. I thought he might be Jewish. Not so. We were a few drinks in but more relaxed than drunk. He told me he had been taken. He could not remember how. He landed in a cell without bars. Said there were others. Said he thought he could smell the sea. Then there were tests that they did using electricity. They put him in a suffocation room. They hypnotised him. Then he came here to work. He wanted to.

Bruce asked, "Were their disappearances reported to the police by friends or family?"

Jaime shook his head. "All these disappearances coincided with apparent work trips. The Canadian was a recent divorcee. Forsberg has never married, just gone from one girlfriend to the next. This next one is a Marinette Mauresmo. As you can read there, she describes a similar experience. What is interesting about her statement is she claims the Iranian physicist, Reza Abbasi, was there at the same time. As you know, Reza's defection to the United States was shocking to both the Americans and Iranians. However, he passed all the protocols to determine he is not a mole. As you know, these protocols are most stringent."

Bruce frowned. "Are you aware of anyone else who has linked these three together or believed the validity of these stories?"

Jaime shook his head. "If you had not come over to see me, I doubt I would have mentioned it. My algorithm program pulled together these three articles as designed. I have not substantiated any of this yet."

The black operations chief understood that a man of Jaime's intellect and curiosity might have delved further. "Is there anyone you identified, any missing persons, you think might be a victim of this?"

Jaime looked at him and said, "Several. An American marine biologist missing for four months. An Israeli aircraft engineer who went missing last year. And most recently, a female translator, a former part-time model from Holland. She was reported missing a few days ago."

Bruce took a few moments to reply. "We cannot be distracted at the moment, so do not extend yourself making the effort. I will throw some pebbles into the water and see where the ripples go. Other than that, we focus on the task at hand."

"Agreed," said Jaime. "Who are you sending?"

"Connor. His Italian is rudimentary and his time in the country sparse. But he's the one who has the best chance."

Jaime sipped his coffee and said, "He is like a Dark Jedi that hunts the Sith. With the charisma of a Han Solo."

"An interesting analogy," said Bruce. "I am not a *Star Wars* enthusiast myself, but to indulge you, let's hope he does'nae turn over to the dark side completely—or meet a Sith more powerful than he is."

3

Carlo Andaloro sat at the end of the Italian bar, enraptured with the football game while still fully aware of his surroundings. His attire consisted of light blue shirt and the white chinos that wrapped around his strong, compact physique.

The scene of the patrons, mostly men, transfixed by the enormous flat-screen, reminded him of a painting he had seen of *Inti Raymi*—an Inca ceremony where they begged the Sun God Inti for the return of the sun. He rubbed his fingertips on his shaved head, and wondered if Juventus's manager would be held in the same reverence as Inti Raymi if his team won the Champions League trophy.

Indeed, it hadn't just been South America he had travelled to in the last two years since he left the French Foreign Legion, but Europe and Asia too.

He had enjoyed the initial few months of unemployment, until a lack of purpose began to settle on his soul. That and his system being deprived of the adrenaline it had been used to since childhood.

Fortunately, a man from his past reached out to make use of his substantial skill set.

An incident in his childhood inclined him to be aggressive and adventurous, and being born in Reggio Calabria combined to forge a youth who had seen more action and danger—and learnt more about human nature—than most humans ever would.

He raised his hand to one of the men behind the bar—who Andaloro guessed to be the manager, given how he directed the other staff.

"Yes, sir?" the man asked.

"A Campari," said Andaloro, referring to the bright red bitter that included orange peel, bergamot, rhubarb, ginseng and herbs.

"On its own?"

"Yes."

The bar manager reached up to the hanging shelves above them.

"Who owns this place?"

"I do," said the man, with a smile that died as soon as it appeared. "Well, I mostly do."

"Husband-and-wife team?"

He shook his head, "No."

"I guess nights like this are stressful."

The owner nodded. "In more ways than one. Here's your drink."

Italian passions rose throughout the bar as it became apparent that Juventus's chances of winning fell further with another opposition goal, putting them 3-1 down.

Andaloro did not mind the tension crackling in the air; a life without danger and action beat a slow, monotonous slide into the coffin.

He thought about the owner's words—*"In more ways than one"*—being such a busy city bar, the prospect of a brawl was to be expected.

After another ten minutes, the bar's collective eyes switched to two patrons' raised voices, squaring up to one another. Andaloro smiled at the posturing peacocks. Though their demeanours were meant to indicate 'I want to fight', Andaloro knew the real intent behind the gesticulating was, 'I am trying to scare you into backing down, because I want to avoid a fight if I can'. Even as a youth, a person touching him in any manner at all aggressively would trigger him to attack.

The doors crashed open, twisting the crowd to face them like a shoal of fish.

Five men. Three were in their early to mid-twenties, wearing dark jackets, designer facial hair and masks of snarling aggression. A man in his early thirties, with cropped hair, had a shotgun tilted back against his shoulder. He barked, "No one move. We are not here for your possessions. Stand completely still and no one gets hurt."

The man behind him—fifties, the lack of sharpness of his jaw indicating his love of good food had caught a slowing metabolism, and who bore a thatch of grey hair—stood by the door, watching the scene without speaking.

Andaloro knew *what* they were without knowing *who* they were—*Società foggiana*, a relatively young, organised crime group by Italian standards, being around thirty years old, and considered perhaps the most brutal, if not sophisticated.

Andaloro's demeanour betrayed no sign of the adrenaline bleeding into his veins. It would be in these first few moments that they would be most vulnerable. He admonished himself—this had nothing to do with him. They were here for their protection money—their *Pizzo*. The landlord was probably late paying and this was the Società foggiana's way of convincing him to be on time.

Andaloro knew the template for low-level mafia extortion very well: indebt the owner with an impossibly high interest rate, smash up his business and beat him when the payments were late. Then, at the point of his greatest desperation, offer to wipe his debt in exchange for a controlling share in his business. Use his good reputation and honest face to launder money through it.

And Andaloro did not have an issue with this—everyone got fucked by someone, eventually.

"Everyone stand back," said the mouthpiece, casually bringing the shotgun to bear on the crowd at waist level.

When they did so, he commanded to one of the men, "Ferrucio, go and turn this shit off now."

Andaloro breathed out through his nose at hearing one call the other by his name—*Idiota del cazzo*.

Ferrucio marched menacingly towards the bar, pistol raised. He would have to pass around Andaloro. When the mafioso stepped within two metres of his space, the former legionnaire turned on his stool and said in their native Italian, "Do not turn the television off. I am watching this game."

The comment momentarily rooted Ferrucio and splashed a mask of confusion on him. His face then twisted with anger as he began to bring his pistol to bear.

Within a half-second, Andaloro snatched and twisted the gun out of Ferrucio's grasp. His shaven head crushed the mafioso's nose before his victim hit the floor.

Plummeting to his knees, he blasted Shotgunner in the chest. The man tipped backwards, his nerve twitch causing the shotgun to fire into the air.

The crowd dispersed in a screaming panic, as Andaloro sprinted for a square pillar. Knowing the two armed youths would have tracked him, he popped his head out from one side for a split second.

He then spun into a crouch on the opposite side, switching the pistol to his left hand and sliding out.

As he anticipated, their pistols were trained on the other side.

He shot both—one in the throat and the other in the face.

He turned to face the entrance, but amid the melee the old man wasn't there. Andaloro shot back behind the pillar, trying to anticipate where he might be.

Satisfied he had left, the former legionnaire skipped over to the nonplussed mafioso lying on his back with his palm cupping his nose. Andaloro snatched a fistful of his black hair and wrenched back his head, before ramming the pistol underneath his jaw and pulling the trigger. A geyser of blood, bone and brain matter spewed out of the top of the head.

The bar now lay empty of its customers.

He ran over to the side of the bar to see the owner and his staff crouched with hands hovering over their heads.

He barked, "Take me to the CCTV room."

They shot him a collective look of fear, and the owner said, "They have been switched off. They made me—since Wednesday. I knew they were coming but did not know when."

Andaloro murmured, "In more ways than one."

"Yes."

He looked down at the staff—the living witnesses—and contemplated his options. If he murdered them, they could not identify him, but the law enforcement pursuit would be relentless in the face of the public outcry.

He would use them another way.

"You," he said to the owner. "Stand up."

When the owner did so, Andaloro pointed to the man he had initially disarmed, and continued, "He went crazy before turning the gun on himself. Repeat it."

"He went crazy before turning the gun on himself."

"If your story to the authorities strays from that you will join him."

Carlo took a napkin from the bar and strolled over to the previous owner of the pistol. He wiped the gun thoroughly before placing it back into his hand.

A skilled and determined investigator could see through the 'mafioso gone crazy before turning the gun on himself' scene he had set. However, with no CCTV and if no one talked, how far would they be willing to go to disprove it?

It was crowded on the path of least resistance.

Ciara walked alone through Brussels' Josaphat Park, buoyed by a sense of gratitude. The sunshine slid past the pink leaves of the overhanging sakura cherry trees to brush her face. Their shadows contrasted with the patches of sunlight on the walkway. As beautiful in its culture and scenery as the Belgian park was, she would have been grateful walking in almost any park—half a year ago she had been close to death.

After she had massacred Albania's most powerful crime lord, his underboss, his chief assassin, part of his security team and over two dozen members of a corrupt fundraising party, she had bundled herself into the boot of the car. The vehicle belonged to the chief caterer Eliza Rexha and although an ally, the woman was clearly terrified. Ciara had wondered, as she had bled freely from the slash wounds criss-crossing her upper body, whether she would die in the dark, or even who would be standing there when the boot lid rose.

Her previously short, blonde-silvery hair had grown down the nape of her neck, promising to touch her shoulders. A black shirt encased her hard figure, with her defined forearms revealed. The stretch jeans finished at her russet, flat shoes.

The Scotsman's voice cut through her thoughts, "Lovely day for a stroll."

She turned to greet Bruce McQuillan, head of the black operations unit she belonged to, The Chameleon Project. He was also the liaison officer between the UK security and law enforcement services.

"All truly great thoughts are conceived while walking," she replied.

"I think the cars and roads were of poor quality back in Nietzsche's day."

The tall, lean McQuillan wore a dark blue suit over a pale pink shirt with a loose collar. Silver streaked throughout the now touching fifty-three-year-old's black hair, a good half-inch longer than the style he had when she had first encountered him at twenty years of age, eight years previously.

"To what do I owe the pleasure of your company?"

"Interpol's European Conference is always an interesting affair. Not a bad place to network."

"So, it is a pure coincidence, the both of us being here at the same time?"

"You know better than that," he said, affording her a smile. "Let's walk and talk."

As they fell into step, she said, "Must be significant for you to come and see me."

She was referring to his habit of now giving her briefs through encrypted e-mails.

"You know, an aspect of air travel is it affords me an opportunity to read without distraction," he answered, seemingly ignoring her statement.

"Oh yeh? What are you currently reading?"

"A book titled *Leading* by Alex Ferguson."

"I didn't peg you for a football fan."

"Twenty-six years of leading any successful organisation is impressive. Besides, he was born and raised in an area not far from where I was."

"Liking the book so far?"

"Aye," he replied, with his Scottish dialect a little more pronounced. "One of his challenges was the subject of who would succeed him."

"Should imagine it was going to be difficult for anyone to replace him. It is like you said, twenty-six years is pretty impressive."

"Which leads me to my point. I don't want a scenario in which I become suddenly incapacitated or die, and the Project is left floundering. And this official position within the government is already stretching my capacity. I need someone to take it over for me."

Ciara understood. "When is he taking over?"

"Who?"

His response confused her. "Connor, surely."

"I can see why you'd come to that conclusion."

"So?"

They reached a denser patch of trees, cooling the air with their shade.

"Connor's family continues to rise, and that will require more of his attention as time passes. Being perhaps the most influential member of a burgeoning criminal empire, along with heading a unit responsible for disrupting terrorist cells and organised crime groups, might prove too taxing for anyone, let alone leading to a conflict of interest. Besides, his strength lies in the field."

"What are you saying, exactly?"

"What I am saying is I want to bring you in from the cold to be my understudy. Bit by bit, you will take on more and more responsibility until it is you who runs the unit."

"You're telling me you want to take me out of the field?"

"Eventually, yes. You can affect more of an impression directing the moving parts."

"Why did you take me on as a field agent in the first instance?"

"Because, in-field experience is invaluable to a director with regards to planning and coordinating. It also helps command the respect of the agents you send. But mostly, at the time, I thought you needed it."

The statement momentarily stilled her. She thought back to when he came to her rescue. She had been looking at a lengthy custodial sentence for manslaughter after killing her mother's former boyfriend and attempted rapist. Bruce came along, and somehow made the whole matter disappear like a dark magician.

And she had wanted to strike back—at anyone wishing to harm or oppress people for selfish desires.

"And you don't think I need it now?"

"I think you can see now it's better to be the one moving the pieces than to be one of the pieces."

"I am not aware of who, or how many agents, are under your charge, but I should tell you now, where Connor and I are concerned—"

"You've slept together on several occasions."

Her mouth briefly opened. "How did you know?"

"The same way you'll be able to—by developing a sharp sense of body language."

"Thought I should tell you in case you thought it would undermine me, if and when it came to giving him orders."

"His respect for you is obvious, for reasons previously stated—he has seen your capabilities in the field, and he has seen you kill. That, in his mind, as it should, gives you more standing than chastity ever would."

"I thought the same. Glad you do too."

He looked at her and said, "Your striking appearance was never going to lend itself to a long-term career in the field. Even though you've grown your hair a little."

"You know, I could always radically change my hairstyle. Maybe take up more running and less resistance training?"

He stopped and turned to her. "If you're saying you don't want it, tell me now."

Her eyes met his. "I want the position."

"Good. I'll keep the option open, in case your services are needed in the field, but I won't be actively looking for tasks for you any more. Instead, I will make arrangements to introduce you to certain people. After that, we'll begin to move you into an official capacity that will act as a cover for you to take over the Project."

"You looking to retire anytime soon?"

"Nah, not for a long time yet," said Bruce. "In the next few days we'll be entering the final stage of our plan for antagonising the two Adriatic rivals against one another."

"Who will you send?"

"Connor."

"And where is the charmer?"

Bruce shrugged. "Probably handling family business."

4

The time on the Ford Focus's digital display read 02.07. Connor sat with Luke, the car hidden in a copse of trees on a hillside. Two hundred metres down the slope lay the country house of Harold Sargent within a vast rural meadow, enclosed by forest.

"We'll wait a quarter of an hour," said Connor, before turning to Luke. "Is that perfume you've got on?"

"Was at a bird's house."

"I take it not the girl you came to Gran's party with?"

"No, mate. Like you said, she's a bit—what's that word you use?—promiscuous."

"You know I was joking."

"I know."

"Then why do you say that? She might be full of virtue, but your good looks and charm could have convinced her down the path of depravity," said Connor, with a hint of a smile.

"Funny you should say that, she said more or less the same. Then she said, 'I shaved my pussy just for you'."

"And?"

"And when I felt down there it was a bit prickly, which means—"

"Means she shaved it for the guy the night before," said Connor, before they both started quietly laughing.

When it died down, Luke remarked rhetorically, "Some house for a politician isn't it."

"He's been on the Planning Permission Inspectorate more times than any other Leeds councillor. He'll flit between posts so it's not obvious, but I reckon you could fill that house with the amount of dirty money he's had. Some of the recreation grounds and parks have disappeared because he approved commercial development plans when he's been chairman of the appeals board."

"I'd love to fill him in," said Luke.

"We're not going to touch him, remember."

"I know. It's just I hate someone like him going around pretending to be an upstanding member of the community, and all the while he's dry fucking the local community, so that he can live like a shit Bond villain."

"Some would say that you—we—are being hypocrites."

"Cos we import and sell drugs?" said Luke rhetorically. "It's high-quality coke and ecstasy to people who can afford it. It's not like we're punting smack or fentanyl to single mums or kids. You remember what Grandad used to say, don't you?"

"That alcohol is the worst drug going because when the damage is done, it can't be reversed," recited Connor.

"Exactly, we only hurt other *grafters*—and only when they force us to. I didn't realise until recently how much Tom gives back to the community—I know it writes some of the tax off, but still."

"I know, we're 'good' gangsters, but we're still gangsters. We shouldn't compare ourselves to Mother Teresa."

Luke looked at him and said, "I've heard she was a cunt anyway."

"Where did you get that from?"

"There're pictures on the internet of where she kept her patients, and they look like Nazi death camps. Said something along the lines of 'there is something beautiful in seeing the poor accept their suffering like Jesus did'."

"She probably did feel like that, took a vow of poverty herself—didn't see her in a flash car or living in an expensive house."

"Fucking awful, mate. They have made her a saint."

"She left a teaching job and opened schools, hospices, orphanages for all the homeless, sick and dying. You can see why," said Connor. "Any other questions?"

Luke thumbed his eyebrow. "OK. Back when your dad was alive, say when you were around eighteen, would you rather sit in a lemon meringue pie and suck his dick, or…eat the cake while getting fucked by him?"

Connor's forehead pushed his eyebrows down. "Can't I do both?"

Luke looked at him and whispered, "Best answer so far."

Connor said, "Run me through the plan again. Including the *Actions-on*."

It heartened Connor that his younger cousin recited them seamlessly

"All right, as Jules Winnfield would say, 'Let's get into character'."

"Who's Jules Winnfield?"

Connor stared at him for a moment. "You're fucking with me, aren't you?"

When Luke shook his head, Connor said, "We'll talk about this later. Let's go."

They donned their black balaclavas, leather gloves and jackets. Leather was tougher to tear and so less likely to leave fabric behind.

They cut through the woods before Connor stopped them both at the edge. Due to Luke not having any military experience, Connor had taught and drilled him in the basic hand signals used by British forces.

"Let's observe for a few minutes. See if there's anything untoward," said Connor.

"I can see the security cameras from here," whispered Luke.

"Good job I've turned them off."

"How the fuck did you do that?"

"Because the *mong* chose aesthetics over reliability. He opted for wireless security instead of wired, probably because it looks 'cleaner' and is easier to install. I came around yesterday when he was out, pretending to be a council ground's inspector—not sure they even exist. His wife let me right in. That's how I was able to put a disarmer on the alarm system."

"You not worried she'll put two and two together? Won't the security cameras have caught you?"

Connor stared at him. "We're looking to discourage them from talking. And no, they are all positioned high up, angling down. A daft cap worked just fine."

"How do you know how to do all this?" said Luke, frowning.

"If I told you, I'd have to kill you," said Connor. "Come on, let's *splinter cell* ourselves down."

He led Luke down out wide, using the sparse trees for what little cover they afforded them.

"All right," whispered Connor. "We'll cut across to the house now. I'll go first with you watching, then I'll signal you on."

"OK," said Luke.

Answering the puzzled expression on his face, Connor said, "It's just so that if I get caught, then you can escape."

He crossed over and checked through the windows. He skirted the property, then the driveway to ensure there were no other vehicles apart from the Sargents'. He returned to the back of the house and gave Luke the 'close on me' signal.

When he sidled up next to him, Connor said, "This patio door is our entry point. This," he said, producing a state-of-the-art lockpick gun, "opens it fine. Again, you remember the 'actions-on'?"

"If he appears, you'll deal with him, while I'll go and secure the wife. If she appears, I'll deal with her while you secure him."

"Good. Put these on," said Connor, handing over what looked like a pair of green-tinted glasses. "I'll signal for you to take them off before I hit any lights on."

Connor unpicked the lock in seconds and stepped into the silence. They cut through the rooms of green-illuminated furniture before Connor tested the bottom tread of the staircase—mercifully quiet.

They crept.

This would be the tricky part. Connor was not sure which room was the master bedroom. He guessed on the right-hand side.

He twisted the knob as slowly as he could. Relief brushed against him, as he recognised Sargent's face. He knew the lump beside him would be his wife. His prior research told him the couple had no children or lodgers or pets. There were no other vehicles, so he was not concerned with any noise that the couple might make.

He stepped over to Harold's side of the bed and took out his commando dagger. He figured the sight of two black-clad men would sear terror into Harold's brain and ensure that he complied with Connor's instructions.

He took off his night vision and held up his thumb. Luke took off his, and switched the lights on.

Harold scrunched his eyes but didn't wake. His wife merely pulled her head further under the covers.

"You've got to be fucking kidding me," murmured Connor, equally amused and frustrated that his plan of instant terror was going awry. He clamped his hand over Harold's mouth and pinched his nose between thumb and forefinger.

It took a few seconds before Sargent opened his eyes and began thrashing. Connor transferred his grip to Harold's throat, put the blade beneath his left eye and hissed, "Shut the fuck up now. If I wanted to kill you, you wouldn't have woken up."

Sargent's eyes beamed confusion for a few seconds before blurring into horror.

Luke now stood on the wife's side and, as her head shook out from beneath the covers, he said, "We apologise for waking you. It's your husband we want to talk to. So, be quiet, and we'll soon be out of your hair."

Indeed, it had not been an accident to accost Harold Sargent in the company of Caroline Sargent. After Connor had reeled off the names and addresses of the Sargents' family members, he knew that in the aftermath, a frantic, badgering wife would convince most men down the path of least resistance.

She sat up, clutching the bedcovers to her throat. Her eyes darted between the two of them. Then her expression changed—to malicious hope. Her diaphragm expanded, and her scream sliced through the house.

"BRIAN, DES, ERIC—"

Luke's punch cut off her consciousness and voice box. Her banshee cry died with the rise of male war shouts from downstairs—Connor remembered they had three other spare rooms down there. Luke's eyes fixed on to his, and Connor sheathed his knife and said to his cousin, one of the most talented bare-knuckle boxers in the country, "Let's stand close to the door, and punch the fuck out of 'em. If it gets desperate, I'll use my knife. Ditch your jacket."

Connor smashed his fist into Harold's jaw, who fell unconscious over his wife. He knew he and his cousin had at least a few seconds, as it would be a brave man to go into a potential fight without at least throwing a pair of trousers on.

They rapidly put on their knuckledusters and converged on the door.

Connor had a mental flash of the Spartans facing what must have seemed like impossible odds at the narrow gates of Thermopylae, and said to Luke, "Do not go beyond this door. Let them come to us."

5

She sat on the hard chair, squeezing her arms into her sides in an effort to stop shaking. Her black hair stroked her collar bones.

Though the goggles deprived her of sight, the awareness that someone else was in the room with her assaulted her senses.

Despite losing a precise sense of time, she knew it wasn't more than a week since she had fallen asleep in her own bed in her high-class apartment in Brussels.

Only snatches of consciousness had been registered since then; the opening of a vehicle's side door. Being strapped to a gurney. Feeling seasick. Waking up in a white room with a side of crystal-clear glass.

Back in her native Holland, she had helped fund her foreign languages degree by modelling part-time. Despite several offers to go full-time she had heeded her father's advice of '*…being able to translate fluently will see you travel all over the world, and make money. Your looks will deteriorate before your brain will. Don't throw away a lifelong career for a short-term one. Time spent modelling is time away for acquiring another language*'.

She had heeded his advice and now years later, was fluent in Dutch, English, German and French, and was a go-to for any meeting, conference or private, between EU delegates.

And yet, she had no recollection of how she had ended up in this strange place and blindfolded.

She flinched as the fingers removed her goggles. Scrunching her eyes against the assaulting light, the man had already sat down before she opened them.

The blue eyes stared through thick-rimmed glasses, momentarily distracting her as to how old he was. The pristine white laboratory coat wrapped around a physique she doubted was that much stronger than her own, if at all. Despite this she felt a worm of fear under his blank stare.

At this frontal angle, his large, hooked nose seemed to perfectly match his ears in length. His patchy white hair stood in defiance to their lost colleagues.

His voice came out crisp, flat and American.

"Your name is Richèl Vergeer. Is that correct?"

"What is this? What is this place?"

His expression did not change. "Your name is Richèl Vergeer. Is that correct?"

"Please. What is this?"

"Your name is Richèl Vergeer. Is that correct?"

Anger pierced through her fear and she cried, "What is this?"

She saw a flicker in his eyes. As he stood, she recoiled. Watching him tap on a black screen on the wall the glass doors parted. Though she hadn't been secured down, her brain fogged its own command to run through the doors.

They closed.

She instinctively knew there would be no white knight in shining armour to rescue her. And then she began to drown in a room without water.

Connor saw in their confident, adrenaline-fuelled haste, that they lacked any sense of cohesion. Still, the first five of them all looked 'fighting aged', big and strong. They attempted to rush through the door as a collective of shaven heads, tattoos and beer bellies.

The cousins, close but not so close to get in one another's way, formed a merciless threshing machine. The first three fell under the tight, powerful and accurate steeled-fisted punches.

However, the men at the back climbed over their falling comrades to get at the pair. Connor could see the numbers to be more like eight, and thus drove forward with a storm of blows to prevent them all getting in at once. If they surrounded them it would be over.

Luke surged forward with him, firing his rapier-fast fists. Bodies fell only to be replaced by more. The tide of brawn forced them back into the room and Connor swallowed the panic rising in his throat like bile.

His creative brain zipped through the calculations of angles so as to not get flanked. The steel knuckleduster encased his weaker left, and he could knock out most men with his right if he hit the jaw or temple. However, the malevolent waves were robbing him of the distance he needed. Connor switched to a peek-a-boo guard—chin down, fists by his cheeks, with his elbows tucked—kept his head in perpetual motion, and fired short punches at the wall of men, now hitting him back. Knuckles dug into his forehand, smashed his own fists into his face and his elbows into his ribs. Fearing death, adrenaline surged through his being, as he used his head to smash the faces.

A grasping hand snatched at his balaclava, pulling it around, obscuring vision in his right eye. More fists chopped through him, and hands grabbed at him. As he righted his mask, a fist slammed the wind from his stomach.

He knew he was about to be dragged down and kicked to death on the floor.

Anger shot through him—*if you die so does your cousin, you snivelling cunt. Keep fighting.*

A hairy arm scarfed around his throat from behind. He turned and sunk his teeth into the owner's face, ragging his head through the victim's screams.

The arm came off his neck, only to be replaced by vice-like hands. Connor unlatched the bite and the man released his throat, stepping back with his hands hovering over the wound.

Fucking idiot.

Despite his weakened state, Connor's steeled left hook felled him.

He looked around for targets—only his cousin stood amongst the carnage, his heaving chest matching his own.

"You OK?" asked Connor, after catching his breath.

"MMAAATTTTEEEE, we just survived death. I'm fucking buzzing."

Connor smiled before counting eleven strewn bodies—*how the fuck did we survive that?*

As relief billowed within, he reminded himself of the Samurai adage—*Once the battle is over, tighten your helmet straps.*

The sound of shivery breaths turned him towards the bed—Mr and Mrs Sargent sat with the covers underlining their terror-etched faces.

Connor walked up the side of the bed with as much nonchalance as he could muster. The couple recoiled like he was a dark spirit.

He picked up and donned his jacket.

"Mate, go through their pockets and see if you can find any ID. And if any of them start stirring, boot their heads."

"Will do."

Connor stared at the fascist leader and said, "Harold—a man's politics is his politics. However, tomorrow you're going to denounce the assault on Jehan Zafar as a cowardly act. I shouldn't have to tell you to speak out against the throwing of paint on a woman. Now—"

Connor saw their train of concentration had been interrupted by Luke's kicking of the victims' heads before turning back to them.

"If you, or any of them, go to the police, it won't just be you or your wife who we go after. It'll be your mother down on Ashton Street, and your wife's sister on King's Royal Avenue. If any of these men are dead, then fair enough—but if not there will be no police involvement. Now, tell me what you're going to do?"

After a moment, Sargent's voice croaked, "I am going to make a public denouncement of the cowardly attack on Jehan Zafar."

"Good." He turned to Luke. "You get any?"

"A few."

"You definitely got everything we came in with?"

Luke checked his pockets as he put his jacket back on and had a scan around.

"Yeh. Everything."

Connor turned to the pair. "All you two have received thus far is a scare and a punch in the face. Don't escalate to a family member's death notice."

Salvatore Mancuso had read and reread both the police and autopsy reports of his half-sister Eralda's rampaging killing spree through the Albanian Mafia's most influential boss, Oso Xhelli's, mansion fortress.

A custom-made and fitted beige suit, complete with a copper tie, contoured the frame of lean, hawkish-faced Mancuso.

Sat across from him was a *Vice Ispettore*—Assistant Sub-Inspector of the State Police in a dark grey suit that lacked style if not expense.

The redwood floors of Mancuso's study were so highly polished they displayed one's reflection back. The oak of the desk contrasted it in colour, and the chrome laptop juxtaposed it in its modernity.

"I thank you for obtaining me these. I understand the risk it must have involved," said Salvatore, holding a pen as black as his full hair. He did not mention the money that went into Giorgio's private account each month. Salvatore always put on impressive acting performances to hide his abhorrence for these uniformed rats—knowing they were the lubricating oil to his organisation, and to himself. As the underboss of the 'Ndrangheta in the province of Reggio Calabria, he had dealt with corrupt policemen and officials all his life.

"It is quite all right. I have friends, not only in the capital," said Giorgio.

The forty-nine-year-old Salvatore feigned being impressed at the overweight policeman's boast, and indulged him further by asking, "It says here my sister died by a bludgeoning to the face. With what instrument was it?"

"It hasn't been fully established but the forensic investigators believe it to be the guard's head."

Even before he had the reports in his possession, Salvatore had been made aware that supposedly a single member—the only surviving member—of Oso's security detail had managed to neutralise Eralda.

"How many people did she kill in total?"

"Thirty-seven. Oso and his underboss. Twenty-five guests and the ten-man security team present in Oso's house—the one responsible for her death succumbed to his injuries soon after."

Salvatore knew the guests were a who's who of financial donors and the political umbrella of protection for the Mafia Shqiptare.

"And the guard who killed her, what is known regarding him?"

Giorgio shrugged. "Not a great deal—he died of asphyxiation from the fire's smoke."

For his sister, one of the most feared assassins in the Mediterranean, to succeed in killing all those people, only for her to succumb to the last guard still alive in the complex, seemed strange. And this, compounded with her killer dying by smoke inhalation, struck Salvatore as somewhat bizarre.

Her use of grenades amid the shootings seemed off-kilter—though tactically sound, in that they could neutralise large numbers of people in a closed space.

Motive had also been an issue. His sister enjoyed high respect in both the two most powerful crime syndicates on the planet, and yet she decided to throw that into the fire?

Salvatore had met Oso a handful of times, and although no one got to his position without being ruthless, equally no one stayed there without being pragmatic. He couldn't imagine what could have set his sister on this path of destruction.

"Do you have any information on Oso's successor? The Albanians have impressively kept that a secret, but someone is running Oso's brigade."

Giorgio's face betrayed triumph. "It is Andrei Faja running that family now. He is likely to be the successor."

At the mention of the name, it fell into place. Mancuso found it impressive that Faja went from a soldier to what the Albanians would call a '*Mik*'—a liaison officer at the young age of around thirty. Astounding he would now be a boss.

"Was there anyone unaccounted for?"

"I don't think anyone who was inside made it out except the kitchen and hosting staff. Your sister's friend must have perished too."

"My sister's friend?"

Giorgio looked uncomfortable, and said, "Yes, a tall, short-haired blonde arrived with her. Many of the remains haven't been properly identified due to the fire. I thought she might have been Serbian."

Mancuso knew the reason for the policeman's awkwardness was his reluctance to acknowledge Mancuso's half-sister's sexuality. An open secret amongst the whispering tongues of the 'Ndrangheta was her preference for foreign women.

"Has anyone confirmed her nationality?"

Giorgio shook his head. "I did not wish to probe."

"My half-sister has died in suspicious circumstances, and you think I care that her preference for women is aired?"

The policeman's sheepish expression softened Mancuso's irritation. He said, "I need you to do all you can to discover the identity of this woman. If there is any assistance you need, just ask for it, but I want to see progress."

Noting the greed in the corrupt policeman's eyes convinced him of his future effort.

"One more thing," said Mancuso. "The killing of Società foggiana members in the backstreet sports bar in their city—what has been the result of that investigation?"

"The local police have closed the case as a murder-suicide. They will be announcing it as such to the media in the next day or so."

Mancuso rose and offered the policeman his hand. "You are a good man, Giorgio. As usual, you will find your payment in unmarked bills in the back of your vehicle."

"Thank you," replied the policeman, and he left.

Mancuso waited a few moments before picking up one of his new pre-paid phones and dialling a number.

"It seems your plan worked. Never return to the province of Foggia. Proceed as agreed. It is time to strike back. And do not allow anything or anyone to stand in your way."

The instructor's attempts at breaking the ash-blond man had so far failed. He was not given the younger man's name, and it had been insinuated he should not ask.

Being one of the most sought-after firearms instructors in the world meant the fifty-year-old had realised the dream of becoming rich through turning his passion into a lucrative career over the past decade. Western military, paramilitary and intelligence organisations contracted him for large sums of money to train and assess their ranks. Now stood on a makeshift black steel balcony overlooking a 'killing house', he had run this Englishman through serial after serial. What had been perturbing to the South African though was the man with the blue eyes and compact frame had made his top five best performing shooters he had ever seen—yet, he didn't recognise him. And on top, in addition to the bruising on the man's face, when he had taken off his jumper, the T-shirt had ridden up to reveal the same on the ribs—so, he could not have been operating at full capacity.

"That's the end of today's practice," he called down to the man. "Go to the room on your right. De-bomb, and then go from room to room with the magnetic hover to pick up the empty casings. Do you know how to use it?"

The man looked up at him. "Yeh," he said, before disappearing into the side room.

The South African flinched as a tall, broad and lean man appeared next to him—blindsiding his usually sharp awareness. He had been briefed the man now next to him would appear, and his name was Bruce McQuillan. The charcoal suit contrasted well with the light blue shirt and grey-flecked black hair.

The man spoke with a trace of Glaswegian. "Mr Hofm, how are you?"

"Please, call me Cassper. I am very well, thank you. I'm *gatvol* of trying to—I mean I am tired of—"

"I've spent some time in South Africa, so I am familiar with the slang."

Cassper smiled, despite feeling unnerved without knowing why.

He said, "That kid—and I am not seeking his identity, but I haven't seen him at any major competition shoots. I've assessed UK special forces soldiers, both your SAS and SBS, for the past eight years. He's British, and you Brits don't have the right to bear arms, so I kinda discounted him firing guns regularly as a teenager."

The shooter appeared from the side room with what looked like a metal detector and began to go from room to room.

"If you're asking me how he's gotten this proficient, I am afraid I cannot disclose that," answered Bruce. "What has the assessment entailed?"

"I've run him through all the serials with several different pistols, Glock 17, a CZ-75, an FN Five-Seven, a P226—timed, snap decision assessment of enemy from friendly, snap commands of firing positions, and had use of 'The Shocker' in place throughout the latter serials."

"The Shocker?"

"A device that straps to the arm and gives a nasty kicker of electricity for incorrect shot selection, inaccurate fire, or if their speed isn't up to par. It's not pleasant."

"Where's the…ahem…emitter?"

"There isn't one, it's all done off the system so fair is fair."

Bruce inclined his head in the direction of the killing house floor. "How many has he received?"

"Three. Everyone receives one in the beginning—we put in an impossible shot selection—and this helps induce adrenaline. The difference between firing on a laissez-faire gun range and in a real-life situation is adapting for adrenaline, complexity and speed."

"What's the record?"

"He's tied it with two others. There have been hundreds run through this since it was built, I think five years ago now."

The Scotsman asked, "Is he done for the day?"

"Yes."

Bruce turned to Cassper and shook his hand. "Thank you for your time today. I can lock up here."

6

Andrei Faja looked over his *Bajrak*—executive committee—knowing what he said and how he conducted himself in his first appointment as Kyre—'Boss'—would be crucial.

The fifteen pairs of eyes staring back at him conveyed different emotions: the thirst for revenge in most and suspicion in others.

"Gentlemen, in the immediate aftermath of our Kyre's murder, I assumed command of the clan as decreed by Oso himself. At that time, the last thing this family needed was an internal conflict regarding power succession while we were seemingly under attack. However, given the nature of his death, coupled with my absence, I understand there might be a thorn of suspicion of my involvement."

There were murmurs of dissent, but nothing too rousing. He held up his hand and continued, "I therefore propose that we should put my succession to a vote. At this time, you do not have to vote for a candidate right now, simply whether or not there should be someone else considered. As you can see, there is a notepad in front of each of you, so put a tick for 'yes, another candidate should be considered', or a cross for 'no, there shouldn't be'. You will fold them and Hasan will collect them before counting them."

Andrei had earlier appointed Hasan Koleka to be the new Mik of the clan. No one had voiced a dissent of nepotism against the former soldier, despite

Hasan and Andrei's close friendship. A Mik—friend—helped liaise with the different members and was responsible for coordinating unit activities.

After a few glances were exchanged among them, Sali Rama—one of the elder members and a good friend to former boss, Oso Xhelli, said, "Surely this is unnecessary. Oso wanted you to take over and you have led us fearlessly since that dark day to this."

Andrei smiled at the older man, while knowing he would be the most likely candidate to jot a tick. It seemed to Andrei that Sali held onto tradition so tightly to counterbalance the fact he had once been a member of the *Sigurimi*—Albania's old secret police. Sacked post-communism, Sali claimed he had always been Mafia Shqiptare and had infiltrated the Sigurimi to gain intelligence. Because Oso had confirmed this was indeed the case, no one ever questioned the narrative openly. Still, Andrei had strong suspicions Oso had thrown the once down-and-out policeman a lifeline in exchange for his unerring loyalty.

"The strength of the leader is correlated to confidence his men have in him, and his confidence in his men. I want this done so we can move forward from a position of strength."

The older man lowered his head. "As you wish, Kyre Faja."

Within less than two minutes, the straight-backed, full-haired Hasan stood clutching the pieces of paper that he had counted. "This Bajrak sees you retain your position, Kyre Faja."

There were smiles and congratulations before someone asked, "How many for and against?"

Hasan looked at Andrei, who nodded, and answered, "Thirteen to two."

"I am glad that is resolved," announced Andrei. "Now we can move on to more pressing matters. Within this six-month period, our organisation has been recovering from the enormous loss of our Kyre, Oso Xhelli. During this time, our differences with the Caucasian crime element in Holland have also been put on hold. Would anyone wish to speak at this moment in time?"

Hasan spoke, "Forgive me, Andrei, but have we discovered the motive behind his murder?"

"It is still unclear. Our friends in Calabria maintain Miss Mancuso acted of her own accord. You see, if the Italians wanted Oso dead, they could have accomplished it more cleanly. If they wanted to make a statement by killing him, our brothers and our benefactors, then why deny it after the fact?"

Sali spoke, "One thing I've always struggled to make sense of is how that treacherous bitch set fire to the place after her death at the hands of Klajdi?"

"The investigators conclude she had already begun the fire before Klajdi heroically accosted her. She stabbed him to death before succumbing to the injuries he had inflicted upon her."

One of the other men asked, "How did she manage to hack the CCTV?"

The private investigators reported the server had been remotely manipulated to play on a loop, thus denying the other compound's security team to be alerted to the carnage in the main house.

"She must have had assistance," conceded Andrei. "However, that doesn't necessarily mean it was sanctioned by Calabria. We all know what is at stake—war with them will cost many lives and substantial amounts of money. If we move on this, we need the backing of all the clans, and we need to be fully committed. If we are, we will rain a storm on them."

Sali said, "I agree there needs to be care taken. A large percentage of our businesses are tied together. Not only that, their money laundering expertise far exceeds ours, and access to that knowledge disappears when war is declared."

Before Andrei could speak, Hasan's voice rose, "In the beginning, they helped us—but now we are kept down by them. Yes, in the aftermath of victory we will struggle and have to fight—but that is in our nature, our blood. We will rise higher than ever after vengeance has been served."

Andrei detected a collective resonance at his underboss's words. He spoke, "Before I approach the clans, I need to know my entire Bajrak is committed to this. We will all be affected. Blood will stain the ground of not only our *Republika e Shqipërisë* and Italy, but through Europe and beyond. All in favour raise your hand."

The first twelve shot up and after a few awkward seconds the last three.

"All agree. I will take this to the council—until I do, I do not wish for this knowledge to leave this room," said Andrei, knowing at least one would not adhere to it. He estimated an eighty-three per cent chance Sali had voted against him and guessed the other. He wouldn't know for sure until he had reviewed the footage from the minute cameras installed in the overhead lighting.

He knew it hadn't been the order of 'Ndrangheta, or even Eralda acting alone, who had assassinated Oso, his security team and a large part of their political and financial lifeblood. It had something to do with Connor Reed—a mercurial and devastatingly dangerous Englishman—who had helped Andrei reach the top position in his clan.

However, Reed couldn't have been the one who pulled the trigger and threw the grenades, as he was in England, dealing with a threat to his own criminal dynasty.

"Kyre Faja, whatever happened to the caterer?" asked the older man.

Andrei didn't let his fear show, and said, "I believe the incident frightened her out of Tirana. Not sure where she's gone."

The older man frowned. "The men on the outer security detail said she was the last to leave. That she went into hiding seems strange to me."

"When we inquired as to her whereabouts, we discovered the restaurant had new owners and they were none the wiser as to her location," Andrei replied, and after a moment's pause, added, "We are done here. Brief your men. And wait."

His Bajrak stood in unison and gave him subtle nods—all except Sali. Andrei knew he would have to be removed from the equation. Not through any searing of his ego—but to protect the mother no one in the room knew was his.

He would need outside assistance.

Connor felt only mild surprise to see his suited boss, as opposed to the firearms instructor, sat waiting for him in the quiet console room. Sweat matted his plain white T-shirt, and his stretch jeans stuck a little.

The kettle clicked off. Two mugs had been set out—one plain and one with a Lionel Ritchie cartoon face on it amid the slogan, "Hello, is it tea you're looking for?"

Bruce McQuillan gestured to the mugs. "The coffee is already in them."

Connor poured the boiling water, handed the plain cup to Bruce and took the swivel seat in front of him.

"He's skedaddled, I take it?" asked Connor.

"Aye. Only after expressing his admiration for your performance today."

"Spent more time in these killing houses over lockdown than a uni art graduate does on the dole."

Bruce McQuillan blinked and answered, "Yes, I heard David Bowie and Alan Rickman were forever in the Job Centre."

Connor knew Bruce sometimes had a mild dislike of some of his flippant comments. Despite knowing him for around four years, he remained impressed he seemed to know a little about everything.

"I'll rephrase—I've been putting in the graft. Treat it as a martial art, somebody told me."

He saw a hint of a smile at that. He continued, "You're looking well. Tanned up. Sunbeds?"

He watched the Scotsman suppress an 'I am not biting' smile with a shake of his head. "I came back from the continent yesterday."

"So, what brings you to the Peak District? You could have gotten my assessment results without coming up."

McQuillan locked eyes on him, and Connor already knew what he was about to say. "It's time to action the second phase of the plan. I understand you have your affairs in order now?"

Connor nodded. "The family's business profits have grown so much in the past six months we're scrambling to clean it."

"That might provide an opportunity."

The Yorkshireman smiled—his boss played on a chessboard where his 'assets' lay on one side, the world's criminal and terrorist groups on the other.

"Can I ask, how exactly are we meant to initiate a war between two of the world's biggest and most ruthless criminal organisations—allies, by the way—when the head of one knows he's being drawn into it via a false flag operation?"

Bruce leant back. "Because, Andrei Faja is an ultra-pragmatist. He has enemies within his own clan, his own *Fis*. I imagine many are suspicious of his absence when the attack wiping out the top three members of that Fis led to his ascent to the top position."

"Still, I shouldn't imagine he'd want his first appointment to be a war with the 'Ndrangheta. I know the Mafia Shqiptare is brutal and powerful themselves, but 'Ndrangheta—fuck me, they have Wrath of God money."

Bruce nodded. "This is true. The alliance between the two is of most concern to us. And you're right, the Calabrese are the scarier of the two in reality—they are the ones who can infiltrate and subvert at the upper levels of global finance and foreign governments. When one organisation's influence grows to that level, a sense of order needs to be restored."

An image flashed in Connor's brain of Liam Neeson's Ra's al Ghul telling Christian Bale's Bruce Wayne something similar—*a bit more poetically though.*

"Why? Isn't there an argument that one ruling criminal group keeps order?"

Bruce shook his head. "When a single entity is allowed to form a monopoly and expands, then any semblance of democracy and good deeds for the sake of good deeds is left in ashes. The earlier you can nip it in the bud, the better."

Connor sipped his black coffee. "So, what you're saying is that, with our help the barbarians of Albania could collapse the Italian Empire to a shadow of itself."

Bruce afforded him a smile. "I am glad to see you read history. A mafia—a true mafia—is almost impossible to wipe out. However, you can weaken them. And I suspect Andrei Faja will accept being the head of a battle-scarred, temporarily weakened but ultimately victorious Mafia Shqiptare that hails him as an avenging saviour. Especially when he knows the alternative will be 'evidence' linking not only him to the massacre of Oso Xhelli and several of the Shqiptare's donors, but that his mother was complicit too."

Connor blew on his coffee. "Let's say he refused. Would you actually draw his mother into this? Not that he has to know if you would or not."

McQuillan answered, "You don't have to know either."

"Well, maybe not anytime soon," Connor responded, before switching to, "You got specific instructions with regards to how we're going to light this fire?"

"Jaime will send you the details to one of your e-mail addresses using the address verify@trustadata.

It'll arrive in your spam folder with the eighth attachment containing the tactical information."

"Another thing I wanted to ask you, seeing as I don't see you often," smiled Connor, "is what protocols are in place should Jaime cream in for any reason?"

"Do you think there aren't any?"

"You know I don't question your professionalism."

Bruce gave him a nod. "There's a man with the appropriate infrastructure to aid us in that event. There would be a time of…a lack of cohesion, but we'd get there."

"You know, if he ever needs an apprentice, my cousin, Charlie, might have potential."

The corners of McQuillan's mouth twitched. "I'll take it under advisement."

"Is Ciara going to be operating with me?"

"What makes you ask that?"

Connor said, "Just asking."

"I also came here to talk to you regarding her, you and the future of the Project."

"You want her to succeed you."

Connor felt a strange satisfaction having observed real surprise on the Scotsman's face for the first time.

"How did you know?"

"Not so long back, you asked me to start thinking laterally—and empathetically—and she would be my choice too. And to be honest, I am glad—for more than one reason."

"Because you enjoy being in the thick of it, and you know your family's burgeoning empire is going to require your time and mental energy."

Connor nodded. "They do not ask me where I go, or what I do when I am not in Leeds—that is the arrangement. But Tom will need my help as it continues to expand."

"I am glad we are in agreement," stated Bruce, before changing the subject. "At this moment in time, it looks as though the powers that be in Albania are pinning the responsibility for the Xhelli massacre on Eralda Mancuso, and her death on a member of the security who died as a result, as planned. If Ciara is seen and jogs someone's fragmentary memory of her presence that night, it could collapse the whole enterprise. She isn't the most unremarkable-looking woman."

To say the least, thought Connor as he nodded his understanding and said, "So. Absorb this tactical package. Head to Italy. Fuck baddies up, and make out the other baddie has done it. Help one baddie batter the other baddie?"

"Eloquently put. Yes."

"When do you need me to head out? I have something I need to put in order at home first."

"You'll have a few days."

7

Tom Ryder raised his hand from the back of the room to help his younger cousin Luke pick him out. The heavy wood tables separated the denim sofas, the smell of cigars filling the air.

The waitresses wore collared eggshell shirts with grey woollen trousers and high heels. Tom watched a pair of them flick glances at his cousin as he walked towards him.

Just shy of six feet, athletic, blue-eyed with bright-blond hair, Luke could turn heads even without the light blue shirt and white trousers. His face displayed only hints of the wild fight he and Connor had been through. The cubic zirconia stud lay confidently in his ear—despite his reckless nature, the bare-knuckle boxer had told Tom more than once that people who buy diamonds "are fuckin' doylems". Luke's employment in the Diaz Jewellery store on Leeds city centre's edge helped him escape the taxman's attention. Not that he turned up much, but his 'boss' didn't care as the 'clean' wages paid to Luke came from his own 'dirty' money.

Now Luke owned the shop, and his former boss—now the manager—had been happy with the over-valuation of the business and his inflated wage packet.

Luke slid into the seat next to his cousin. No sooner had he greeted Tom, than a shapely waitress came over.

"Hi. Can I get you anything?"

Luke asked Tom, "We drinking?"

"Afterwards," said Tom.

Luke turned to the waitress. "Just a Coke for now. Lemon and ice."

"And you, sir?" she said to Tom.

"Another pot of tea, please."

Smiling, she sauntered away.

"Did you see the news?" asked Luke.

"Course. I don't think the newsreader could believe what he was saying. I reckon it's done his cause more harm than good, to be honest," Tom responded, flicking invisible dust off his shirt. "Thought you said Connor smacked 'im? Was expecting to see a mark at least."

"Think he caught him sweet on the jaw," answered Luke. "Who were those blokes? They were pouring into the room like giant, pissed-off ants."

"They were heads of various groups who were going to a protest the next day—but something put them off going. They were dropped off by coach and were going to be picked up by coach too—that's why there weren't any other vehicles in the parking area."

Luke said, "Thought we were gonna die. Lucky we brought those dusters or Connor would have got out his knife and then it would have been murders."

"Life in prison or be killed."

"Yeh, hopefully the fat Nazi doesn't have a change of heart and go to the authorities."

"The longer he leaves it, the better the chance he won't. The issue would have been the reaction to his U-turn from his followers—but seeing as you and Connor smacked out most of the dangerous leaders means they've probably all agreed to keep quiet."

"Connor made me take any IDs I could find on them. I don't know where he's put them."

Tom shrugged. "Anyway, how you getting on?"

"Good." Luke nodded. "More nervous for this than I am before bare-knuckle matches."

Tom smiled—a good sign, as this meeting they were about to have could constitute a major turning point in the Ryder business. "I know. Things have gone banzai this last half-year, the money is coming in faster than we anticipated. We need this hotel to clean it."

Luke frowned. "In Skipton though? I'd have thought you'd want a hotel nearer the city centre or up in Harrogate."

"People come from all over the world to Skipton, and I mean even from Australia and the States. It's 'The Gateway to the Dales'. There's the market, Craven Museum, Bolton Abbey, Skipton Castle and all that."

"You were going to tell me the full extent of our laundering operation."

Tom nodded. "Yeh, you need to know in case something happens to me or Connor."

"Where is our illustrious cousin?"

"He's coming up later, after the meet," said Tom.

The waitress returned with their drinks and Tom caught her giving Luke another look.

He said to his younger cousin, "Tell me what you know so far about how we clean our money."

"We place it into things so when it comes back, it looks like profits from legitimate businesses."

Tom shook his head. "You've skipped ahead a bit. There're three phases. I'll tell you how I started. John Stratton had a car pitch in Yeadon and takes me on as an employee—so every morning I am there learning to be a mechanic, like Uncle Greg tells me to.

In the afternoons and evenings, I am grafting elsewhere. I give Stratton my money, and he pays an official wage after taking a percentage off it for the risk of vouching for me should the coppers or even the CPS inquire. So that money is 'clean'."

"And did they?"

"One time they came around, but I was in that day. Besides, he could have always told them I was out picking up a car from an auction."

"All right, then what did you do?"

"During my few years of apprenticeship, I am putting money into a savings account, an amount that would mathematically be possible for me to save should I be some sort of cyborg of frugality."

"Which you are," said Luke.

Tom ignored the playful barb. "As you know, you can't just buy something really expensive without having the figures to back it up should you get pulled into court. Anyway, I bought the garage. Stratton lent me half the money, and I paid him back over time. Once I had the garage, I started to bang in moody invoices. Not too many though, and the garage legitimately makes a profit. Nothing more suspicious than a business producing a healthy tax return but is always empty."

Luke sipped his Coke. "Like all those discount and pound shops in Bradford."

"Probably," replied Tom. "Do you see how it all has to be 'slowly, slowly, catch the monkey' in the beginning?"

"Yeh, I do," answered Luke. "Then what did you do?"

"So, it gets bigger and bigger. We've got that online betting firm that hands us out a 'win' for twenty per cent. They came in handy but you can't do too many of them, obviously. We had certain car dealers give me cars where the invoice shows a knocked down price due to faults and damage that doesn't exist. I pay them the full price from my dirty money. Then I make up a false repair slip before selling them, either to grafters at inflated prices before giving them cashback off the books, or straight-goers at standard prices. Again, that's clean money."

Tom's eyes flicked around and he continued, "Then that money is invested in businesses and the trick is repeated. The Buxton Arms has many ghosts drinking there. Then came your idea about the watches. Although, you'll have to explain to me again why you don't look out for Rolexes."

Luke answered, "I do but Patek Philippes they keep their value more over time. I have a few of them stashed."

Tom sipped his tea and said, "Eventually, we contracted a few accountants to clean our money, but things have got to the point we're going to have to expand. Hence this bid on the hotel."

"Imagine if we got this," said Luke. "Just us working-class lads who went to a comprehensive school owning a massive hotel."

Tom looked at him. "We'll have to go beyond this hotel too, cos the money is coming in waves. We'll discuss it with Connor once he's here."

Luke nodded. "How's Uncle Ryan and Uncle Lee? I haven't seen them for a while."

"They're all right, enjoying the quiet life now. Lee likes running the Buxton, and I reckon Dad lost the taste for this life after getting his jaw fucked up. How're our younger cousins getting on?"

Luke said, "Getting their confidence back slowly. The aggro on the estates seems to have calmed a bit. The thing is, how long is it going to be before Curtis starts wanting to prove himself again. Fact is, though both are a bit handy, they're not fighters—and I know they've bunged lads from Chapletown and Seacroft a few quid for heavy lifting before. Our Charlie isn't arsed about having a reputation—think he'd be happy just being a hacker nerd—loves all that. But our Curtis can be a liability."

"We'll keep an eye on it," Tom replied, before leaning forward. "Now, you've seen I've involved you in everything recently?"

"Yeh, I've noticed."

"Do you know why the Italian mafia is still here?"

Luke shrugged. "Because there's loads of them and they are ruthless cunts?"

Tom smiled. "It's because there's no law enforcement agency that could take enough of them out at the same time to make it collapse. And another is they are in with the right people."

"What are you saying then? We should all start having kids? Because, my dad and your dad are both semi-retired? And if me, Charlie and Curtis are worker bees, then that means whoever only has to take out you and Connor, and that's the Ryder family fucked now, isn't it? I mean, I know we have good people around us, but not blood."

Tom nodded. "Pretty much. I am not saying we can become a White Rose mafia, but there're things we can learn from them. One is making the right relationships. Now, this is what's going to happen. I'll lead this conversation with the sellers. Every so often

I'll turn to you as if to get your opinion. Now, if I wink my right eye—on their blindside— then you give a little nod. If I jut my chin, then give a little shake of your head. Got it?"

"Yeh, you wink, I nod a bit. You tip your chin, I shake my head a bit."

"Cool."

"Why we doing this?"

"Because if I do ever get murdered, I want people to take you seriously, to think you know what you're doing. In time, you will do," said Tom.

"Well, not just murdered," said Luke. "If you get banged up for life. I am guessing it isn't just local police looking at us now."

"There's always that," replied Tom, before looking up. "Right, they are here."

Kathryn Bainbridge felt a hint of relief when the meeting broke up. The Head of Scotland Yard disliked these interagency meetings with the intelligence community. The objective behind them was to ensure the left hand was aware of what the right hand was doing in the protection of the citizens of the UK.

However, she had regularly found them warped with subterfuge and mistrust.

The Cabinet Briefing Room A—COBRA—reminded her of something a Bond villain would use given how sterile it was. Known to the public as the place where the Prime Minister would be advised in times of national emergencies, the rest of the time it was used for meetings such as these.

The hints of grey in her otherwise black bob matched the hue of her suit.

She stood up with the other three.

"Thank you, Georgina, Kevin," she said, shaking the hands in turn of the younger MI5 and MI6 representatives as they were leaving. "Bruce, do you have a few moments?"

Bruce McQuillan, officially the liaison officer between MI5 and MI6, remained much of a mystery to her despite their co-operation over the years. She had heard rumours of his exploits in the world of black operations and had mused on how much of this was mythologised.

The tall Scotsman had perhaps given her the most professional aid of anyone, including within her own organisation.

When they were alone, she said, "I haven't seen you for a while and so wished to thank you."

"What for?" asked the still broad and lean fifty-three-year-old. His answer had been predictable.

"For the breadcrumbs that led to my taskforce discovering a factory holding within it enough carfentanil and other drugs to turn thousands of UK drug users into desperate zombies."

"Surely you should be thanking the detective work of your team?"

She smiled. "Oh, I have, and they have worked awfully hard. Still, certain pieces of evidence seemed to fall into our lap not long after our conversation in which I referenced my concerns."

His face did not give anything away as usual, but he said, "I am glad you got the result you wanted."

"Well, there were no arrests, as the place was empty. And there was evidence of a firefight—no bodies though," she said. "Still, it was a major win for us, and has given us some political clout, so to speak."

Her thoughts drifted off to her most pressing threat and to her astonishment, he said, "Why don't we take a seat and you can tell me what's on your mind."

"How did you know there was anything?"

"Sharp observation."

They descended into seats facing one another and she said, "You trust our privacy in here?"

"Yes," he said, with a confidence that transferred to her.

"You know, you asked me once, what was my most pressing professional concern, and I had answered, the Albanian Mafia, the real one."

"You said 'the criminal element out of the Balkan region', and I said the Albanian Mafia."

She gave a chuckle. "So I did. After that conversation, I thought about the question more deeply. And I realised it wasn't them per se—it was how these groups were managing to clean their money. A hundred billion pounds a year of dirty money is cleaned by criminals operating in this country alone. So, I set up a small team dedicated to tracking how, who and how much."

"And how has your 'Al Capone-ing' been going?"

"It has been going very well until it hasn't been. We have tracked millions, seized millions, chased several brokers and have strong cases pending."

"What's bothering you, Kathryn?"

"It's a small fraction, Bruce, most of the big players take their laundering abroad. I began reaching out, and that's when the problems started. You see, the Russians, Chinese, Ukrainians, Israelis and many others are all masters in this, but there is one organisation that kept coming up."

"The 'Ndrangheta in southern Italy."

Her mouth fell open. "How did you know that?"

"I do my own research," he said. "Who's been stonewalling you?"

"Bruce," she said, her hand picking up a tremor. "I haven't had the support I expected from friends in Lyon, that I usually receive."

His grey eyes met hers. "You're considering the possibility the 'Ndrangheta has penetrated Interpol?"

"A possibility."

"That's not ideal," replied Bruce in his Glaswegian-edged accent. "What specifically do you believe has been happening regarding the Calabrian organisation?"

She tapped her fingers on the table, and said, "I suspect their expertise in this area is as such, that many of the larger criminal organisations both here and in Europe pay them a premium to help clean their money."

"You know," began Bruce, "A man once told me of the importance of identifying the single aspect that would make the most difference. If you're right then we are lucky."

"We're lucky?" she asked.

"True mafias are almost impossible to destroy. But if the 'Ndrangheta can be sufficiently undermined, then whatever organisations rely on them for laundering will be sent into a panic. And you'll be able to capitalise on that."

"Do you have an idea with regards to how to do that?"

The man smiled without baring his teeth. "I'll set the birds off into the air. You shoot them down."

Her smile mirrored his. "Maybe capturing them would be a better euphemism."

"Maybe."

"You didn't answer my question with regards to if you had a plan or not."

His answer came without any tone of arrogance. "I had a plan a month ago."

8

Connor felt surreal as he spied his two cousins through a glass window of the huge, stately country house. Harrogate's Ashington Hall was a place where the social elite of the north of England met, and his cousins had grown up on housing estates in Leeds and never tried to deny their roots. Connor was brought up mostly in the more affluent area of Roundhay in Leeds, but used to spend the weekends with his dad a short drive away in Harehills, or his grandparents in Burmatofts, or various other places in Leeds with his uncles on his father's side.

After a career in the Royal Marines, and a few years spent away from West Yorkshire on operations with The Chameleon Project, he felt a warmth at being close to his cousins again. They had united to come through a torrid time.

The dark clouds began to fleck his three-piece suit made up of light and dark blues, and he made his way inside.

The pretty, raven-haired hostess asked, "What name is it, please?"

"Connor Reed."

Her face slowly turned into a frown and asked, "Connor Reed?"

"My cousin probably put it under Connor Ryder. Still doesn't understand a man can have his mother's maiden name on his birth certificate."

She smiled. "He did indeed. Please follow me."

As she navigated him around the tables, Connor took in the subtle indications of wealth amongst the patrons: custom rather than brand clothes, beautiful teeth, hints of surgery, upright postures and the clarity of their speech. There were no credit cards on display. Connor knew they'd all have a line of credit with the country club which they would never dare renege on, else they be banished from it. He and his cousins were considered *Nouveau Riche*—new rich—but as long as they behaved, paid on time and remained discreet, this place could offer respite to their dangerous lives.

"Here he is," said Tom.

The hostess asked Connor, "Is there anything I can bring you?"

Connor turned to Tom and asked, "Did it go well?"

When Tom nodded in reply with a massive smile, he turned back to the hostess and said, "In that case, if you have a bottle of the 1978 Lytton whisky, could you bring it with *drei Gläser*."

He held up his thumb, index and middle finger to specify 'three glasses' like a true German.

"Certainly, Mr Reed." she smiled. "Anything else?"

"I think we'll go the full cliché and get three Cohiba Siglo Vi cigars, please."

She left with a nod and he slid into the seat opposite Tom, next to Luke so he had a view of the patrons and entrance.

Luke looked at him. "Think you should be pretending to be the German SS officer in here, even if I did love that film?"

"One, if you loved Tarantino's *Inglourious Basterds* you'd know I was impersonating how the British officer should have impersonated a German SS officer. And secondly, not all wealthy people are Jewish. Anyway, congratulations, you two."

Tom shook his head. "Congratulations to all of us. Aziz must have reached out to Jehan Zafar because it turns out she helped grease the wheels for us."

"What do I keep saying?" said Connor, turning his palms to the ceiling. "It's the physics of the universe."

Tom spoke, "See you got her to use your mam's name."

"There's a reason why I go by my mum's maiden name."

As soon as he said it, he knew his cousins would pick up on it.

"Maiden name?" said Luke. "I thought Uncle Greg and Auntie Rebecca were never married?"

Connor began to shrug off his suit jacket. "I don't know how Bond fights in a suit. I can barely move in mine."

"Come on," said Tom. "What did you mean by maiden name?"

Connor sighed and said, "They were married—abroad and in secret. I found out just before I carved the Kanji into Derek's forehead."

He was referring to their uncle, now deceased, who had been banished from the family.

"How did you find this out?" asked Tom.

"Aziz. Him and his wife were there as witnesses."

Zain Aziz was perhaps the most influential crime lord in Bradford, the city next to Leeds. He and Connor's father had met in Armley prison around a quarter of a century ago. And the Ryder criminal dynasty re-established relations with him.

A frown briefly shadowed Tom's forehead. "I am not saying Aziz is lying but how do you know for sure? I mean, why would Uncle Greg have Aziz at his wedding but not his own family?"

Connor shrugged. "I've seen the pictures—they weren't photoshopped. And he has no reason to lie about it."

"Have you asked your mum?" asked Luke.

"No, they obviously kept it from me for a reason," answered Connor.

The hostess arrived with the whisky, interrupting whatever Tom was about to say. She poured the glasses and left.

Connor held his glass up. "We are now owners of our very own hotel. It wasn't long ago we were struggling to survive, in more senses than one."

Tom smiled before saying, "We didn't get anything off it though. Full whack we had to pay."

Connor and Luke caught one another's eyes and simply smiled at their elder cousin's notorious thriftiness.

"Christ, Tom," said Connor. "I bet you complain about bald kids jumping the queues at Disneyland."

Luke laughed. "His war-cry is, 'How much?'"

Tom smiled before saying, "You're right. This helps secure our family, and that's priceless."

They clinked glasses and took a sip.

As the smooth, subtle blend of flavours convinced Connor he would not buy cheap whisky again, he realised this was how 'the good life' enslaved you.

"Can't say I am a whisky expert but that's mega," enthused Luke.

"Now, this is your tutorial on how to smoke a cigar."

Connor showed his younger cousin how to use the sharp cutter and how only to cut the first cap off.

"Don't go further than one cap or all you'll end up with is a mouthful of tobacco bits. Wipe this and you cut yours."

When Luke followed suit, Connor said, "Right, hold your cigar to the flame at an angle like this, but don't let the flame touch it. Just rotate the cigar until a bit of smoke starts evenly around it."

When he had done so, Connor continued, "Right, initially gently blow out—it'll get rid of ammonia and any bitterness. Then take a slow draw—for fuck's sake don't inhale. You'll end up coughing up your lungs and you'll never touch one again."

Luke went through the routine and gave a small cough. Connor and Tom laughed.

"Take your time with it. Take a puff a minute and just rest it in the tray when you've had enough."

The three enjoyed the cigars for a minute.

Connor leant forward, looking at Luke. "Listen, Tom and I have been speaking. We all know we had a lucky escape not long back. That could have been our entire family wiped out."

The Ryder family had survived a war on two fronts with elements of the Liverpool mafia and Albanian organised crime.

"Yeh, but we did survive."

"Uncle Michael didn't survive," interjected Tom. "And Curtis got shot and not to mention before this all kicked off my dad got hospitalised."

"What we're saying is we want to grow into the type of organisation where threats like that can be brushed aside."

"Tom was talking about that before you came," said Luke. "Though I remember you telling me constant growth makes an organisation hard to control. Something about the Roman Empire having to be split in two and then it all going to shit."

"I said it could do. And I said 'type' not 'size'. But you're right, we're going to need to grow."

Connor looked at Tom who said, "And we're going to need to restructure. This is the new order—it's us three at the top, anything Connor and I know, you'll know. We'll make the major decisions together."

"How…how come you're letting…why me?"

"You've gotten a grip on yourself this last half-a-year. Bill says when he went on holiday for a couple of weeks and left you to watch over the various operations, that everything was running smoothly when he got back. You've knocked the pissing-up on the head too. You'll continue to shadow me and learn."

Tom referred to Bill Hopkins, a man who managed several trucking companies the Ryder family were silent partners in through shell companies.

"That's good to know. You did tell me that transportation is the most important area of this business."

"Yeh, I did," said Tom, before shrugging. "Well, that and the laundering."

Luke blew out, and Connor could see the gravity of what he was being told was hitting him. He put his hand on the back of his neck and said, "Congratulations, Luke. You deserve it. Remember, this is just the beginning—don't fuck it up by slackening off. This is a rest-of-your-life thing. It's going to require your constant attention. We don't want you slipping back into bad habits. By all means have fun but remember, don't take recreation past the point of restoration."

"'Don't take recreation past the point of restoration', who made up that quote? Bruce Lee?"

Connor smiled. "That's a Connor Reed original."

Tom said, "The operations side is larger than you think, Luke. There are various transport companies and people we employ to make sure things run smoothly. Bill Hopkins is up here, but we have quite a few 'Bill Hopkinses' around the country and Europe. Like we keep saying, our first challenge is going to be laundering."

"I understand," said Luke, before taking another puff of his cigar. "What about the rest of the family? Aren't they going to be fucked off I am now in the inner circle?"

"Your old man is happy running The Buxton Arms, mate. And my old man is semi-retired—he doesn't want the aggro now. He's happy doing a bit of running up and down the country, making sure things are tickety-boo."

"What about the twins?" Luke asked. "I know Charlie is sound, but Curtis is going to be mardy, to say the least."

"The things Charlie can do with his computer are amazing, and some of the contributions he has made have been a massive help," said Tom. "As for Curtis getting upset, that's his own fault. I trusted him with running the drops down south and he's fucked that despite me telling him exactly what to do."

"How? Unless it's none of my business?"

"It is your business now. This is the whole point, you dingbat," said Tom. "I told him umpteen times to discipline the lads to drop during work traffic hours. And only to use business insured vehicles. He can't get it into his head that lads with records going through the ANPR cameras at daft times at night and early morning are begging for unwanted attention. And he's not once used Yo-Yos. I think he's dead from the neck up sometimes."

Yo-Yos, Connor knew, was one of Tom's favourite tactics for large and dangerous transports. He would 'tip-off' the police to trucks going through hotspots, particularly on county lines. These trucks would be pulled over only to be found legitimate, allowing the 'loaded' ones to pass through without incident.

Luke's head creased. "Why did he say he did it out of business hours?"

"Fucking…he said he was taking the opportunity to collect as much cash as possible for the family. I've told him until I am blue in the face making big money over a long time under the radar beats quick money we can't spend as we'll be in the nick—unless it's on solicitors. Even with the discount Caris now gives us."

Robert Caris was the family's main legal fixer based out of Liverpool.

Connor said, "Grandad told me having an ugly girlfriend signifies a lack of confidence. Maybe he needs more time?"

"Can't see how that's true," said Luke. "Curtis is arrogant as fuck despite his bird having a face like it's been drawn by Michael J Fox with his left hand."

They laughed before making an effort to quieten down, given the environment they were in.

Tom then said, "He's had time. Like Luke said, it isn't a lack of confidence."

"What's happened then?"

"I've taken him off that and given it to Mark Briggs to run. He's an old and steady hand and knows what I expect."

"Can't imagine Curtis took that well—even if Mark has known the family since when Grandad ruled the roost."

"I softened the blow by putting him in charge of running the girls at the escort agency. There're less moving parts with that."

Connor interjected with, "You sure about that, Tom?"

His elder cousin shrugged his shoulders. "It's the nearest legitimate illegitimate business we have. The only thing naughty about it is running 'phantom' girls through it for laundering purposes—you know the crack, 'Jolene' has been taken away for a week to the South of France by 'Rupert', the successful businessman. But even then, Curtis can take the piss, which is why you need to supervise the books, Luke."

"Me?" said Luke. "He'll get a *cob on* taking orders from me. But I know—it's my role now."

"Exactly," said Tom.

Luke replied, "I never actually asked before, but I always pegged it as you run the business at home, and Connor runs it abroad? Very 'Johnny Aged Five' way of looking at it, but I thought that was basically the way it is."

Connor looked at him and said, "Tom is the CEO, and I am his operations manager for foreign imports."

Tom shifted in his seat. "Don't listen to him, Luke, he's the leader of the family. I just run the West Yorkshire Urban Area part of the operation."

"Let's just go with your original assessment, Luke," said Connor.

Luke took another puff of his cigar and asked, "Since I have been brought into the inner fold, can I ask what your next move in foreign operations is going to be?"

Connor leant forward. "Do you know what the biggest challenge for crypto-currency is?"

"That it's not legal?"

"Not much of what we do is legal," said Connor. "It's the mining of it takes a lot of time and energy—specifically electricity. Some of these miners fuck off to countries with lower electricity prices, which shows how determined they are."

"What's that got to do with us?"

"Well, one of the things that's like gold dust to them is graphics cards. And our partner in Ukraine has a line on them. And there're guys in Craiova who are thirsting for them."

"Where's Craiova?" asked Luke.

"Romania. It's a town renowned for its cyber thieves and IT geeks. There are naughty people there who'll pay big money. Money that needs to be laundered—we haven't that type of expertise, but we've got to get it somehow."

"How?"

"Well, being new to being this…profitable, that's the part we've got to figure out. Then we might live in something grander than a house."

The castle stood as a beacon to Andrei even at a distance of half a mile, framed by the blue sky and wisps of cloud.

The physical comfort of the passenger seat of the Bentley Continental GT dabbed his stomach with anxiety. Money did not hold an allure for him with regards to the possessions it could buy, it was the power it could obtain. However, he knew he could not shun the game—a game that necessitated he could not arrive at a castle to meet with fifteen other Kyres without his mode of transport symbolising his newly acquired status.

As the Bentley cruised the ascent on the smooth road, Andrei could make out more of the castle's features. The difference in tone between the base and it's cylindrical, monolithic top indicated its refurbishment back in the nineties, though the original was built centuries ago.

Ritual respect within high council conferences like these meant Kyres could only take one other person—a driver. Still, every one of them took a trusted bodyguard to drive and not their regular drivers.

As Hasan deftly manoeuvred the €185,000 vehicle, he said, "Can I ask you a direct question, Andrei?"

Hasan's use of his first name was not out of disrespect but out of familiarity—they had come up through the ranks together, and it had only been in the last few years that Andrei had ascended more rapidly. Despite this, Hasan never displayed any resentment.

"Yes."

"Are you confident of gaining their backing? Forgive me, but they may not be able to see merit past your youth."

"I will show them all the respect their age deserves."

Hasan smiled briefly before asking, "Might the Italians have them all in their pockets? Just because our clan has been hit, doesn't mean they will sanction total war. Another's burden kills the ass."

Andrei never wanted a confidante but calculated he needed allies, and Hasan was valuable.

"Our Mafia Shqiptare is an organisation of family and honour. You know this. Oso Xhelli had many friends, and those donors who were killed helped support the organisation."

"This is what I cannot understand, my Kyre," said Hasan, as the castle loomed closer. "Why would they want to destroy us, as they seem to be wanting to do?"

"That's another mystery."

Hasan slowed the car at the gate. Three suited men, each armed with the beige and black FN SCAR-H assault rifle, stopped them past the gate in a triangle formation. Andrei caught the glint of a sniper scope from the castle turret.

The guards inspected the car, including the boot, and waved them through to the parking area.

They disembarked to the sound of crickets. Their suits were mercifully light as the heat of the sun set the vast scrubland plain shimmering.

They ascended the chalky steps. The pillars guarding the entrance were sculpted with giant snakes slithering up them.

Andrei entered the vast hall—the last Kyre to do so. All eyes were on him and he gave the collective a cross between a nod and a bow.

The circular table meant no one Kyre could sit at the head of it. However, most of their eyes furtively glanced in the direction of the silver-haired, clean-shaven, immaculately suited man whose seat afforded him the most direct view of the entrance. Tefik Mesi headed one of the most feared clans in the entire organisation, run out of the town of Shijak in west-central Albania. Due to his strategic mind, contacts, ruthlessness and vast experience, he held the most influential position on the council.

"How was your journey, my brother?" asked Tefik.

"One cannot complain when riding in a Bentley Continental and not even having to drive. I should imagine you get used to it quickly."

Smiles broke out amongst the fifteen Kyres and their bodyguards surrounding the room.

"Before we begin," announced Tefik, "we have been informed the members of your Bajrak have confirmed their wish for you to succeed Oso Xhelli as the Kyre of your Fis."

"That is correct, brother," replied Andrei, still standing.

"Though it had not been unanimous."

"It was not. Thirteen to two."

"A couple of dissenters is natural given the circumstances. The vast majority supports you and that is the most important thing."

Andrei knew this was Tefik's hawkish but subtle way of asserting his dominance; to highlight there had been dissenters, only in his next sentence to dismiss them spoke of the man's cunning.

"The vote here is done in the open and has to be unanimous, Andrei. Each man in turn states 'Yes' or 'No' to permit your ascension. I will begin by saying 'Yes'."

Andrei gave him a subtle nod of thanks, before feeling his stomach tighten like a ratchet, as his anxiety-prism slowed the vote. All had said 'Yes' as it came to the last man—the Kyre of Elbasan, who looked Andrei in the eyes with a sombre mask.

"Andrei, you know I respect you, brother." Andrei's heart dropped in his stomach as the man continued, "Which is why my answer is 'Yes'."

Hoots of appreciation at the Elbasan Kyre's joke rose from the others, rapidly followed by their congratulations to Andrei.

"Take a seat, Kyre Faja," said Tefik.

Andrei felt as though the chair came up to support him with its power rather than he sitting on it.

Tefik continued, "If you are unaware, each Kyre brings to the council any concerns, opportunities or requests, and they are discussed in turn."

Andrei nodded his understanding. He was aware of this and that he—being its newest member—would be last. And that was bad; he had read studies showing court judges were less lenient in the afternoon of a full day than the morning due to decision-fatigue. It was why the US President's full schedule was mapped out for him, even down to the tie he wore for the day.

After nearly three hours—albeit punctuated with short breaks—it came to him.

"Gentlemen, my Kyre, members of our family and our friends were ambushed and murdered without warning or provocation. I have spent the months in between reaffirming and forming alliances, gathering intelligence and helping to restructure the Tirana clan. I am asking for your blessing to strike back at the 'Ndrangheta."

Silence seared through the room. Finally, Tefik spoke, "As you are aware, Andrei, the Calabrese has not claimed responsibility for the attack. Whispers suggest Salvatore Mancuso is convinced his sister—and their organisation—has been scapegoated and that the massacre was a result of internal politics."

"I would suggest Mr Mancuso would say that to avoid the ramifications of war with us, or consequences at home if indeed his sister did act of her own volition."

The Kyre of Kamëz called out, "Our partnerships with the Calabrians are interwoven and vital. They provide laundering, have helped being guarantors for our largest shipments with the Colombians. They have—"

Tefik cut him off, "None of that matters in the face of our murdered kin."

The Kamëz clan boss stopped talking as if he had been slapped, and Tefik continued, "However, you are correct. War with them is not something to be taken lightly. Therefore, it is my suggestion you send an emissary, Kyre Faja, to see if Mancuso is receptive to remuneration. If he is, then honour is spared and a costly war is averted."

Andrei hid his frustration. Certain members of his clan would see it as a weakness he could not garner the support necessary for war.

"And what if he refuses?"

"If he refuses then we must do what is necessary," said Tefik. "We should vote."

"There is no need for the council to vote on this—it should have been my first course of action," announced Andrei. "However, I would like to be the one who chooses who the emissary is. He must come from my clan."

After a few moments silence, Tefik said, "As a compromise, Kyre Faja, the council shall vote on who will go, but the man will be a member of your clan."

"I would like Hasan to go, Kyre Mesi."

"We respect your clan's Mik—his talents are well known—I would prefer someone less…intimidating. Sali Rama would be my choice."

The low murmurs of agreement indicated to him the outcome of such a vote.

"Unless the other Kyres have any other suggestions then I will accept your nomination since it comes from a man of a wisdom born of vast experience."

Andrei knew Tefik himself would be unmoved by such flattery, but the game was there to play. A game he could not lose, for both his and his mother's sake; he could not afford mistakes if he was ever able to bring her back from hiding in Greece.

"Thank you, Kyre Faja. I am sure Sali will fulfil his purpose to you."

9

Daniel saw Connor in the far corner of the high-rise London restaurant. The white of the disappearing sun, the dark blue of night and the lights of the city framed his older-by-a-year cousin regally.

"May I take your jacket, Mr Ryder?" asked the pretty, raven-haired hostess with a hint of an accent.

"Please," he said, as he slid off the navy-blue Tom Ford piece.

Her words, as he handed it over, jolted the investment banker. "Mr Reed is waiting for you in the far corner, as you can see."

That his cousin had been able to procure a table in a restaurant such as this had been a surprise. For him to do it on short notice, a shock. And now the way the hostess said 'Mr Reed' with a taint of reverence, hinted at unreality—*What has he become now?*

She handed his jacket to a clerk attendant with a command of "Mr Ryder", before leading him across the shimmering polished floor, threading a path through the quietly chatting patrons.

Connor stood to greet him. Dan held envy for his effortless style; the collared cream shirt's rolled-up sleeves, revealed tan, striated forearms, one with a silver-faced, brown leather-strapped watch. The jeans were so dark and uniform in colour they could be mistaken for trousers at a glance.

Dan stuck his hand out only to have it met with his cousin's open arms and derisive words of, "Fuck off, you dickhead, I haven't seen you in years."

Dan smiled as they embraced. "Sorry, been in London for too long."

As they broke, Connor said, "You'll be liking rugby union over league next."

"Already do. Thought you kept an open mind?"

"Sell it to me," Connor said as they sat.

"Us northerners like to think everyone and everything is harder up there, but the rucks and mauls in union make it a harder game to play. Fact is, league has become largely amorphous roid-monsters running at full pelt straight into each other five times. That's before booting it with barely any room for cerebral gameplay."

"I'll wind my neck in." Connor smiled. "Do you know what you want to drink?"

"Are you drinking alcohol?"

Connor shrugged. "I don't normally but it's a special occasion. Do you like red wine?"

When Dan nodded, Connor turned to the hostess and said, "Una bottiglia di vino rosso di cui mi ha parlato prima, per favore."—*A bottle of the red wine you told me about earlier, please.*

She laughed. "Molto bene, non ci vorrà molto."—*Very well, it won't take long.*

As she walked off, Dan asked, "Do you know her or something? How did you know she was Italian? And how do you know Italian?"

They sat and Connor answered, "Could you not hear she has an accent?"

"Yeh, but it was that faint I didn't know what it was," said Dan. "Then again, you must be a dab hand at languages, I remember you conversing with the Asians in Punjabi that night on Manningham Lane."

Connor gave a nasal exhale of laughter. "Was a good night. Luke told me some of the Pakistani birds are starting to be seen out, and in make-up. And in his words look 'banging', although he used to mix them up with Indians."

Dan smiled. "How is my younger brother? I am glad you and Tom are looking after him."

"He's good, he's less reckless and a lot more responsible now."

The hostess came back, even though there were no shortages of waitresses, and placed the bottle of red wine on the table.

"Spero vi piaccia."—*Hope you like it.*

Connor replied, "I hope so too. Or you shall feel my wrath."

She laughed, placing a stroking hand on his shoulder. "Would you like to order yet?"

The two men did so. Connor ordered an Atlantic salt cod and vegetables, and Dan a medium-cooked fillet steak and a sparkling water.

"Just to dilute the alcohol," said Dan.

"Don't know why you'd drink sparkling over still," said Connor. "Tastes like I imagine TV static does."

Connor turned to the hostess and they had another exchange in Italian, which lit a smile on her face before she left.

Dan shook his head with a laugh. "I was going to ask you when you were going to settle down, but I can see why you wouldn't want to."

"How is Angela? Heard she had a bad episode not too long back."

Dan sighed. "Stress aggravates her Crohn's, and when you're one of the CPS's top prosecution barristers, that's not good."

"Is she ill now?"

"Nah, she's managing it quite well given the case she's on."

"I won't ask."

"How come you didn't tell me you were coming down? You could have stopped at mine."

Connor smiled. "We both know the enterprises I, and the rest of the family, are allegedly involved in could cause you embarrassment with Angela."

Dan shook his head. "She doesn't judge me…she might judge you, but not me."

Connor smiled before saying, "What you worried about? That the stress could cause another episode, or is there something else bothering you?"

Dan felt a jolt of surprise at his cousin's guess.

"Most organised crime elements—the ones with any sense, at least—know not to touch members of the prosecution. Aside from increasing the law enforcement scrutiny and aggression towards them, it's a futile endeavour, as the caseload along with all the evidence would just get passed to another barrister—the best one the CPS could find, as then it would become a crusade."

Connor tilted his jaw. "What's the problem then?"

"Under the leadership of Kathryn Bainbridge, the NCA has had a series of victories against mafia elements. Angela says they have been producing concrete evidence and it's been helping to get results. Keep what I am about to tell you quiet, mate."

"All right."

"There's been a series of suspicious deaths of people associated with the cases involving this group."

His cousin's eyes remained fixed on his. "Who?"

"That's the question. They think it's a renegade Turkish group but they've tracked some of the communications back to Italy—weird."

"Where in Italy? Toe, midsole, mid or top of the boot?" asked Connor.

"They don't know," said Dan. "But it's like I said, these deaths are 'suspicious'—one died from a heart attack, one a heroin overdose who had no previous known history of drug use, and another drowned in Egypt while scuba diving."

Their meals arrived and once the waitress left, Connor asked, "I take it since she's told you all this, Angela thinks the three have been murdered?"

"She doesn't know for sure, none of them do. Still, it doesn't look good."

"I can put a discreet security attachment on her. Professional outfit, before you ask."

"I've already looked into it. She won't have it, mate. Discreet security might be able to intercept a knife-wielding manic or maybe a gunman, but to prevent your food being poisoned or whatever would require your security to be scrutinising everything. I am doing well now, I can afford it even with the trial's length, but she says, 'I refuse to show them I am scared, and if everyone else is going without security then I am going without too'. I pointed out to her not everyone is the chief prosecutor—"

Dan stopped as he felt emotion press on the back of his throat.

Connor reached to grasp his wrist and said, "Hey, get a grip, we haven't even finished one glass yet."

Dan smiled despite himself. "I just don't know what to do."

"This is what we're going to do. You're going to impress upon her the need to continuously change her patterns. Walking up to someone—even today—and shooting them isn't that hard. Making it look like an accident is—that requires a tremendous degree of planning. And planning involves gathering intelligence—they'll need to nail a routine. The routes she takes to work, the times she sets off at, the places she socialises, the garages she fuels up at—everything will need to be constantly switched up—"

"I already know she'll say she has enough on her plate without—"

"Hey," barked Connor with a sharpness that cut through him. "The day you put your girlfriend's feelings before her life is the day you can pick another gender—there are sixty-three others to choose from, knock yourself out."

"All right, point taken," said Dan. "Although, are you saying being a 'man' is the only gender that would put a person's life over their feelings?"

"Can we put my northern ignorance aside and focus on the task at hand?"

"Of course."

"If she starts or refuses, then move out. Doesn't matter if she screams, cries or threatens you. Pack your stuff and fuck off. Remind her if she is being targeted because of the case she is on, then people are counting on her to succeed. It's inconveniencing herself for a few months, that is all—she won't be Viktor Frankle-ing it."

"OK," agreed Dan, nodding. "You said, 'we'?"

"I'll worry about what I am going to do."

Dan's heart dropped. "Connor, please, I came down here to get away from all that. I just wanted your—"

"If these people want to assassinate Angela then you have to ask yourself if her life is more important than your morality. In fact, you don't have to ask yourself that."

"Why don't I have to?"

"Because I don't have to ask myself that question," said Connor, taking a sip of his wine. "You haven't done anything wrong. Just do as I say, and in a few months, this should all be over."

"You know, the reason I moved down here wasn't that I am ashamed of my family. It was just that, you know."

Connor shook his head with a smile. "Dan, I am proud of you for not towing the party line. You and I know you're better suited in the line of work you're in. You're good at it. I've seen many men who, in attempting to become something they're not, piss away what they might have been."

"So, you don't hate me, then?"

"Where the fuck did you get that idea from?"

Dan shrugged. "I know you all went through a rough time in the aftermath of Derek. I won't ask if we're ever likely to see him again."

"Probably wise," replied Connor. "Why? You missing him?"

Dan shook his head. "There was always something about him, wasn't there? Like he couldn't relax without letting people know he was the big man. Grandad was never like that, neither was your dad."

"He reeked of insecurity and it came out in bragging and bullying. If you don't know, I won't tell you, other than it was a lot worse than that, Dan."

"That fact Gran doesn't seem upset he's missing speaks volumes."

When Connor said nothing, Dan continued, "I haven't even asked you what you've come down here for."

He saw Connor take a breath and say, "The family business has grown at an almost exponential rate. We need to pay tax on the money efficiently. I'll be taking a flight out of Heathrow in a couple of hours to Europe."

Dan frowned. "Couldn't you have gone out of Leeds-Bradford airport?"

"Thought I'd work it so I could spend part of the evening with my cousin."

There were a few moments of silence before Dan spoke, "There's this guy—"

"Don't do it, Dan. I am perfectly capable of finding my own without you. There're all sorts of laws your bird could get you on," his cousin said with a wink.

Angela Bromley sat at her office desk, trying to massage mental energy into her temples. It had been a long day—like all the days for the past four weeks. She knew she had come to her point of diminishing returns.

She turned to look at her view of London from her high-rise office. Instead of admiring the view as she always did, she caught sight of her dark roots coming through her blonde bob, and winced.

Her phone lit up as did her face upon seeing it was Dan.

"Hey, you," she said, answering on loudspeaker. "Had a good time?"

"Yeh, always do. He's a character."

Angela kept a happy tone. She got with Dan knowing full well who his family was. She either accepted him, warts and all, or not at all.

"I'll have to meet him one day."

"I wouldn't put you in that position."

She felt relieved. Angela had high aspirations—indeed, she had quit her highly lucrative law practice to ply her trade in the CPS. She had accepted the risk of dating Dan despite who his family was. However, it was manageable, as Dan had never been involved in crime.

The rest of his cousins were a different story; upon researching Connor Reed, she had discovered he had done a custodial term in HM Prison Wetherby as a youth, and had served a brief stint in the Military Corrective Training Centre (MCTC) in Colchester before being released from the Royal Marines.

He, his cousin Tom and a notorious South London gangster named Louis Allen, had all been found not guilty of various offences that saw several doormen in a Manchester nightclub savagely beaten. The incident was caught on multiple phones and had gone viral.

"Well, we can't put my meeting them off forever, Daniel. Maybe once I've gotten this out of the way."

"That's what I wanted to talk to you about, Angela. Have you requested security for yourself yet?"

She had hoped he would forget about it.

"Not as yet." She sighed.

"Well, I am going to. If these people are as dangerous as you say, you owe it not just to yourself, but all those vulnerable people you're trying to protect by bringing these people down."

He has me there—she thought.

"We've discussed this. I do not want them slowing me down—prying into all aspects of my day. You know that I am sometimes here, there and everywhere."

"They can remain discreet. As long as you switch your patterns—ways you go to work, the places you go."

She massaged her temples again. "I'll think about it."

"Well, you can think about it in the house on your own. I'll be in a hotel until you decide to see sense."

She bolted upright. "Excuse me?"

"You heard me fine, Angela."

With that, the line went dead.

Damn him—she thought—*this is all I need. If he wants to spend the night in a hotel then I won't get in his way. One meeting with his cousin and he's cock of the north.*

She knew she was not going to get anything meaningful done now.

She stood and packed her things, still thinking about Dan's stance—*Good, I get to starfish in bed.*

By the time she had made it down the second flight of stairs, her attitude was already softening. He was simply looking out for her; she would call him from the car and tell him not to be so silly.

She hit the dark underground car park. Though the hour was late, she recognised both wandering security guards and another in the booth on the far side, which calmed the raising of her antenna.

As she shut herself into her silver Mercedes, she began to hook her phone to the car's Bluetooth.

She decided to wait until she was free of the London inner city to call him—she did not want to take her frustrations regarding the traffic lights out on him.

The barrier released her only for her foot to stamp on the brake in a gasping halt.

A youth—she guessed his ethnicity to be Middle Eastern—walked out in front of the car. His rubber-gloved hands held up a bucket and sponge with a huge smile. Immediately, he began to wash the bonnet, seemingly oblivious with his ears hidden by oversized headphones.

You have to be bloody joking. At this time of night?

Feeling a tinge of guilt, she knew she was just going to drive off as he started on one of the sides.

However, as he did so, he left the bucket in front of the car and her patience snapped. She ripped her purse out of her handbag, grabbed a couple of twenties and wound the window down. When he failed to respond to her calls, she got out of the car with the money held out towards him. He did not seem to notice her, absorbed with ensuring her wheel arch was spotless.

"Excuse me. Excuse me," she called. Finally, he looked up at her, stood and punched her hard in the abdomen.

Her hand flew to her stomach as she fought for breath. The youth fled to the distorted shouts of the security guard from within the underground parking lot.

Her legs sat her down without waiting for her brain's command to do so.

She looked down in horror to see her hand covered in diluted red paint—only for the metallic smell to tell her it was blood.

She became aware of the security guard next to her as her vision began to fade.

10

It took Tom a moment to register the vision of a broken man in the hospital corridor as being his cousin, Dan.

Luke—Dan's younger brother—and his dad, Lee and mum, Stephanie, immediately rushed over to console him. Tom looked on with the left side of his chest listing under the weight of pain he felt for his cousin.

Pain, but also a seething rage.

He had had to reconcile himself to the fact that though a deep love of his family was the driving force in his life, it would always conflict with the inherent danger of their business.

However, Dan had always shunned a life of crime or even naughtiness. He got his head down in school, went to uni and then moved to London.

Though he had physically distanced himself, he regularly called, especially Gran, and Tom felt close to him.

Tom approached as the huddle seemed to loosen, revealing his bleary-eyed cousin.

"How is she?" asked Tom.

"They say it's going to be touch and go for a few days. They are keeping her sedated. Lost a lot of blood."

Stephanie spat, "The fucking bastard, whoever did this. Probably some little immigrant scrote from—"

"Auntie Steph, calm down. We don't know what's happened yet," said Tom, firmly. His aunt nodded with a hint of contriteness before rubbing her elder son's back.

"Sorry," she said. "I am just het up, that's all, she's such a sweet girl—salt of the earth—and she's laying in this…"

As her voice broke, Tom said, "Uncle Lee, why don't you take Steph for a coffee."

Lee looked at him for a moment. "Yeh, OK. You'se all want 'owt?"

"Yeh," answered Tom. "White coffee, no sugar."

Luke opted for the same, and Dan declined.

When Lee and Stephanie were out of earshot, Tom asked, "Did they take anything?"

"No," answered Dan. "That's the first thing the police told me. Strange as well, it wasn't in the parking lot like I thought. It happened literally just past the barriers. I can't understand what possessed her to get out of the car."

"The police not given you any other details?"

"No, they can't yet."

Luke murmured, "Why stab her if they weren't going to take anything."

Tom and Dan looked at one another, and Tom said, "You're going to have to tell me who her case is targeting."

He could see the vengeance dance in his cousin's eyes before Dan slowly shook his head. "I can't do that. She's a leading Crown Prosecution Service solicitor, and I am coming up for partnership in the investments firm. If it came out my family attempted to strike back, that would be both our careers down the pan."

Tom could see Luke's frustration in his peripheral vision before saying, "We're here. Whatever you need or need doing."

Dan said, "These people, Tom. They would eat our family."

In that moment, Tom realised Dan did not know the extent of the family's growth within the criminal underworld in the past eighteen months. When he heard Luke take a breath—presumably to educate his older brother—Tom silenced him with a hand gesture.

Lee and Steph returned with the coffees. Her hand returned to rubbing her son's back.

Tom said, "Just got to make a call. I'll give you some space."

As he walked away, he was mildly surprised to find Luke following him.

When out of earshot, Luke said, "Tom, we're going to fuck him off with that not doing anything plea, aren't we?"

"You heard what he said—it's their livelihood."

"Listen, I would never go against what you say. But they've fucked with our family."

Tom regarded his younger cousin's flashing eyes. "Don't suppose it would hurt to find out who was behind it. He might change his mind."

Luke took a moment to reply. "Got any ideas who we start with?"

"We need a guide."

"You got a man in mind? A friend of yours?"

"Well, he's more of a friend of Connor's."

"Are you telling Connor?" asked Luke.

Tom shook his head. "He said under no circumstances was I to get in touch with him until he got back."

Sali Rama waited until the scrum to depart the ferry died down. His habit for years, he could not abide queuing or having anyone behind him if he could help it. He and his bodyguards sat on the upper level as the passengers swirled down the stairs.

He'd spent the five-hour journey alternating between the Ismail Kadare novel *Chronicle in Stone* and his thoughts regarding Andrei Faja.

He found it surreal that just prior to the ferry docking in the southern Italian port city of Brindisi, he had reached a point in the World War II story where Italian fascists hung several Albanian rebels.

He thought of the quagmire The Brotherhood now found itself in—sharpening their claws for war with their once closest Italian ally. A voice in his mind whispered too quietly for his concerns to be clear.

Unlike the Camorra, Sali never felt the men of the 'Ndrangheta looked down on him or the Mafia Shqiptare. Their underpinning virtues of family, honour and discipline mirrored one another.

Barring a few skirmishes, the partnership between the two had been mutually beneficial. The Mafia Shqiptare had been given access to their money laundering expertise and the ports of Europe. In return, the Calabria-based syndicate passed over the security of their product's transportation, so that the media and law enforcement fallout from any drug war violence shone on the 'blood-thirsty' Albanians and not suited Italian businessmen.

So, it was a pleasant surprise Faja had chosen him to negotiate for remuneration, and with it a de-escalation of war before it began. However, from being selected to now, he had felt a grinding pressure build—what if he could not succeed?

How had things got to this point?

He thought of Andrei Faja, and realised he had been troubled by the young man's rise to power even before he claimed the title of Kyre. To get to the position of Mik—a liaison and coordinating officer—so young, had raised his eyebrows. For Faja to now sit as head of the most potent mafia clans in Albania puzzled and aggrieved him.

On hearing he had been passed over by Oso for his young nephew made him mad—but not as seething as when he discovered the amount of support Andrei held.

Finally, the downstairs voices floated away.

His hard-eyed bodyguards stood with him, one in front and one behind. Their manner and postures reminded him that although he had made this journey to a liaison with their Italian counterparts, this time he could be stepping into an ambush.

"Sir," said Vaso, his chief protector. "I will go on ahead and check."

"Vaso, no one knows of my arrival. I do not expect that there has been a 'shoot-on-sight' policy as yet," he said, but on seeing the big Tirana native's expression, added, "Thirty seconds. Then I will be coming down."

Vaso smiled before spew-spitting a cupful of blood and bone into his face. Sali's feet refused to move as Vaso's claret-mashed lower face collapsed with its body.

In a moment, his brain told him his second bodyguard had been shot in the face too. The pouring back to reality made him focus on the ferry staff's uniform, only the wearer of it seemed more western European—German, Dutch or British.

He never found out the nationality of the man with the ash-blond hair. The bullet tore through his face, taking his life with it.

11

Bruce McQuillan walked into a corner office of Interpol Headquarters in Lyon, France.

Chen Zhao, the president of the multi-agency, stood to greet him.

Bruce admired the Shanghai national's eclectic sense of fashion. Today he wore a grey formal business suit with the mandarin collar matched by the white shirt beneath.

An inoffensive bright cream paint covered the walls, and the white blinds were half shut. A standing lamp-sized flag with the Interpol emblem stood to Zhao's side.

The organisation's remit was to support and promote co-operation between police forces worldwide, irrespective of the political relationship between nations.

Not long back, Bruce had inserted Connor into the least tourist-friendly parts of Ukraine to locate and rescue a British national. It turned into the saving of numerous children held by a madman intent on pitting Russia and much of the Islamic world against one another.

Chen had sheepishly admitted he lacked any sort of assets in the region, and Bruce had rectified that.

A professional relationship was born and Chen, despite a diary Bruce knew must be crammed, always made time for him.

"Bruce, good to see you," said Chen with seeming sincerity. Bruce suspected the Chinese native's flawless English had even more clarity to a British ear than Bruce's own.

"You too, Chen."

"Please, take a seat."

They sat facing one another across the polished desk.

Chen spoke, "Never in any of our meetings have you stayed long enough to enjoy your tea, so I hope you do not take it as impolite."

"Of course not."

"So, what would you like to know?"

"What are your current challenges today?"

Chen tapped his fingers on the table. "All types of cybercrime are major concerns. Economic globalisation has made corruption borderless. Crimes against children have been exacerbated by the internet—though in some regards, offenders are easier to catch. Money laundering is getting more and more high-tech."

"What about specific groups?"

"Italian mafias tend to have their hands in most things, although for some strange reason we seem to be experiencing some mild relief in that area."

"How?"

Faint lines briefly appeared on Chen's forehead. "One of our major challenges came from the alliance formed by the 'Ndrangheta and the Mafia Shqiptare. The Albanians' ruthlessness and cunning, combined with the Calabreses' expertise in money laundering and criminal finance. However, for some unknown reason, they seem to be at war with one another."

Bruce feigned the absorption of this information as being new to him.

"Can you ascertain who has the ascendency at the moment?"

Chen shrugged. "Due to the secrecy and expanse of both organisations, it is difficult to tell. If my life depended on it, I would say the Albanians."

"Why is that?"

"Intelligence has always indicated the general basis of the relationship was one of the 'Ndrangheta guiding them in the ways of high-level laundering in exchange for the Albanians' heavy lifting. This was to reduce their exposure—indeed, when the world thinks of Italian mafias they think of the Sicilians and some maybe the Camorra—they have always been less discreet and there is even a television show depicting them. But this reliance has worked against them. The Albanians know the routes, safe houses, drop-off points because they protect them."

"Surely the Albanians will struggle in the long term when they can't clean their money?"

Bruce liked to feign ignorance on certain matters and occasions.

Chen's chest briefly expanded. "They are not ignorant on the subject. And they can survive on more of a subsistence level—at least for a while. And there're other European financiers out there. People who will not say 'no' to money, however obtained."

"Any concerns regarding potential replacements in the power vacuum that may follow? Is there a possibility of destabilisation causing even more misery than previously?"

"There are always entities ready to fill the void, as you are aware. But monopolies are extremely dangerous and that is—or maybe if we get lucky and this continues—was the case with the 'Ndrangheta," he said, taking a breath. "I would not ever say this out of present company, but the ideal scenario would be for both to decimate one another to the point of mutual weakness. And the more they kill one another, the greater opportunity it gives us for arrests."

"I am not against fulfilling quotas per se—as long as they are legitimate."

"Let's hope their conflict remains between them."

Bruce stared at the Interpol emblem for a moment.

"I wanted to ask you something, but must caution you not to get excited, as it's very much hearsay, perhaps nothing more than an internet rumour."

Chen turned his open palms up. "We are just talking."

"Heard anything about certain people going missing and being sent to a facility—perhaps an island—to be indoctrinated before being re-employed elsewhere?"

Chen looked to be in thought for a few moments. "No. I haven't heard anything specific. However, I have been aware of certain highly skilled people disappearing for a few weeks only to reappear in places you would not expect."

"If it is true, what would be your thoughts as to whoever was behind it?"

Chen's eyes unfocused themselves in thought for a few moments.

"Wealth and global reach—deep as well as wide—would go without saying. I would presume a great degree of subtlety given the targets involved, so I would initially rule out Central and South American cartels. Tight security and strong organisation."

This correlated to Bruce's own thoughts, who said, "Do you know the identities of the missing persons?"

"I am sorry, but because none have broken the law, I have not remembered names or specifics, Bruce."

"Could you find out?"

"Of course. Check your e-mail by the end of the day."

Bruce stood and held out his hand. "I appreciate it."

They shook hands and he left.

Salvatore stared back at the various members of the Camera di Controllo, displaying a mask of obedience. When he had first been present at a Camera di Controllo meeting over two decades ago, it had been ten men stood in a circle smoking, as the San Biagio Festival in Puglia danced, sang and cheered around them.

Now, over thirty men sat stone-faced with self-importance around an enormous, highly polished mahogany table in a palace outside of Rome.

Like any business, a few made most of the money, and some of the men present were not amongst them.

Still, it would not be long until Salvatore would be able to bend them to his will without the need for a politician's smile or subterfuge.

The meeting had gone as predicted; commiserations on the death of his sister, proclamations of understanding for his striking back at the Mafia Shqiptare and finally, a request to ceasefire.

Salvatore stood. "Our collective interests must supersede any one man's desire. Please pardon me for any transgressions of mine regarding this matter. Of course, I will parley for peace."

He fought against sneering at the expressions of avuncular forgiveness on some of the cowardly and weak men.

With a bow, he left.

Raphael Del Piero approached the gathering before the Brindisi policemen cleared them away to enable him to enter the cordon.

Raphael guessed the policemen knew who he was. As one of the most aggressive investigative officers in ROS (*Raggruppamento Operativo Speciale*), the principal investigative arm of the Carabinieri, dealing with organised crime and terrorism, he had been dispatched to the triple murder scene on the ferry.

There had been a brief struggle as to whose jurisdiction this came under; three Albanian citizens dead on a ferry owned by an Albanian company. However, Raphael's boss's connections ensured the vessel's swift commandeering before the Albanians could physically intervene.

He recognised his point of contact, a respected crime scene investigator, and introduced himself with a smile. "You must be Mr Zaniolo."

The older man with a full head of grey, replied, "And you must be Mr Del Piero. You must call me Ciro."

"Raphael," he said, as they shook hands. "Any witnesses?"

"One of the female staff thought she saw the back of a man she didn't recognise walking away from the stairwell from the upper floor. He was wearing a staff uniform. She is the one that discovered the bodies."

"Where is she now?"

"Still on board. I guessed you would want to speak to her."

Ciro's feet clunked up the stairs in front of him.

The staff were dispersed throughout the first floor and were being spoken to by Ciro's officers.

"Let's go upstairs," said the ROS officer.

The scene greeting Raphael was of the three dead men with smashed lower mandibles. However, his eyes caught the rotten leaf placed equidistant between the corpses.

"A symbol for the 'Ndrangheta," he remarked.

"Yes," replied Ciro. "Shot in the mouths? Informants?"

"Maybe. Or maybe the assassin shot them through the medulla. As you are aware, it causes instant paralysis—particularly useful when dealing with armed guards."

"To shoot them with such accuracy would mean he'd have to get close. Maybe they knew him?"

"Or maybe he's that good?"

Ciro kissed his teeth. "That would make him a remarkable shot. The bodyguards' attention would have been on him immediately, so the speed of the shots would have been rapid, and the distance from the toilet or stairwell—his only two points of entry—are both almost twenty metres. Especially impressive with a suppressor."

"The Calabrians have plenty of killers to call on. Maybe they knew the difficulty of this and hired an outsider?" pondered Raphael. "CCTV?"

"I sent two of my most trusted officers. The footage is distorted beyond the point of use. The strange thing is, the real-time clarity is perfect, it's the recordings that are blurred."

Raphael shook his head. "The 'Ndrangheta have a proven ability to infiltrate the upper echelons of government and finance, so local port security wouldn't have been too much of a challenge. And no threats or promises on our part will persuade them to talk."

"So, what can we do?"

"You can decide if there is anything in it for your department. If so, then you can take it, if not, I'll be happy to accept ownership."

The older man looked at him. "I am happy for the ROS to take this."

Raphael had guessed as much. "Good, because I have a feeling this is the first salvo in a coming storm, and whoever this assassin is, he'll be highly sought after by those who want people killed."

12

Connor Reed felt almost childlike in relation to the size of the bed.

"Making this bed must be a workout. You bought it for orgies or something?"

Long fingers flicked the jet-black hair aside to reveal the beguiling face of Monique Bayer next to him.

"I have a maid."

"Of course you do."

The room felt palatial to him. The long, heavy, rich chocolate curtains swept down from their white-painted frames. Towering cream pillars at the foot of the bed held up the roof. White rugs cut into shapes of interlocking swirls lay beneath a long dressing table. Above it were pictures and ornaments—his eyes were drawn to a painting of a woman flying with a shoal of winged fish over a seaside town. A lamp of black feathers hung from the ceiling.

He knew being one of the world's leading violinists had helped the thirty-six-year-old Italian-Austrian become a multi-millionaire.

However, he had been shocked at the size and grandeur of the temple-style mansion on the outskirts of Rome. Last night, as he rode up the long marble path on a rented Honda Goldwing, he had initially thought it to be a communal abode. The balmy trees were watching him, as lights on the tiled roof highlighted the cylindrical pillars manfully holding it up. Foundation sculptures edged the white, smooth stoned driveway. He rode around the back to park the black Goldwing out of sight, only to be astonished at the Olympic-sized swimming pool, enclosed in white marble with statues at either end.

"Can I ask you a personal question?"

She turned to him, propping her head on her hand. Looking at her face provided evidence for his theory that the more naturally beautiful a woman, the less make-up did to enhance her attractiveness. Monique seemed just as striking now as she did when he first met her at a social function over half a year ago.

"You may."

"Well, you're—according to Google—one of the most talented violinists on the planet. I read somewhere you are 'proof that God exists'."

She smirked and nodded her head playfully. He continued, "And you have model-like good looks and don't feign modesty."

She simply shrugged her shoulders. "What is your point?"

A knock at the door interrupted his response. She covered her breasts and called out, "Entra e lascialo sul tavolo della toeletta. Grazie."—*Come in and leave it on the dressing table. Thank you*

A maid stepped in, placing a tray of drinks, cold and warm, as well as a plate of Italian baked eggs and sausages, and a frittata Florentine—an Italian omelette.

Monique turned to him and said, "Why did you do this?" before mimicking the way he flinched.

"Just a left-over reflex from pulling women in Leeds and having their kids walk in the next morning."

She blinked twice. "Maybe your humour will improve once you have eaten."

It especially impressed Connor, as it had been a late hour when he rode in, when Monique had nonchalantly asked what he would like for breakfast. As she got out of the bed, he got to admire her. The twin grooves running either side of her spine and the soft lines shaping her calves and shoulders hinted at good genes. The softness of her hips and ass told of her Italian love of food and drink. Her hair intrigued him as it seemed almost unnaturally black.

When she brought back the tray, she seemed to sense his awareness not to mark the sheets and said, "Do not let a material that can be replaced stop your pleasure of your food."

Her Italian accent had a soothing allure. And his omelette did taste superb. In between mouthfuls he asked, "My point was—before we were interrupted—how come you're not a household name? I mean, I know you're famous, but I thought you'd be known to young and old across the western world and beyond…apologies, I got a bit carried away there."

Connor fixed his eyes to her face as she answered, and not her bare tits.

"I had many offers around a decade ago. But if the corporate machine gets hold of an attractive woman they use her until her beauty fades, then she is left out in the cold."

"Then you could argue you should strike while the iron is hot, so to speak."

"You could but you would be wrong," she said, stretching like a cat. "The system grips young girls, squeezes everything out of them—*insensata* interviews where they are asked the same questions over and over. Photographic shoots that last for hours and where you are ordered around like a trained dog. It is all exhausting and while all this is to be going on, your time and energy are being used up, when it could go to what made your talent in the first place."

Connor digested this and asked, "All right, if you've turned down all these offers and opportunities, then how—if you don't mind me asking—are you able to afford a rotation of maids, a home that Caesar could live in and a chauffeur-driven Bentley?"

She frowned. "How do you know it is chauffeur-driven?"

"Come on." He laughed. "You're only a dainty woman."

The force of the back of her hand colliding with his face balanced between spite and playfulness. "Sexism will not be tolerated in this bedroom."

"That intolerance will be the Austrian in you."

She ignored the barb with, "Ahhh, so you should know my Austrian side—my practical side—comes from my father, who is an investment banker and taught his only child from a young age. Almost two decades of intelligent investing, and here we are," she said theatrically, raising her arms, and her tits, proudly.

"If you could impart anything in the brief time we have together, what would it be?"

"So, I am to be your teacher?"

"I am always open to learning."

She sipped her coffee and said, "You will need a notepad."

"No, I won't."

"Why is that?"

"A man in my profession needs a mind sharp enough to remember without needing to take notes."

"And what profession is that?"

"And you're far too sharp not to have guessed."

She remained quiet for a few moments before she said, "My father made me a limited company for tax purposes. People whispered it was silly as I was barely sixteen years old. The very next year, the company received an anonymous five-figure donation. Naturally, my father had been curious who had sent it. Having the influence he had, he eventually discovered it had been Van Der Saar."

"What's your point?"

"My point is, he has become like family to me, and I have never seen him show as much warmth and respect to a man as he does to you. Can you explain that?"

Connor shook his head. "Sometimes people just click."

"Like us?"

"No. I am just using you for the knowledge of investing you have yet to give me."

She slid further into the bed before turning to him and patting the pillow next to her. He mirrored and faced the dark pools of her eyes.

She began, "Firstly, you will attack any personal debts you have—business debt is a very different thing, you need that to live into the future—but personal debt is a form of slavery, with mortgages being the worst. Because a person pays it over decades, they are not aware how much it costs them—like the frog in the pot allowing itself to be boiled as the temperature is increased very slowly."

"I see, so I've eliminated my credit cards, car finance and mortgage—what next?"

"Next are your investments. They need to be diverse for two reasons. One is you must not put all your eggs in a single basket, you know why?"

He frowned. "Because if you drop your basket you break all your eggs—it isn't a saying exclusive to Italians, Monique."

"OK. Also, different investments have different time frames and risk." She sighed with a smile. "But you already know this, so why don't you be a man, and tell me what you really want to know?"

He looked at the ceiling. "OK, why can't someone tickle themselves? And for what purpose do men have nipples?"

She looked at him quizzically. "What?"

"Nothing. I'll google those answers," he answered before turning to her. "What I need to know is whether there is anyone here in Italy who would be willing to guide me in the building or acquisition of a business."

"Why would you want to build one in Italy? Why not at home?"

"Tax purposes."

"You know you are playing a dangerous game attempting to set up a business here for 'tax purposes'. There might be interest from organisations you may not want to be interested."

"Or maybe I would."

She peered into his eyes and said, "I believe that you will not be changing your mind, no matter what I tell you."

"I am aware of the dangers."

"Then what are they? Just so I know that you know."

"The worst danger would be members of my family getting raped, tortured and killed while I am forced to watch, before I get raped, tortured and killed."

"It isn't just your family. It can be anyone close to you."

"I know." He mock-sighed. "All I wanted in life was to be afforded the opportunity to eat a great omelette in massive bed without having to worry about staining the covers. If I go down this road, this will be taken away from me."

She laughed through her nose. "You are a strange man."

"Handsome though."

"Your looks are a little above an average man," she said. "Your personality makes you attractive."

"And I'll never lose that."

She ignored him to say, "There is a man who may be able to help you. I can arrange an appointment."

"Maybe it's best that I see this person without an appointment. Then there is no link to you."

"He wouldn't see you without my recommendation."

He remained quiet for a few moments as he stared at the painting, before saying, "If that's the only way, then I'd appreciate it."

"It's good to have friends, isn't it?"

Connor looked up at the feathered lamp.

"It certainly is."

Louis Allen lay on his lounger, staring out into the beautiful turquoise sea, as a cool breeze feathered along skin that, already dark to start with, was looking only a few shades off being as black as an eye's pupil.

His mild frustration danced with his contentment. Frustrated, because St Lucia was just as lush as he thought it would be, and he was now feeling vaguely bored with the place—*if I can't fully chill here, where will I ever be able to?*

Happy, because he knew he was not going to lapse into softness. He had seen that repeatedly during his rise in the London criminal underworld.

He could not understand how some guys, thirsty to have the freedom to make their own moves, endured danger and strife to make that happen, only to grow soft when on top, before finding themselves taken out by a version of their past selves.

He knew now, that would not be him—he buzzed off the cut and thrust of it all. He looked down at his phone. He had promised himself a rest from it when he had started his holiday. That promise had lasted nine hours, but he had been limiting it.

Louis had thought of how his already successful business had received an injection in recent months. His friend—his Oppo—Connor Reed, had warned him to discontinue the EncroChat network he had all of his guys on. He did so, reluctantly, as it meant a complete overhaul of his businesses' communication network, and reaped the benefits of several of his competitors being taken out of action as the police raids came.

He cracked and flicked on his phone. After a few minutes, his interest spiked as he got to a message sent by 'T'.

He dialled the number of his Oppo's elder cousin, Tom Ryder.

Connor sat on the vast, blue-matted area in the lotus position. The Roma Lupo Brazilian Jiu-jitsu Academy lay on the city's edge and was its premier competition club.

He had resolved himself to training in the Gi for the past six months, at first with George Follet—a UK MMA legend contracted by Bruce to train his agents—and a club in south-west Leeds, who graded him a blue belt.

He recalled Follet's cockney accent clarifying the benefits of training wearing the Gi: 'If you're pinned in the *Kimono*, you can't facking slip out with sweat, you have to use your technique. Remember, people can still fight with broken limbs, but no facker can scrap when they are unconscious—and the Gi reminds ya to protect your throat, as people go for these ropes,' he'd said, pulling on his own Gi lapels before continuing, 'And people who say it has no application on the street don't know what they are talking about—all right, maybe you won't be doing the *Berimbolo* on some heathen in a pub, but the first thing any facker does when they're on the floor is to start grabbing whatever you're wearing, so you need to know how to negate that.'

Though NoGi (as in without the Gi) remained Connor's preference, he knew way above blue belt level in the Gi.

The heavyset instructor with a thinning pate and thick black beard barked out a few Italian sentences and the class lined up at one side. They began a series of movements from one side to the other to warm up until finally the instructor shouted, "Ottieni un partner."—*Get a partner.*

Connor turned to the brown belt next to him and asked, “Hai qualcuno?”—*Do you have anyone?*

The man stood a touch taller and broader than Connor, who put him in his late forties. He shook his head and asked, “Di dove sei?”—*Where are you from?*

“Inghilterra.”

“I can speak English very well, if you prefer,” said the man, whose full head of grey hair softened to white around his ears.

Connor smiled. “Thank you. I was getting to the limit of my Italian vocabulary.”

The man smiled. “My name is Alessio.”

“Connor.”

For the next half an hour, the instructors demonstrated various sweeping techniques from *the guard* position. Though Connor used a mental sequencing technique to remember the steps shown, Alessio gave a few pointers throughout when they practised.

The technical absorption part of the session came to an end, and the instructor announced it would be free rolling.

Without asking, Alessio lay on his back in a manner of a father about to play fight with his young son. Connor hid his smile.

The timer sounded, and Connor stepped one foot forward. As anticipated, Alessio swung in for the De La Riva. Before he could set up a sweep, Connor’s sublimely executed long step struck the casualness off Alessio’s face, as only the Italian’s steel-like frame prevented an immediate pass.

Connor eventually whipped around to the other side of Alessio’s torso and secured the pin. The higher belt escaped, and a battle ensued for the rest of the round. Using an *IBJJF* competition point tally in his head, Connor had Alessio edging the round.

At the end of the five minutes, Connor stuck out his hand and said, "Grazie, good roll."

As Alessio gripped his hand, he said, "Do you want to go again?"

Connor nodded.

The remaining five times five-minute rounds were hard fought. Connor kept a neutral expression to disguise any effect the pace was having on him. Alessio could not hide the heaviness of his breathing. At the end, Connor's mental scoreboard had them even on rounds. Neither had submitted to the other.

Connor caught some of the glances directed towards them. In between heavy breaths, Alessio's smile turned into a laugh.

"You are not a blue belt, my friend."

The Yorkshireman returned the smile. "I've done a lot of judo, NoGi and wrestling."

The Italian laughed again before clapping Connor's knee and shaking it. "Thank you for telling me. My ego feels a little better."

Connor noticed that although the instructor had lined up the class, presumably for a summary of the session before dismissing them, Alessio made no attempt to join them. The instructor made no attempt to make him.

"I like how you insisted we complete all six rounds together. Shows you have a thirst for competition. I'd like to see the business advisor."

Alessio smirked. "I guessed with your name being Connor that this was not a coincidence, Mr Reed. Monique must have told you that I would call you though. I am a little disappointed she told you my name."

Connor shook his head. "She dialled the number in front of me—for some reason she doesn't have it saved—and I memorised it. Then I put it through a number recognition scanner and it came up with 'Letta, Prodi and Zaia Investimenti'—and since Monique referred to you as a 'he' and—assuming their genders— Laura Prodi and Camila Zaia are women, I guessed it was you Monique was referring to."

Alessio flicked his leg behind and over the other, and began stretching his glutes. "So, you followed me here?"

"No, I tapped your name into Google. Seems you've made a name for yourself on the jiu-jitsu scene over here."

Alessio regarded him with a nod. "I can see you tomorrow. Ten a.m."

"Thank you." Connor nodded. "Could you maybe not tell Monique we are going to meet?"

"You want me to lie?"

Connor nodded. "The less she knows about my business the better."

He felt a hint of relief when Alessio said, "I understand. There will be no talk of this. I will tell her to say no to you—capisci?"

"Capisci."

"You know who I represent? Specifically?"

"I have an idea, Mr Alessio—I'll say mid-boot —and I am fully aware of the…seriousness of the organisation."

"Good," said Alessio, standing up. "See you tomorrow."

13

Salvatore Mancuso painted on a wry smile at Mario De Filippo's vulgar joke. The Camorra's boss always did like the sound of his own voice.

De Filippo and Vincenzo Loi—the Camorra's underboss—had arrived five minutes ago with their security. Five minutes ago had been seven minutes late, and the casualness of De Filippo's 'Sorry we are late' had been noted by Mancuso. He accepted it, while noting the customary embrace/pat-down had been more thorough than last time. Vincenzo's apology seemed more sincere.

They sat on opposing benches, separated by a wood table stained by drink spillages and cigarettes, in an outdoor picnicking area of Appennino Lucano - Val d'Agri - Lagonegrese National Park. The snow-patched mountain overlooked the park, which was due to close in three minutes. The dark-jacketed security teams—each party brought their own—watched the smattering of visitors wandering the park, seemingly oblivious to the high-powered meeting going on at the table. The small car park opposite Mancuso, and behind De Filippo, contained the vehicles that the four and their security had arrived in. The shine of De Filippo's black Bentley reflected the entire scene back at Mancuso, which gladdened him, as he hated not knowing what was going on behind him.

Italo Mauro, the nearest equivalent the 'Ndrangheta had to a *Capo dei capi*—Boss of bosses—sat to his right, opposite De Filippo. Salvatore sat across from Loi.

When the laughing settled, Mario spoke, "Italo, what the fuck has happened? Word on the street is you've declared war on them, and they ain't happy."

Mancuso hated how Mario thought he and Italo were equals. Mario was forty-four years old and had been in the top position for barely three years. And he revelled in his own notoriety.

The seventy-two-year-old Italo had steered the 'Ndrangheta for nearly fifteen years, after being a key member for decades. He fostered loyalty, made sacrifices, looked after the right people and shunned the shallow pleasures of money and fame. Instead, he had expanded quietly—turning the 'Ndrangheta into a superpower.

Mario bemused Mancuso with his inquiries into the situation between the 'Ndrangheta and the Mafia Shqiptare. A commonality with the 'Ndrangheta and the Cosa Nostra, was a *Casus Belli*—case for war—would usually need to be agreed on by their respective councils; and this was not the case with the Napolitans.

"There has been confusion."

Mario laughed with an edge of derision that made Mancuso seethe. The Camorra boss said, "What's the confusion? You sent our friend's here"—indicating to Mancuso—"sister to take out their biggest boss and many of their financial backers—a spectacular success, and you have our condolences."

Mancuso would have found the subtext of Mario's nonchalance offensive if it hadn't been predictable.

"Thank you, Don De Filippo."

Mario spoke directly to Italo, "Is there anything you'd like to tell me?"

Ordinarily, Italo would have put the upstart in his place with a verbal lashing even as advanced in age as he was. However, he had counselled Mancuso on the drive over—"Let us not show this peacock neither supplication nor disrespect, each would feed his ego. Let us make him feel like an equal. If his uncle was still boss, there would be no doubt of Naples' loyalty towards us in any conflict with the Albanians. This upstart has no such honour."

Mancuso felt a mist of unease as he observed the bodyguards in the black paintwork's reflection—*why are some looking to our table? They should be scanning the walkers or looking out.*

Salvatore spared Italo the indignity of answering the disrespectful Neapolitan. "We have not made any moves against our friends in Tirana. We are still investigating the circumstances. They say my sister was responsible but they have no knowledge of any motive."

"It wasn't their 'story'. The police over there said she went on a murdering spree."

Mancuso kept a neutral expression. He hadn't understood why De Filippo had ascended to the top position when it had been first announced. Vincenzo Loi held five times the respect than the braggart.

In time he understood; De Filippo would form a lightning rod of Italian law enforcement, and a soothed ego didn't vent as much vindictiveness. Another reason that took the shine off the crown was if a boss faced severe charges, he was less likely to be able to inform his way out of dying in prison—if he is the highest and most publicised prize to the justice system, why would they seek leniency in exchange for the lesser-knowns?

De Filippo might have a type of animal cunning and a capacity for violence, but insecurity seeped out of the young Don.

Mancuso spoke, "Our Albanian friends' infiltration of their police force exceeds even our own. Our own investigation into what transpired has been slowed by our separating the reliable from unreliable intelligence."

A young couple meandered down, before walking past. The 'Ndrangheta underboss noticed a fidgetiness in the Camorra bodyguards.

"Are you heading that up?" asked Loi.

Mancuso's anger barely showed as a simmer on his face—but it did show.

"How we conduct our business is our concern."

"I am just saying. A policeman wouldn't be allowed to conduct an investigation into anything to do with his own family, would he?"

He has me there.

"Are you questioning my honour?"

"No one who knows of your reputation would question your honour, Salvatore."

Mancuso, peering into the paintwork, noticed the heads of De Filippo's close protection all looking to their left. It dawned on him—*they are waiting for that couple to disappear.*

His eyes shot over to observe De Filippo nodding an affirmation to his men.

As Mancuso violently pushed Italo to the floor, he screamed, "Draw your weapons."

One of Mancuso's measures had been that the security teams for the 'Ndrangheta leadership received regular and hard close protection training from the best. Italo, in his old-school attitude of wanting to keep the business separated to any influence from outside forces, had initially resisted. However, Mancuso had persisted and not only had things run smoother from a security perspective but had been of benefit when the guns came out.

Amid the cracking wasps, he ripped his Beretta M9—fifteen rounds, iron-clad reliability, 9mm calibre—from where he had taped it on the underside of the table; one of the benefits of arriving to a meet early. And Mancuso could hit a bird at thirty metres.

He scrambled for purchase with his feet, diving to shield Italo. The closing assassin squad had become target-fixated on the 'Ndrangheta bodyguards.

Mancuso's first shot hit the closest in the chest, with his second grazing a half-joker smile as the assassin fell. He drew a bead on his next target, only to see him fall under a hail of bullets.

Curses and grunts spun his head around to see Loi wrestling with De Filippo, gripping the wrist in which the Don held a flick knife.

Mancuso understood— De Filippo was trying to kill Italo.

With the assassins neutralised, Mancuso stood, whipped around the table, and placed his Beretta against De Filippo's head. "Either your brains or blade will be on the ground in two seconds."

De Filippo released the blade, and Mancuso snatched it up. Italo stood by his side as their security closed in—there were two missing.

"Where are Gianluigi and Francesco?" asked Italo.

One of the bodyguards said, "Gianluigi has been hit, Francesco is attending to him."

Italo nodded and looked to Mancuso. "We don't have much time."

"Hold him down," said the underboss.

"By Mother Mary you'll all die," screamed De Filippo.

"Pin his head," commanded Mancuso, and a pair of knees wedged the thrashing mafioso's head, along with several pressing hands.

Under Mancuso's grasp, the tip of his own flick knife pierced both left eyelid and eyeball. The sound De Filippo made was like a blend between a trapped wild animal and The Joker's laugh. After two minutes, Mancuso said, "If you run, you will die."

"I won't."

The 'Ndrangheta underboss gestured to his men to release him, before saying, "I know you have only one good eye. You can either live the rest of your life with one eye or completely blind. Why did you attempt to take us out?"

"The Albanians. They sent an emissary. Offered me millions and said all their business dealings would go through us from now on."

"How were you going to explain it was just us that got hit and none of your guys?"

"I'd have told people we left before you. The Albanians were going to take credit anyway."

Italo spoke, "And you thought it would remain a secret?"

"They would have had to keep it."

Loi barked, "Do you think I would have?"

De Filippo's good eye scrunched. "It was your idea."

Mancuso levelled the Beretta at De Filippo, who cried, "You said if I told, you'd let me go. Where is your honour?"

Mancuso smiled. "I said you could either live the rest of your life with one eye or completely blind. I didn't say how long that life would be."

"Please, on my sacred honour, I will—"

"Your word means nothing," were the last words De Filippo heard before three bullets destroyed his face.

The breeze combed Connor's hair as he sat at an outside table of a Rome café. He enjoyed watching people criss-crossing the square while diners looked on from the many street cafes.

His dark blue suit jacket wrapped around a light blue shirt, with a white collar, from which sprang a tie that matched his jacket. He'd polished his sunburnt oxfords to impress but not dazzle.

He smiled as the young, dark-haired waitress presented him with his coffee. Ordinarily, he shunned milk but felt compelled to buy one owing to this café's well-known 'cappuccino animal art'. The intricacy of the cat's whiskers and ears impressed him to the point of almost not wanting to drink it.

"Se Leonardo Da Vinci preparasse il caffè"—*If Leonardo Da Vinci prepared coffee*, he said to the waitress, forming an 'O' with his index finger and thumb for 'Italian' emphasis.

She laughed and asked, "Qualsiasi altra cosa ti serve?"—*Do you need anything else?*

He noticed she, like a number of women in the country, had amber eyes.

"No, grazie."

She left with a smile. Connor liked Italy; the way its women dressed, the language, the easy-going ambience, and the food.

The thought occurred to him that he had never been abroad with any of his cousins, and how fun it would be to do so.

He resisted the urge to contact any of them. He enforced his own rule of not contacting or seeking any of his family while away on missions for Bruce McQuillan. Any distraction on an operation might prove fatal, which was partially why he had avoided pursuing a permanent girlfriend.

He briefly thought of Grace—the flame-haired surgeon, full of adventure, intellect, humour and sex appeal. And he purposely steeled himself, dousing any curiosity of how she was getting on.

She should have been the one, he thought. *Stop it. You've got a meeting to attend.*

14

Raphael recognised the man, despite the bone shard pulp where a face used to be.

He had swum through the swathe of crime scene investigators who were snapping photographs, taking swabs from the corpses, examining where the rounds had impacted, and the ground for signs of evidence.

The local officer in charge gestured to the dead body at the table and said, "There's no identification as yet on this one; no wallet or phone. The rest of the bodies are members of the Camorra."

"That's Mario De Filippo."

The officer frowned. "How can you tell?"

"The top of the left ear is missing. Bitten off in a bar fight back in 2005."

Seeing the officer fidget, Raphael added, "It's my profession to know these things, and Naples isn't your jurisdiction."

"There's going to be a storm when this gets out."

Raphael could sense the jangling of the officer's nerves. Years ago, encountering this attitude shocked him—*why be in law enforcement if you weren't willing to do whatever was necessary to uphold it?* As time went by, he understood—though for reasons that hardened his resolve, whereas others shied away.

"After the first stage evidence has been collected, you can hand them over and we'll take full responsibility for the case. You may inform the media accordingly."

Relief briefly appeared on the officer's face, before he nodded. "Do you have any ideas at this early stage? A hit?"

"A hit gone wrong, I think."

"Gone wrong? Seems like there's plenty dead to me."

"The dead bodyguards belong to De Filippo, but the arrangement of their bodies is important, I think. See? They are facing him. They've been shot at distance, whereas he has been executed at close range. There're a couple of your people over there—my guess, they've found blood."

The officer looked at him quizzically. "So, what do you think, exactly?"

Raphael looked around, selecting in the theatre of his mind the scene that fit the best. Ordinarily, he kept his thoughts to himself but decided to throw the officer a bone.

"I reckon this was a high-level meeting hid in plain sight. This part of the park is quite secluded with no cameras. De Filippo was sitting in front of his intended target, or he might have had a companion sat beside him who planned it. I reckon the target's, or targets' security, were positioned adjacent—a mirror image of how De Filippo's team were set out."

Raphael gestured with his head for the officer to follow him as he began circling the murder scene. When they had a side-on view, he said, "I think the Camorra team must have given something away to their opposite number. A shootout took place. I am unsure why it seems the unknown team outfought De Filippo's team—maybe something distracted them, or luck, or they were simply better. Let's get a closer look at the meeting table."

They wandered over, and the forensics team moved away under Raphael's polite request.

"OK. Someone was sitting next to De Filippo but not now. This could mean they let him escape. If he's been allowed to sit at a high-level meeting by the Camorra Godfather's side, there could only be a handful of people who it could be."

"So, that's a good thing, yes?"

"It remains to be seen if any of this will be a good or bad thing. What it will be is a storm of upheaval."

In the distance, he could see the black Alfa Romeo Giulia of a team from the ROS.

Raphael thought about the ferry murders, and his instinct told him they must be connected.

The officer asked him, "What now?"

"Now," began Raphael, "we will take over from here."

"My boss will have something to say about the case being handed over."

Raphael shook his head. "When I inform your boss of who it is I think it might be, he's going to beg for us to take it off his hands."

Connor sat in the waiting lounge of 'Letta, Prodi and Zaia Investimenti'.

The greyish-blue felt seating curved in a semi-circle, looking out onto the urban streets of Rome. A black glass table, supported by red oak, inverted pyramids formed the centrepiece.

A bespectacled and suited woman of around fifty sat on the edge to his left, and a man in his early thirties, with a tie and slicked black hair, to his right, a little closer in.

Connor took one of the business cards from a chrome holder and used his pen to write on the back.

The wall-mounted television appeared to be purely screen and no edge. It curved around, enabling it to be viewed from anywhere in the entire room. It hadn't been the flickering images of a murder scene that had initially drawn his attention to it, but the two receptionists whispering, nudging and subtle gestures towards it.

His Italian was proficient enough to decipher an assassination of a mafia boss and a contingent of his men had taken place in Appennino Lucano - Val d'Agri - Lagonegrese National Park. His mind located the province of Potenza of Basilicata, where the murders had taken place, and he guessed it to be nearly four hours away. His heartrate quickened a little on hearing the name Mario De Filippo.

Connor knew the Camorra's structure differed to the 'Ndrangheta and Cosa Nostra in that instead of having a pyramid of hierarchy, it was more a horizontal conglomerate of formidable families from the Neapolitan region. However, he was also aware Mario De Filippo was the head of the most powerful clan, and his slaying would have far-reaching consequences.

The reception phone rang, and one of the women answered it. After a moment, she put it down and called out cheerily, "Signor Reed. Può entrare adesso."—*You can enter now.*

Connor stood and made towards the door. As he came level to the receptionists, he turned to the taller of the two, and said, "Mi piace molto come ha fatto i capelli."—*I really like how you've done your hair.*

She beamed him a smile, her hand hovering as if to touch it, and said, "Grazie."

That's it, thought Connor, *compliment them on their effort, not their natural gifts.*

Connor refrained from knocking as was his habit and entered.

The view of urban Rome filled the entire right side through glass so clean only the seams between the panes indicated it existed. A painting of a black horse peering through white mist was the sole interest in the otherwise plain, beige wall.

The lack of any other furniture or storage stood out to Connor.

Alessio looked even more impressive in his woollen grey and blue striped business suit, with a dark tie.

Looking at the suit reminded him of something Bruce had told him once. "*Wealthy people not in the public eye don't shop for clothing brands, they have their clothes custom-made.*"

"It's good to see you, Mr Reed. Please take a seat."

When Connor did so, Alessio asked, "How can I be of help?"

"I have a heavy goods transportation company that delivers from Ukraine to all over Europe. My knowledge of managing my financial assets is, of course, rudimentary in comparison to yours, but I understand the importance of diversification, and that includes advisors."

"So, you have an advisor back in your homeland but wish to have others?"

Connor knew he was fishing; he wanted to know just how many he had, so he could gauge the size of the Englishman's operation.

Instead, he answered, "I believe the term 'don't put your eggs in one basket' is used over here?"

"I know the saying."

"Then, you'll know part of the reason why I am here."

Alessio subtly leaned back in his chair. "Different baskets could be found within your own country."

"True, but the further the baskets are away from one another, the harder it is for someone to find and break all your eggs."

"I understand," said Alessio, his fingers giving the table a tap. "However, I look after the investments of people here who require my constant attention."

"Maybe you should diversify," Connor replied. "Besides, I am not looking for anything too dynamic. Just something stable and long term. I am not looking to get in early on the next Apple or Facebook."

Alessio looked at him without speaking for a few moments. "Do you have any ideas yourself before I suggest my own?"

"I could bring cash to you, and you could put it into an investment which I would pay my government tax on. I was also thinking about becoming an avid collector and seller of fine art. I hear there're many talented artists in Italy."

Connor had already experimented with buying and selling art as a means of money laundering. Because its value was subjective, if the seller was willing, the piece's invoice could be marked as being much lower than the money he paid—the surplus being paid in 'dirty' cash. The piece could then be sold on at its intended price, thus presenting a 'clean' invoice to the taxman.

"You don't need a financial advisor to guide you in the world of Italy's art world."

He wants me to say it.

"True, but I need an advisor to guide me in handling the money I obtain after selling the pieces."

Alessio steepled his fingers. "Am I correct to think you want your money to be tax-efficient?"

"That would be a correct assumption."

"I have a large amount—roster, I think you say—of clients, and —"

"I am sure the fees you will charge me will compensate for the extra time and effort."

"What I was going to say was that my current clients might not wish for me to take on others at this time."

"They might not. Perhaps you can ask them if there is anything I can do to ease their concerns. With me being a foreigner, I could be useful."

"That might not be a path you would wish to journey on."

"Or it might," said Connor. "Be that as it may, my businesses are suffering from the opposite most are—there's too much cash flow and not enough possibilities for reinvestment."

He kept his back straight. This was his way of telling Alessio he was a criminal without telling him.

The Italian said, "Of course, I have done my research before you came. Information on you is difficult to obtain. However, I know of your involvement with Signor Raymond Van Der Saar.

The Dutch are indeed more open than the Italian businessmen who make up much of my client base; however, it is good to have references."

"Good to know."

"Any more ideas?"

"Yes. There're a few wind farms dotted around Europe I have been prospecting. I have them on a digital file for you to look at. I would like to invest my money in alternative energy since that is the future."

Alessio showed a hint of a smile. "And I guess none of these farms are in the United Kingdom?"

"The European Union is very forward-thinking in its grants towards these types of altruistic endeavours, and I would like to take advantage before the door is fully closed to me."

"As I have stated previously, though I own my business there are…silent partners I will have to discuss your proposals with. It may take a while to get you an answer. Are you staying in Rome for a while?"

"I won't be far away."

"How do you like our Italian food?"

"Superb, as to be expected."

"Any particular favourites?"

"I am a fan of the frittata Florentine. And I indulged myself in a couple of tiramisu crepes that were special."

Alessio nodded before asking, "Is there a way to contact you?"

Connor reached into his jacket pocket and removed the business card.

"My details are on the back."

Alessio subtly nodded. "Forward-thinking. This is good."

Writing a name and phone number on the back of his own business card, he handed it to Connor and said, "This is one of Rome's best tour guides. Book yourself on for Saturday. I may meet you there. If I do not, then your proposal has been rejected."

Salvatore sat outside, overlooking his rural estate. He nursed a glass of red wine grown from the vineyard in the distance to his left. The farmland before him stretched out for half a kilometre before dipping into the valley. In the far distance, the mountains threatened to fade into the sky.

His grandfather had once tilled these soils as a teenager. That was until he decided he wanted ownership. It had struck Salvatore how one man could ignite a fire of change. The Mancusos had been peasants for generations preceding his grandfather's birth. And now, here Salvatore was, a mere two generations on, arguably the most powerful man within perhaps the most influential outlaw enterprise on the planet.

Italo was still the boss of bosses—*Capo dei capi*—but Mancuso wielded the greater influence. The likelihood the old man would ever venture out beyond Calabria again in the wake of the assassination attempt was virtually nil in Mancuso's estimations.

For the past ten days, 'Ndrangheta-controlled ports and transportation routes had been continuously hit by Albanian ghosts, costing the organisation significantly in finance and reputation—the South and Central Americans already expressing nervousness.

This had caused *La Santa*—the secret society within the 'Ndrangheta—to request Salvatore be called in front of the *Camera di Controllo*—the 'Ndrangheta's Board of Control.

La Santa was still a highly controversial committee within 'Ndrangheta, as it included state representatives who joined through Freemasonry—with whom fraternising was strictly against the wider 'Ndrangheta code. However, it was this committee—whose roots could be traced to the sixties, and whose real birth came after a brutal and bloody civil war in the seventies—that had helped give the Calabrese crime organisation the security and intelligence to turn itself into a global superpower.

Due to their divisive nature, they only called meetings for matters of extreme seriousness. And though the Camera di Controllo comprised only members of the 'Ndrangheta, Mancuso knew he would have to do something to assuage both their concerns or—despite his power—his life would be in danger.

He heard the quiet footsteps of one of the housemaids behind him, and asked, "Is he here?"

"Yes, Senor Mancuso."

"Send him into the dining room."

She left.

Salvatore did not wish his place of private reflection sullied by the presence of the corrupt policeman. He drained off his glass, tucked in his finely woven shirt and made his way in.

He found Giorgio sat, drumming his fingers impatiently, on one of the table chair's armrests. Salvatore watched his face in a mirror from the shadows—a mask of impetuous arrogance. However, when Salvatore came into view, Giorgio's face instantly transformed into an expression of congeniality.

Fucking serpent, he thought, before realising the hypocrisy; he kept the disdain off his face every time he met with the corrupt officer.

"How are you, Giorgio?"

"Life is a gift."

"It is a gift that was taken from Mario De Filippo two days ago. Have you heard anything regarding that?"

Giorgio shifted in his seat. "The Camorra are forever involved in blood feuds. They're a collection of street gangs."

"The Camorra has been listed as the fourth most dangerous organised crime syndicate to the United States, according to that nation's reports. They are not simply a collection of street gangs, as you term them."

"Maybe my wording is not appropriate, but the sentiment is true. We know they are constantly at war, and De Filippo has many enemies."

"Who is in charge of the case?"

"Raphael Del Piero—he's an officer in the ROS."

Salvatore's stomach tightened on hearing the name.

"So, why did you request a meeting, Giorgio?"

The policeman's lips drew back to reveal his cigarette-stained teeth. "I have some interesting news regarding your sister's death."

"Proceed."

"It seems my guess of the nationality of your sister's companion the night of the massacre was woefully incorrect, according to the security team. She may have been from the United Kingdom."

Mancuso kept his face impassive. "How have you drawn that conclusion?"

"Picked up on ROS wiretaps three days ago. Those files are closed even for me, and I can't dig without arousing suspicion. The information has not been released to Albanian law enforcement as yet, and probably never will."

"Because they fear the exposure of whatever agents they currently have over there," replied Mancuso, rhetorically. "Could you have been misinformed? There has been no reaction from the British."

"I haven't found any information regarding a British woman being identified at the scene."

"So, you're suggesting she survived? Would seem strange she was not recorded on the security cameras leaving?"

"There was one vehicle that left before the fire. The only visiting vehicle allowed onto the property, and it belonged to the caterer."

Mancuso's eyes narrowed almost imperceptibly. "Her name?"

"I haven't been able to obtain that information yet."

"Why?"

"Because prying into other people's investigations always carries risks, and those in other countries even more so. It takes money to grease the wheels."

Mancuso feigned an expression of consideration. The reality was, he would pay whatever he needed to obtain even a shred of evidence regarding the truth of events that night. And he knew Giorgio knew he would. It was not the policeman's request for money that angered the 'Ndrangheta underboss—it was the blatant revealing of his greed, and it would be that voracity for cash that would begin to drown him. And most drowning men would grip anything to help pull them from the water, even a poisonous branch. Mancuso seethed—he had allowed his own eagerness to show, and now this pig was attempting to take advantage.

"How much do you want?"

"Double our current arrangement should suffice."

"The intelligence you provide had better be of the highest value if you wish for the doubling of your compensation."

Giorgio opened his arms in a gesture of transparency and mild offence. "I always try to provide you with the best."

"That you do, Giorgio. That is why I reward you accordingly."

Watching Giorgio leave, he hoped the others he employed could be relied on to give him what he needed.

15

As Hasan peered through his binoculars at the 'Ndrangheta protection team, he saw the cleverness of Andrei's plan.

He and his team of five had arrived in Bavaria two days before. This had been his ninth time in the country, and apart from a brief visit to Munich, his first time this far into the Bavarian Alps.

His team, along with several others, had spent just short of two weeks continuously hitting 'Ndrangheta targets without taking a single casualty, despite the Italians increasing their security.

Hassan lay high up, clad in camouflage fatigues, hidden in the treeline, overlooking the trucking depot. Through the condensation of his breath he could see the seven men's Calabrian blood did not like the cold.

In the wake of Sali's murder, Andrei had made it clear to him an attempt to strike back in their urban heartland of Reggio di Calabria would be futile—they would be identified before they could take any action.

Instead, his plan of attack had revolved around disrupting their drug transportation routes. Most were known intimately by the Mafia Shqiptare, as it had been they who were protecting them.

Now that war had been declared, the 'Ndrangheta sent soldiers; but as Andrei had told him, they wouldn't have enough hardened professionals to cover them all—and weak links were there to be attacked.

In the distance, Hasan watched the tiny beacons of vehicle lights, and a scan with his binoculars confirmed that there were three trucks, and right on time—*just as Andrei said they would be.*

Indeed, Hasan had been impressed by the recent, unerringly accurate intelligence Andrei had supplied him. Strange though, as Hasan now held the title of Mik—the clan's liaison and coordinating officer—and thus traditionally, it would have been the Mik's role to supply the Kyre—boss—not the other way around. That said, Andrei's position just prior to assuming the role of Kyre had been the Mik of the clan, as opposed to being the second in command—the *Kyretar Ramiz Suxho.* Since both Oso Xhelli and the Kyretar had been killed in the massacre, even Hasan had pondered whether or not Andrei had been complicit.

However, evidence had trickled out via various voice recordings that Eralda Mancuso had acted on the orders of the 'Ndrangheta. With his innocence proven, Andrei was the ideal choice—not least because Oso had decreed him to be in a letter released by his most trusted lawyer.

Hasan whispered into his radio, "Thirty seconds."

He had one of his men with him, and the other three on the opposite hill.

In answering Hasan's desire to steal the trucks, given they were loaded with cocaine, Andrei instead ordered him to kill the men and burn them and the trucks inside the depot.

"Fires bring the fire service. The fire service brings the police. Police bring Interpol, who bring a pressure that will affect our enemy, whose base of operations is in the EU, more than us."

The man is a tactician.

Hasan noticed his adrenaline had not spiked to the degree of some of the earlier ambushes. He knew this was due to the natural physiological response to repeating the same dangerous task without any harm befalling him.

He heard it—a crunch to his left. He made out the shadow approaching through the trees. He slowly rolled onto his side and pointed his weapon in the direction of the threat.

He quickly decided this was some type of security patrol and not an ambush, as they were moving too fast to ensure stealth.

He cursed under his breath. His team's Beretta ARX160 A2s remained unsuppressed.

He whispered into the radio, "Enemy approaching. When the firing begins, Bravo team focus your fire on the truck."

"Acknowledged."

"Alpha Two," said Hasan, referring to the call sign of Gjon, the second member of his fire team. "When I fire, swing right around so you can flank the threat. The number is unknown as yet."

"Acknowledged, Alpha One."

The face appeared from the trees—and disappeared in a burst of pink mist in the same instant.

He fired bursts in the general direction to suppress whoever might be in support. Rolling to change his firing position, as rounds zipped overhead, he *snurgled* behind a huge tree and kept firing.

He resisted the urge to radio through to Gjon for an update, not knowing the enemy's proximity to his favoured soldier.

The weight and accuracy of the returning fire increased. Despite this, he chose to keep firing back as opposed to hiding entirely behind the tree. Chunks of bark skimmed down as the earth kicked up around him.

His earpiece crackled. "Alpha One, making my sweep."

Hasan emptied the rest of an almost full magazine in a continuous long burst, before rolling behind the tree and reloading.

Hasan's fear dissipated. Gjon had a renowned ability as a soldier. He would cut through whoever it was.

Unable to fire now that Gjon was sweeping through, all he could do was observe his arcs for *squirters*.

The firefight seemed to peter out into a steady exchange.

His radio crackled, the voice garbled.

"Alpha two. You are difficult. Over."

'Difficult' was a term he had learnt studying Voice Procedure—it meant it was difficult to hear what was being said.

Further garbles.

"Alpha Two. Come in, Alpha Two."

Silence.

He spoke again, "Bravo Team, what is your status."

A knee and muzzle of a weapon pressed into his lower back and his skull, respectively.

"It is difficult for dead men to speak," a cool voice said in Italian—the second most widely spoken language in his native Albania. Years of watching

Italian television and visiting the country had given Hasan a fluency that bordered on native.

Still, he said nothing.

"Fully unload your weapon and throw it to your right, and the magazine to your left. If you stay alive, then you have a chance to seek vengeance. Unless, of course, you do not trust yourself not to talk. And, please, include the bullet in the chamber when you unload."

Hasan said nothing but complied. The voice spoke the truth—he was of no use to The Brotherhood dead.

The knee and muzzle left him.

"Slowly kneel up. Remove your webbing and throw it in the direction of your magazine."

Hasan complied.

"Before you answer my next question, be advised if I discover you have answered untruthfully, I will remove the trigger finger from both of your hands. Nod if you understand."

Hasan did so and the man asked, "Do you have any other weapons on your person?"

"A small switchblade disguised as a torch in my pocket."

"Throw it in front of you."

And when he had, the voice said, "Shuffle around and face me."

He turned to see a man dressed in a blur of dark greens, olives and brown. The chest rig held several magazines and a small radio attached to one of the straps.

His stocky build belied his average height.

The three-colour camouflage cream broke up his facial features and took the shine off his bald head.

The dark eyes stared at him with an alertness that scrubbed any thoughts Hasan had of attempting to escape.

"Your skills are good. I had to observe more than one of your ambushes to work out your tactics. Your success bred an arrogance—using such a small team. But your failure to leave the ambush sites with the stealth you entered them has led to you and your team being identified. Not just this team, but the other teams you briefed in the bar in Munich. Careless, Hasan."

The sound of his name stabbed him, and although his expression had been brief and subtle, the man caught it.

"It comes to us all in this life, my Albanian cousin."

He heard the crunch of the undergrowth behind him in the now still air.

He did not attempt to struggle against the hands seizing him. Hands that not long ago belonged to allies, and the Albanian thought of how quickly things in life could change.

Bruce walked out of Vauxhall Cross with his eyes scanning the cars driving along the A3036 roads to his immediate front, and the people walking beside the embankments opposite.

With the breeze buffeting his charcoal cashmere overcoat, he began the walk to his car, parked a few hundred metres away—he always did this in order to identify any potential watchers.

He thought about how difficult he would find it to hand over the reins to Ciara. Though the process would be slow, ultimately he would have to take a complete step back from The Chameleon Project or else stymie her leadership development and create confusion amongst the ranks.

In time, he would request for her to take tasks but leave how she chose to accomplish them entirely up to her. She would have her own through Jaime also.

His desire for freedom and control protested against these thoughts but his rational being asserted itself—*this has to happen.*

His phone vibrated in a way subtly different to 'ordinary' calls.

He answered it. "Are you all right?"

"I am fine," replied Jaime, meaning *'I am not under duress.'*

"I understand this is not a priority," began Jaime. "But the Canadian architect who claimed to have stayed on the island we spoke of is in London for a few days. I guessed you might want to speak to him."

"I do. Send me the details," said Bruce before ending the call. Intelligence had always been the most valuable weapon in war.

Louis enjoyed these meetings with his retained solicitor, Shola Aysha. Some of London's white-collar elite frequented this restaurant, and most gave him more than a passing glance.

And he knew there were different reasons for it. The Londoner of three-quarter Nigerian and one quarter Irish stock exemplified 'tall, dark and handsome' with a muscularity evident even in loose-fitting clothes. His pleasure at being eyed lustfully by women—and more than a few men—simmered over the years, as he had become accustomed to it.

Another was due to racism. Shola, mixed-race herself, her glossy black hair flecked with grey and cascading over her shoulders, told him that all her black and mixed-raced clients got some of the same stares. Louis found it amusing that while her other clients were straight-goers who came to her to sort the legalities of legitimate business deals, he was a gangster through and through at the head of one of the most profitable distribution networks of coke, ecstasy and marijuana in the United Kingdom.

Shola regarded him from across the table. "Are you in trouble?"

Louis shook his head with an amused smirk. "No."

"You just enjoy our meetings here then?"

"Yeh. One day I might find myself locked up for a long time, so I might as well see and experience as much as I can. And nice places with nice people lifts my mood, ya get me?"

"One's sphere of observation determines the state of the mind," she murmured.

"Exactly."

"So, what brings you to see me?"

Louis sipped his coffee and said, "This stabbing the other day. Did you know her?"

The widening of her eyes momentarily confused him before he realised. "Shola, you know I would never give the OK for something like that."

Her face softened. "Sorry. It was the way you said it. And I came across her a few times, yes. A lovely lady outside of the courtroom, and a dragon in it. What happened to her is a tragedy."

"Well, that is what I wanted to talk to you about. Heard a rumour she was preparing a case against some big players."

Shola shrugged. "She's an exceptionally talented Crown prosecutor. She'll be going after some big fish. Why do you ask?"

Louis thought about lying to her. Instead he said, "She's close to someone close to me."

He watched her blink a couple of times.

"You know it would be highly unethical for me to discuss a case."

Louis frowned. "It's not your case."

"It makes no difference. I can't be discussing sensitive cases with my clients. Especially as you've inferred what I might tell will be passed on."

"I get ya. It's a pity how some people thrive on their lack of ethics."

She looked at him for a few moments. "A lack of ethics for me would be telling you about cases. Stabbing a lone woman trying to play her part in this broken thing we call the justice system would be unethical for let's say, Turkish-Cypriot mobsters based out of your neck of the woods."

Louis nodded his appreciation.

16

The tour guide's enthusiasm amazed Connor. At the beginning of the walk he told the group of nine this was his eighth year hosting the Colosseum, Roman Forum and Palatine Hill tour.

His bald pate and scraggy neck reminded Connor of an ostrich.

They stood within the monumental entrance, jostling with the other tour guides.

Connor listened intently while keeping up his counter-surveillance. The birds flew around the corner, where the sand-like upper edge descended back down to two levels created as a result of earthquakes and stone robbers, so the guide said. It stood in testament to how things lasted longer than now—*especially me watching Hentai porn*, thought Connor.

"So, you see," announced the Ostrich in his heavily accented English, "many of Rome's aristocracy liked'a food and drink. They became much too fat and unattractive. So, their wives would pay the guards and have…alone time with the gladiators because they were very strong and good-looking."

The guide theatrically flexed his near non-existent biceps to laughter.

Bet a lot of them were ugly as sin too—thought Connor. Although, he had a theory that most men, if they got in shape, had a bit of a tan and got a decent haircut, would be halfway there on the physical attraction scale.

He tuned into the guide's voice again.

"You see, Romans did not just have lions against the gladiator, they had animals against other animals. One fight during the reign of Claudius happened between an elephant and a very angry rhino. The elephant was victorious by picking up a broken spear and blinding the rhino with it."

Connor murmured, "Fucking awesome."

The lady beside him gave him a look of bemused disdain.

After the riveting tour of the Colosseum, which included stories of naval battles and famous gladiators, the guide took them around the Roman Forum, and finally they made their way to Palatine Hill. A few locals and small food stalls broke up the throng of tourists. A small boy sat on a ruin step, just watching the tourists—*may be a pickpocket.*

Connor listened as the group stood in the remnants of the Palace of Domitian.

"And this was one of Emperor Domitian's many architectural projects and was used as the official residence for the following emperors. Rome had a wide variety of different emperors—and some known for their love of pleasure. Now, who has heard of the Vomitoriums?"

Murmurs of affirmations came forth along with a few noises of disgust.

Using his hands for expression, the guide said, "Judging by the look on your faces, it seems you have been taken in by the myth. Vomitoriums were passageways behind the tier of seats in a stadium or amphitheatre, so the crowd could exit rapidly after the show was over. They were not rooms where the ancient Romans went to vomit their food during feasts so they could eat more. A vicious rumour."

The group laughed, and the guide concluded, "Now, this is where we finish. If you liked the tour then please, please, please put a review online. If you did not…then please remain quiet."

More sounds of merriment as the group broke up.

However, Connor forced his laughter—Alessio was nowhere to be seen.

The Ostrich approached him and asked, "Did you enjoy the tour?"

"Very much. I was going to ask you how you keep the same passion for it year upon year?"

The guide smiled. "I love the history. Besides, I only do this for three months of the year. Are you familiar with Roman history?"

"I reckon I have more knowledge than the average man from my country has, but it'll pale in comparison to yours."

"Where did you get your knowledge from?"

"The internet, YouTube, a few books—there's an author named Conn Iggulden whose books I like."

"So, who is your favourite emperor?"

"My favourite is probably Julius Caesar, but in my opinion Augustus achieved a lot more."

The guide looked at him with a frown. "Why do you say that?"

Connor replied, "His longevity stands out. Julius Caesar ruled for a handful of years, whereas Augustus ruled for over forty. A better politician too, in declaring himself 'First Citizen' instead of Emperor—which he was—he possibly didn't make the Senate feel threatened in the way Julius did, probably why he died at an advanced age—for the time at least. He expanded the empire, and his rule began that two hundred years of peace—Pax Roma or something."

The guide laughed. "I could spend time telling you of all the reasons why Julius Caesar has the better legacy. But, my friend, I like the term in English 'there is an elephant in the room', and there is one here larger than those Hannibal attacked with. Do you know what it is?"

Connor ghosted him a smirk. "That it was Julius Caesar who named his great-nephew as his successor. That if he hadn't adopted him as his son, Augustus would not have been able to succeed him, as his family was not wealthy."

The guide waved his hands in the air. "Then why are we arguing this?"

Connor shrugged. "I don't know. I guess it's because I've seen and heard about so many men being given an opportunity only to fritter it away. Suppose I like it when a man maximises his opportunities."

The guide looked at him strangely before saying, "Our organisation does too. Mr Letta believes we should also give you an opportunity."

Connor stood still for a moment and chastised himself. Of course, Alessio would send someone else. He would never have expected this guy though—*which was the point.*

"I am glad he does."

"You are aware tensions have arisen between our organisation and our cousins in Naples."

"No, but I am aware of the murder of a Naples boss."

The guide nodded. "Our organisation is involved in a delicate matter at present and cannot be distracted at this time."

"What's your plan?"

"A group, who the media name 'The Black Axe', has been at war with Naples for years over territories on the northwest coast. For a year, an uneasy ceasefire has been in place."

"A Nigerian crime organisation," stated Connor. "What if I have won a money prize over there and need to give them my bank account details?"

The guide frowned. "What?"

"Nothing. Bad joke," said Connor. "Anyway, you would like to see this ceasefire shattered?"

"You are intelligent," replied the guide. "If not funny."

"OK."

"The Black Axe is a collection of groups under one mast. However, there is one man who has more influence than anyone else. His name is Okemiorukaye Akintimehin. A very elusive man. His business interests in Europe keep him in motion."

"And you want him gone?"

The guide smirked. "It is true his death may result in meeting our objective. A better…trigger would be if The Black Axe were attacked in their own fortress…in his presence."

"When is he supposed to be in Castel Volturno, and how reliable is your source?"

The guide's eyebrows arched. "Very reliable. He is there in four days."

"Quite a short window of time," stated Connor, thinking about not only the travelling, assimilating all the relevant information, performing a thorough reconnaissance of the town, but also if Jaime could guide him to an armourer, and if he could find a place to zero the weapons.

"I'll accept," replied Connor.

"Accept what?" answered the guide.

"The mission and the memory card you're about to put into my hand."

The guide shook his head. "I will not be handing anything to you."

Abruptly he walked away. Connor opened his mouth to speak but closed it.

He turned to walk in the opposite direction, not sure what had just transpired.

He began down the hill and began to rebuke himself—*there's a time and place for daft jokes, and negotiations with one of the world's most influential mafias is not one of them.*

Connor spotted the boy he had pegged as a pickpocket in the reflective corner of his blue-lensed sunglasses. He was jogging towards Connor, who decided a 'Chinese burn' would be the most appropriate form of punishment.

However, the lad slowed and called out in accented English, "Mr Reed."

Connor turned around, and the lad threw him a plastic case containing a memory card.

Luke watched Louis alight from the passenger side of a mauve BMW M8 and lamented on how cool he looked. Tall and broad, he moved with the relaxed awareness of a man who knew he could handle danger. He wore a black, knitted sweater underneath a dark grey woollen jacket, dark blue jeans and white trainers. Luke could not see any jewellery, apart from a Hublot Big Bang Evolution watch which Luke knew to be worth the cost of a deposit on a decent house in some parts of Leeds.

Louis, half a foot taller, clasped Tom's hand and leant down to 'bro-hug' him. The Londoner then turned to Luke with an outstretched hand.

"You must be 'Cool Hand Luke'. Connor talks about you all the time."

Luke frowned while grasping the strong grip. "Does he?"

He was also surprised Louis knew his familial nickname.

"Fuckin' loves you, don't he," stated Louis. "Didn't you throw down with some bare-knuckle gypsy boxer in a scrap yard and beat the brakes off 'im in front of all his family?"

Luke shrugged. "Yeh."

Louis laughed. "Gee."

Tom interjected with, "Get anywhere with our request?"

Louis looked at him. "It isn't good, bruv. It's the Turks from my end. I'll tell you the truth, we don't get involved with that lot—they are bad news. We don't work with 'em but I try not to aggravate them either. They're the same with us."

"We're not asking for your help, we're—"

"Connor's like a brother to me. I'll give you any help you need, but it has to be *sneaky-beaky* and I can't get any of my lads involved, it isn't fair on 'em."

Tom said, "I understand completely. You've done more for him and our family than we've done for—"

"Connor's done more for me than you know. Why do you think I let him get away with his militant jokes?"

Louis and Tom laughed.

"What sort of jokes does he say to you?" asked Luke, bemused.

Louis tutted. "All sorts, mate. He sent me a WhatsApp picture of this Colonel Sanders statue that had been pulled out of a Jap river after twenty-four years. Connor put something like 'I am glad to see this insult to your culture has been rectified'—you know how he is with his big words."

Luke laughed. "And you're all right with those sorts of jokes?"

"Listen, Man'dem, jokes are jokes, we all tell them. It's what a man does that counts. I'll *spin you a dit*, back when Connor and I were just sprogs in the corps—we weren't even close friends back then—I mention in front of him—not directly to 'im— how my old boxing gym might have been getting closed down. That gym got more black boys off the streets than any other youth project in the area but the council had cut funding, and the gym's gaffer was lax with the fees, as he knew some of the lads couldn't afford it. The local community gathered around it the best they could, but the council said they wanted the year's rent upfront—scandalous."

Louis's eyes narrowed seemingly in the memory of it, as he continued, "Anyway, leave came around and I fucked off on holiday. Comes back and hear it's been sorted. Asked Virgil, the coach, what had happened. Apparently, Connor walked into this gym—doesn't tell anyone 'is name, but cos Virg' is a spotter who knows everyone who is anyone in UK amateur boxing, recognises 'im straight away. Trained with the lads—impressing everyone—before dropping Virgil a cheque for eight grand. When I see Connor again, I keep my mouth shut, reckoning he'll lord it that he saved the boxing club. Never mentions it to me—ever. In fact, I don't even think I've told him I know."

"He did that?" exclaimed Luke.

Louis nodded. "So you see, bruv, I couldn't give a fuck what jokes he makes. And that's just one thing. So, you don't ever have to fret about reaching out to me."

Luke felt a deep familial pride towards Connor. He swallowed and cleared his throat.

"Fair enough," answered Tom. "Might not come to anything. Our cousin Dan insists we're not to go there."

"Why did he say that? He still has faith in the justice system after this?" said Louis, with a hint of disdain.

"The world needs crusaders. But it's not just that. If our involvement becomes knowledge to certain people then both his and her professions go up in smoke.

"Then how come you're making these inquiries?"

Tom shrugged. "I always like to have the option."

Louis lifted a USB chip from his pocket. "James Bond would laugh at it, but it has some of the names and faces of the key players in that mob. Some of their whips and hangouts. Should get ya started. If you need a safe house, I have that covered. That's as far as I can go."

Luke felt an expanse of gratefulness in his chest as he and Tom shook Louis's hand, before the Londoner strolled back to his car.

Carlo knew Hasan would be tough to crack. The soldiers of the Mafia Shqiptare lived by the *Kanun*—a code that had been passed down for hundreds of years as a means of governance amongst northern Albania villages. Their Mafia, as with the 'Ndrangheta, had a bedrock of familial loyalty, honour and a severe protocol of internal discipline.

However, Carlo suspected many within their brotherhood would not welcome war if they knew the catalyst behind it was a lie.

Though he had Hasan stripped upon detention, he had been re-dressed in traditional Albanian clothing, which included a beige sleeveless *Xhamadan*—a type of woollen vest, a golden and red patterned *Fustanella*—a pleated kilt, and a pair of white *Opinga*—art sandals.

They were in the basement of a Munich brothel. Hasan sat with his wrists bound to the armrests of a comfortable, leather chair. Carlo sat on an identical chair facing him.

Small black pyramids of acoustic foam made up the ceiling and walls to soundproof it. Positioned at the back was a metal table with a first aid box on top—this was so the room could be explained away as a room to administer first aid in, and not where the bouncers mercilessly beat any non-payers or unruly customers.

Carlo spoke in Italian, "Hasan, I am aware your Italian is superb while my Albanian is rudimentary."

Hasan said nothing.

"I am also aware the amount of time and effort it would take to 'break you' would be immense. You are a hard man, Hasan, and a superb soldier, as I have witnessed. You are also a respected member of a brotherhood that understands the meaning of *Omerta* more so than even other Italian organisations—others, but not ours. That is why our organisations have always done great business, Hasan. Which is why I will not be asking you any questions of tactical relevance."

Hasan's face betrayed a ghost of confusion, but he remained silent.

Carlo continued, "Now, you believe Eralda Mancuso—'El Kuq'—was ordered by our organisation to murder Oso Xhelli and the financiers at the fundraiser he was hosting. My first question to you—which I do not expect you to answer—is why would we do that? To teach you a lesson? That would be a stupid action and you know we are not stupid. A lesson is one thing, severing a highly lucrative relationship is something altogether different—a business relationship which earns both parties millions and millions of Euros to be thrown away for a war that would cost us both millions and millions of Euros. Does that sound logical to you, Hasan?"

Hasan said nothing.

"I bet you can't find a single witness who would point the finger at Eralda Mancuso. Now, I know what you're thinking—she killed them all. Convenient isn't it, Hasan, that she ended up dying herself—with her supposed killer dying too?"

Hasan's eyes briefly creased from the bottom.

"Loyalty comes in more than one form, Hasan. There is the blind loyalty of a dog. Wonderful animals to be sure, but domesticated nonetheless. Or, there is the wolf's loyalty—though hierarchical, their loyalty is to one another to ensure the survival of the pack—not the loyalty of a master and pet. I wonder what type of loyalty your new Kyre thinks you have, Hasan? Strangely, the person who has benefitted the most from all this is Andrei Faja."

Hasan's eyes seemed to glaze and Carlo continued, "Strange too, that apparently Eralda was accompanied by a woman—tall, beautiful with short silvery-blonde hair. Oso's outer security team remembered her. I wonder whatever happened to her, Hasan?"

Hasan raised his head. "She died in the fire."

Carlo hid his joy at Hasan breaking his silence, and asked, "Where did you get that information? We know she was—or is—British. Yet, I am guessing there have been no inquiries from the British Embassy in Tirana."

Hasan said nothing.

"I am going to release you, Hasan. I have no malice towards you. I do not ask anything from you except you look into your Kyre's eyes and see if they can convince you of the truth. See if the cause is justified, or if he has engineered all this to take over and then solidify his position, with the belief he can win a war with us."

Carlo took out his Maserin French Foreign Legion blade and Hasan's reaction, a subtle flick of the eyes but nothing else, impressed him.

He stepped around behind Hasan before cutting his hands free. He put his hand lightly on the back of

Hasan's neck, and said, "Don't try it, Hasan. D'Artagnan and the Three Musketeers could not defeat me in a knife fight with their swords."

He let go, and said, "What we want is the security footage of that day. Or, in the least, a still picture of this woman. Then we will take it from there, Hasan. Here is enough cash to buy a phone and a hotel for a few nights. If you believe the cash is traceable, then go ahead, give it to the homeless."

He dropped a banded bundle of 1,000 euros in his lap.

"Go ahead, Hasan. The door is open. The flight of stairs will lead you to reception, where you may leave, or indulge in one of the girls if that is your wish."

Hasan slowly rose, and took a few steps before turning. Carlo waited for what he was going to say or do. Instead, Hasan turned back and left.

17

As Connor walked around the coastal front of Castel Volturno, he had to remind himself the place hadn't just experienced a natural disaster or military war. Instead, the evidence of neglect from a community that either would not or could not help itself, and a lack of local government, lay all around him.

He sat on a smooth log with his back against a ruined wall, looking out onto the dark sea. He kept his awareness heightened, listening for any sounds of approach, despite the hypnotic rush and break of the gentle waves.

It had been an exhausting few days. Jaime, Bruce's technical support guy, reminded Connor of an Arthur C Clarke quote he had once heard from a world-famous engineering entrepreneur:

"*Any sufficiently advanced technology is indistinguishable from magic.*"

Connor had not known how, but within two days Jaime had arranged his required combat kit, cached inside a securely locked garage in the town of Ceccano, which lay en route to Castel Volturno.

The tactical package included highly advanced body armour, a chest rig which held not only fragmentation and smoke grenades, but two sets of spare ammunition; a set for the FN Five-Seven pistol and a set for the HK G36c assault rifle. Both were the weapon systems he had asked for. Though much more expensive than its Glock and Sig counterparts—which was not a concern for him, the Five-seven held a twenty-round magazine, was highly reliable, easy to strip and operate, and the recoil was not as hard as some of its 9mm counterparts.

He had enjoyed shooting the HK G36c on the ranges, though had not fired one in a firefight. The German-made rifle was light, ambidextrous and had an easily manageable recoil. He counteracted the lack of texture, and thus grip on the pistol grip, with a couple of rubber bands. Though it fired a smaller 5.56mm round as opposed to the 7.62mm, Connor had noted in the intel report Jaime had sent him, The Black Axe—due to their dominance of the area—did not wear body armour.

He knew carrying out days of reconnaissance was out of the question. Being neither Italian nor Nigerian meant he would get noticed by the wrong people if he hung around for too long—the municipality of the Campania region was far from a tourist hotspot.

Indeed, Jaime was a magician; however, an organisation and location that lacked technology could nullify that magic. The bane of Jaime's work would have been an organisation that made use of 'dumb' phones, person-to-person message transference and written messages.

Though there was a distinct lack of CCTV in and around the town, Connor knew the only people who did not own smartphones were the various hunter-gatherer tribes worldwide.

He looked out to the sea, which reminded him of being a young marine in a sentry box on the Scottish firing range of Barry Buddon. The lads had often pondered how many masturbation sessions had occurred in the wooded boxes looking out onto the beach and sea. He smiled as he remembered catching sight of a message on the right-hand side that read, 'Look Left'. When he did, another scribble instructed him to 'Look Up', only to be told 'You're Gay'. Even then, he had been impressed by the correct spelling of 'You're'.

He envied the lack of remorse—either through naivety or youth—he had back then. He would fight whoever his government told him to fight. He was not thoroughly discerning regarding the justification; he had joined for the action, adventure and camaraderie.

When he felt morally justified, Connor felt a heady pleasure when hurting and murdering bad and evil men. If he doubted the wickedness of their natures, he lost interest—and he knew he needed to be engaged.

He decided to take a walk around the town's periphery to get a feel for the place.

Andrei Faja felt it the moment he embraced his old friend—an awkwardness.

Maybe he believes I blame him.

"I feared you were being tortured or were dead, my old friend. I am happy you are alive and appear unharmed."

They sat opposite one another in what used to be Oso's private study. Hasan wore a traditional Albanian dress, while he wore a white shirt, open at the collar, with grey, cotton trousers.

The fire warmed and lit the desk, dark blue and gold patterned carpets, and landscape paintings. A small, polished table separated them.

"My team is dead. I will have to live with that forever, my Kyre."

"They were soldiers, Hasan, who died with honour. You have done more to undermine our enemies than anyone else in our brotherhood. Your success encouraged my prolific use of your team. If anyone is at fault, it is I, Hasan."

Andrei caught the hint of a subtle nod before Hasan said, "I was the man responsible."

Realising this could continue, Andrei asked, "How did you escape?"

Hasan straightened his back. "I didn't. He let me go."

"Who did?"

"The man who captured me. He must be a specialist. I have seen and been around soldiers—military soldiers—all my life. And I have been around outlaws all my life too. This man is both. I have only seen his kind twice in my life."

"Did he tell you his name?"

"No."

"Description?"

"He was not tall. Compact build. Olive skin. Shaven head."

Andrei tapped his fingers on the table once. "And what reason did he give for letting you go?"

Hasan's eyes beamed onto his. "He wanted me to ask you for the security footage of the massacre here."

"Did you ask why?"

That he needed to pry the answers from Hasan disconcerted Andrei. That, and the way he was looking at him. When his Mik shook his head, Andrei asked, "Why would he ask for that? Surely, if they could insert a false loop, they had the ability to record."

Hasan stared at him. "He wanted to know what happened to the woman who Eralda attended with."

"Incinerated in the fire."

Hasan tilted his jaw. "I spoke to the security, Andrei. They believe the woman was British. They heard her speak English with Eralda on the audio."

Andrei became more aware of the door being ajar.

"Perhaps it was the only common language they spoke."

"Gezim has spent a lot of time in London. He says she was British."

"Interesting," said Andrei. "In that case, I—"

"Gezim told me that he told you he believed she was British. He said you asked him to keep it quiet until you spoke to me about it."

The air cooled.

Andrei did not speak, and Hasan continued, "I have been your friend for a long while, Andrei, even when it was dangerous to be so. I defended you against certain whisperers who suggested you might be behind the massacre—not only out of my faith in your character, but because it seemed stupid to wipe out a large segment of our organisation's funding that you could have used when you took over. So, I am confused as to why you have not come to me—your closest confidante—regarding this matter."

Andrei could see the conflict in Hasan's eyes. He would not believe the truth, and Andrei would consider him stupid if he did. Explaining how an unknown agency was behind it and had blackmailed him into beginning a war with the 'Ndrangheta would mean having to trust Hasan with the information. Hasan would believe him—probably. However, if he did not, he might seek the advice of one of the other clan Kyres—Andrei might then be 'questioned'. No man holds out forever. He would never give his mother up, but nor could he protect her dead.

Hasan was his friend and ally. An ally whose help was highly useful, especially at this time.

"Hasan, as you know, tomorrow is the day I meet again with the high council to request assistance in this ongoing war. I would like you to drive me there. Your success has given me leverage," he said, sincerely. "I have not told you the entire truth of this matter—I have not lied—but I needed to discover some truths before sharing them with you. It is after this meeting I will know certain realities. And then I will tell you everything, Hasan. Will you at least afford me this for the sake of our friendship?"

His friend's eyes failed to hide the conflict in his brain. After a moment they hinted at an affectionate relief.

"Of course, my Kyre."

Despite a distance of over forty metres, the three black prostitutes called out to him in Italian. Giving him a twirl, he especially admired their big, peach asses held back by dark stretch pants.

Though Connor had indulged in prostitutes and escorts in the past, only a couple had been good enough actresses to convince him of their interest. If they could not convince him, they could not turn him on—*How could a woman be attracted to a man who's paying her to fuck him?*

Connor knew the pimps could not be far away. *Where would I be if I was tasked to watch over my commodities?*

He spotted the car immediately. The black Dodge Charger SE stood out for its expense in this part of the world. That and Connor guessed it was what a Nigerian Mafia enforcer would drive.

Connor thought of his options. He could not follow the car. The rented Moto Guzzi V7 motorcycle, which lay in a secure garage on the outskirts the town, would be conspicuous to all but the most docile.

He possessed the tiny tracker Jaime somehow had placed for him in a securities box in Rome. However, getting close to the vehicle without the occupants knowing would prove difficult. The windows were tinted, but he guessed a two-man team sat in the front seats.

What if you're wrong? You'll be fucked.

Adrenaline began to press into his system—it was like his body knew the decision he would make before his mind did.

More is lost by indecision than wrong decision.

He walked on for a couple of minutes before rounding back on the opposite side. As he staggered towards the car, he swilled saliva around his gums to trick his nervous system into taking the edge off the adrenaline.

He stood behind the car, used his hand on the boot to support himself and feigned pissing.

Immediately, the door opened and a pair of chunky legs clad in white cotton pants flew out. Before their owner could stand on them, Connor whipped around, caught sight of the scarred face's jaw and smashed a knuckle duster-reinforced fist into it. Astonishingly to Connor, it took three punches to put out the heavyset Nigerian, which gave his lithe and nimble colleague time to draw his pistol.

Connor darted back, but instead of running off, slid around the back of the vehicle again. As the passenger alighted from the Charger, Connor fired the three-pronged taser into his throat.

As his victim dropped, the convulsing caused him to fire off his revolver across the street from his outstretched hand.

Connor knew the place would be swarming with The Black Axe within a minute or so. He rifled into his pocket, removed the tracker and stuck it under the wheel arch before running.

After sprinting a couple of hundred metres, changing direction through the alleyways, he slowed so as not to attract attention to himself.

He knew the general layout of the town, based on his map studies. However, some of the buildings had been thrown up by the African immigrants, and it took Connor longer than usual to plot a path.

With relief ballooning inside his diaphragm and throat, he reached his cache.

Shouts behind him went up like clapped pigeons and he cursed. They must have a *dicker* system.

Knowing they had identified him anyway, he ragged on the webbing and re-secured the daysack, before running, while inelegantly fastening the webbing to his frame.

Connor did not want a scenario to occur where he would be forced to kill people, but he knew he would not martyr himself if it came down to them or him.

If he walked he would be caught. If he kept running, witnesses would continually identify him.

After putting in a reasonable distance, he swung his bag off his shoulders and around to his front. His hand found the smoke grenade; different from the British military issue that took a number of seconds to build and was relatively harmless, this version exploded into a cloud of vision-obscuring and choking smoke. Trials had indicated although the smoke could not realistically kill a healthy adult, a lungful could cause death to someone with a severe chronic pulmonary disease.

Fuck it, if one of them had that, they wouldn't be able to run to the front of the queue of this mob, if run at all.

He ran on as the shouts grew in number. He couldn't keep running for ever—as fit as he was, eventually one of the fresh chasers would catch him.

He saw his opportunity.

He took out his Five-seven and fired down the alleyway to discourage anyone from sticking their heads out. He pulled the pin and let fly the canister. It landed just over thirty metres away.

The plume of smoke reminded him of the grainy video of the Hiroshima bomb in miniature.

Connor watched from behind the stack of rotting fruit boxes and pallets. He sat, gripping his pistol between his legs, back hunched, looking through a small gap. He did not want to make any movement to retrieve the G36c from the customised daysack with his pursuers so close.

The mob thundered past like a herd of dark velociraptors. After a few moments, he could hear the sounds of spluttering coughs, as his would-be assailants underestimated the effect the smoke would have on their lungs.

A dark thought occurred to him—*walk out and kill them all, reach your motorbike and that's the job done. If they had caught you, you'd have been lynched.*

Despite being on the precipice, he could not do it; some might be kids caught in the excitement, or men forced into this life. He knew who his targets were.

He would have to wait. Even donning a disguise, he would still be recognisable as an outsider and thus accosted.

The good thing about places like Castel Volturno was that the sounds of gunfire would be a regular occurrence—not the sort of thing that would excite the residents enough to stay up all night. After a few hours, the furore might have died enough for him to slip away.

The adrenaline hangover added weight to his eyelids—*don't be a fucking mongchild. Stay awake.*

The previous night, after parking his rented motorcycle, he'd snuck into the town on foot. After carrying out a recce, he found the place to cache his gear. He had struggled to find a place to sleep, not trusting any of the 'hotels' in the area. Eventually, he had found a little cove on the beach, but being in enemy territory meant he slept fitfully, hence his now weary state.

He had experience of this. Every British soldier knew of the temptation while shrouded in the silent cold darkness of sentry duty, to rest the front edge of one's helmet on his *SUSAT*—rifle scope—and drift off for a few moments. A few moments almost always turned into being woken by someone else. If you were lucky, it would be your Oppo, if not it would be the staff or a higher rank. He had never fallen asleep on sentry—the lack of discipline to stay alert was a cardinal sin in the British military—and he remembered the 'beastings' some of the recruits had had to endure for being caught while he, and the others, felt a congratulatory relief swim through their veins.

However, he also knew a person could get to a level of tiredness that meant sleep was inevitable if they remained still over too long a length of time. After a military exercise, while still a recruit, the Training Team would not let them sleep until they *deserviced and reserviced* all their field kit. He remembered scrubbing his field mug with wire wool in the chair by his *pit space*—bed, and waking in the same position three hours later.

Wake up! There're a bunch of ruthless Africans looking to skin you.

He knew he needed movement to keep himself from sliding off.

Perhaps adrenaline too.

As quietly as he could, he checked the tracker. The car had moved—and Connor guessed who would be at the location it was now parked. No civilians—just Black Axe members.

He thought of the suppressed HK G36c. He had managed to zero it in a forest on the way over. He had his night vision—they looked indistinguishable from sunglasses, with turquoise lenses, but turned night into day with only the smallest amount of ambient light.

Shut up, you mad cunt. You're not going to mount an assault just because you can't be fucked keeping your eyes open after only a few nights of lost sleep.

For some reason, Grace, a girl he thought he could share his life with, crept into his mind. He wondered what she was doing now. Probably seeing someone. Someone steady. She would not feel about whoever it was like she felt about him, but she would not have any of the aggravation he brought, either.

She was awesome in bed. Remember when—stop.

His hypothalamus tried dragging him off to slumber once again—he shook his head like a St Bernard.

He thought back to a book by Steven Pressfield titled *The Tides of War*, chronicling the Peloponnesian War fought between the Greek City states of Sparta and Athens from 431 BC to 404 BC. A friend had recommended it to him. In it was a description of the differing mindsets. The Athenian mindset is one of *thrasytes*—a boldness born of great ambition. The Spartan philosophy being a manly enduring of what must be endured, and doing what must be done, known as *andreia.*

And Connor had adhered to this; hours and hours of high-speed range work, punishing MMA, Gi and NoGi jiu-jitsu sessions, flexibility work, strength training, language acquisition, and his constant studying of terrorist organisations, criminal organisations, global issues, physiology, warfare, history, general knowledge, geography, culture and many other subjects until his brain felt raw.

He had thrasytes too—his instinct, skill and luck had rescued him when his boldness had plunged him into danger. That had happened several times in his life. Pressfield had said Alexander the Great was one of the few in history who had both andreia and thrasytes. And he, too, always found luck on his side in battle.

You comparing yourself to Alexander the Great now? Get your head down.

He listened for another minute—the voices receded far down the alleyway, chasing his phantom.

A voice in his head—not his own—shook him from his creep into slumber.

The man who can ally Athenian thrasytes with Spartan andreia can rule his world.

He took out the G36c, fit the suppressor and left his hiding place.

18

The huge Okemiorukaye Akintimehin paced around the disused warehouse in a rage. His soldiers, twenty-two of them—stood, wide-eyed and fidgeting—witnessed the spectacle of Okemi pointing his blood-stained charcoal axe at them for emphasis, and Ade's chopped up corpse lying next to him. It seemed to focus their attention. The man proved more useful dead than alive.

"This is one man—if he was more, he would not have run like a rat. And he will be hiding somewhere in this town—our town, like a rat. He cannot escape—you have promised me no vehicles can come in or out without us knowing. I do not care what weapons he has, or what magic tricks he can perform. I want him brought to me—alive would be better, but dead if he must be—before sunrise. Or, there will be more of you who will fall under my black axe. Any questions?"

They shook their heads.

A sound—like a quarter deck of cards being riffled. Then the garbled and panicked calls of his men, two floors below. It took him a few seconds to realise.

He bellowed, "We are under attack. Move!"

His men dispersed in wild expectation. Then the lights went out.

Connor crouched in a splintered doorway fifty metres across the street. He watched the two sentries smoking in the entryway of a large, three-storey, derelict warehouse. Large openings in the sides were covered by what looked to be thin wire mesh. The largest of these gaps opened into the second-floor corner overlooking the road, big enough for two men to get through—the wire mesh had been torn away and Connor wondered if anyone had been thrown out of it.

That he had managed to creep down to this point without being noticed indicated their lack of awareness.

A disused dumper truck lay on its side halfway down his side of the street—*how the fuck has that gone onto its side?*

There were cars of various expenses, and differing states of repair lining the streets.

He could see the various Black Axe mafioso with pistols tucked into their hips. Some had different AK variants dangling from their slings.

What the fuck are you doing, Connor?

He now wore a Type 3 bulletproof vest; a Chinese development capable of stopping 7.62mm rounds. It was heavy but not nearly as heavy as it should have been due to a material weld technology and lack of side protection.

Still, body armour or not, the last thing he wanted hitting him was a 7.62mm round.

His mind began to whisper—*They might be criminals but so are your family. These Africans come from abject poverty, and maybe see this as their only way out. And you're going to murder them.*

He stopped himself, and countered—*Everyone can justify their actions with a sob story. This needs to be done. It's for the greater good. You've seen this town—The Black Axe don't bring anything good. You're doing the world a favour.*

The two sentries' faces snapped in the opposite direction at the sound of a speeding car. Connor took his chance to cross the street.

Hugging the walls of the run-down holiday shacks, he crept down to the pair.

The nearest sentry only noticed his movement at five metres away. They both fell with a pink mist skimming off their heads.

Connor rolled on through the door with the suppressed HK G36c on aim. Rapidly stepping in and to the side to remove himself from the 'fatal funnel', he scanned the corners.

The closed space—not much larger than an average western living room—surprised him, as he had expected to see an expansive floor. The space had two doors, one situated adjacent to the entry door a foot off the stairwell leading upstairs. The second down a short hallway to his right. Both had several deadbolts on his side of them. He surmised one might have led off to a basement and the other to an extra storage unit of some type.

A voice in Nigerian pidgin—a creole English—called down, the owner presumably ignorant of his two comrades' deaths. Connor heard the clatter of footsteps and, guessing the numbers to be greater than three, switched the firing mode selector to automatic.

He stood at the bottom, but off to the side, of the stairs. He wanted them all down. As the first came into view, he opened fire.

In British military doctrine, a snap ambush needed a three-to-one advantage. However, Connor's positioning, accuracy and the enemy's lack of weapon handling discipline allowed him to scythe down all four, who tumbled down the stairs like bloodied, stringless puppets.

He rapidly negotiated the bodies, realising he might have compromised himself. The shout from somewhere above confirmed it.

Rolling around to face up the stairs, he saw that halfway up, the electrical fuse box's plastic, cracked door opened like a wave of invitation.

Tyche must be looking down on you.

As he slid his night-vision glasses on, he hoped the Greek Goddess of Fortune would stay with him tonight. Flicking down the row of trip switches, the building plunged into darkness.

He heard running feet and panicked creole, from some kind of expansive room up on the first floor. A vague feeling called to him from the back of his mind, telling him he should now be terrified—but he wasn't.

In a semi-crouch, he ascended the stairs to reach a hallway on the first floor. He shot two more enemies bounding out of a door to the left.

Connor knew killing all the building's occupants was a nigh on impossible challenge—no matter how poorly trained they were, sheer numbers would overwhelm him. Still, he had several advantages: surprise, night vision, operational experience, tactical expertise and an ultra-high proficiency in weapons-handling, and firing honed by several thousand hours of high-speed, pressure-tested range work.

And he did not need to clear the entire building. He just needed to cause enough of a 'Pearl Harbor' to disintegrate the fragile peace between The Black Axe and Camorra.

The stairs stopped at this floor, even though he knew there was one more storey above. He quickly decided the building must have been designed to have the stairs on alternative sides despite the size.

As he peered around the door with his weapon on aim, he saw fortune had favoured him once again.

The entire first floor, almost the size of a football pitch, had no furniture or any other obscuring items. His theory regarding the layout was proved correct; the members of The Black Axe were pouring towards him from the doors on the opposite side like screaming ants.

Connor reached inside his webbing pouch, pulled out a grenade, removed the transit clip, pulled the pin, waited two seconds and threw it underarm into the swarm.

The explosion reverberated before being swept by the screams. He rifled into the same pouch and repeated the exercise.

That'll do.

He fired off a burst through the door to deter, even for a few moments, would-be followers until he had expended the clip.

The rounds fired from the stairwell below caught him spinning back around mid-magazine change.

19

Andrei remained quiet throughout much of the journey until the castle appeared.

"I appreciate your faith, Hasan. I might not have been so patient given the evidence you have been presented."

Hasan smirked. "You're the most patient man I know, Andrei. You would have given your oldest friend the benefit of an afternoon."

"I thank you anyway."

"Besides," said Hasan, "if you wanted to kill me, you could have arranged it while I slept."

"A man who kills those who risk bringing him hurtful truths will eventually hear nothing but soothing lies."

With a vague sense of déjà vu, they alighted from the Bentley, walked into the castle and the conference—all the members present and seated in the same positions as before.

Tefik rose and smiled. "Kyre Faja, have you grown tiresome of being chauffeured in the Bentley yet?"

Andrei answered, "I believe it might take many a full moon to pass before that happens."

He turned to Hasan, whose smile mirrored the rest and said, "I wonder if I'll enjoy it more when I am the one driving on the way back."

Hasan's face scrunched into puzzlement just before the tip of a ten-centimetre spear punched into the point where his jawline met the neck. Andrei gripped the back of his neck as he ragged the switchblade from side to side, before pulling it free.

Blood drained through his clasping fingers, leaving a mask of anguish.

Andrei spoke, "You forgot your honour for money."

His friend opened his mouth to speak but instead collapsed.

As the pool of dark claret expanded, the face lost its expression, before freezing into a chalky mask. That the blood spread so far it began to stroke the shoes of the closest Kyre did not elicit any response from them. Instead, their expressions conveyed faint approval.

Andrei cleaned off the blade on Hasan's face and clothing, before retracting it and putting it back in his jacket pocket.

Tefik rose. "Betrayal in our brotherhood is mercifully rare. Some say tolerance is a mark of a civilised society. That may be true, but it is also an insidious sign of weakness. This committee recognises your strength in extinguishing this traitor's life."

Andrei answered, "I've known him for many years. I do not know how I did not see the signs. His actions have led to the deaths of people close to some of you—indeed, when one of us is taken, it hurts us all."

Tefik waved his hand dismissively. "You are young. You have had this position thrust upon you. Other harsh lessons will await you, as they do even the most experienced of us. Oso Xhelli was amongst the wisest of us, and even he fell prey to being too trusting. You have dealt with it."

Tefik gestured to the empty chair. "Please, take your seat amongst us and tell us of your findings and proposals."

Andrei nodded and sat. He felt the blood of his friend drying on his face. The young Kyre presented the 'evidence' of Hasan's 'betrayal' that had been requested through his digital backchannel to Connor Reed. What he received had been so convincing that for a moment he wondered if it was true. Of course, Hasan had not been guilty, and Andrei kept off his face the sorrow and revulsion at what he had done.

That he did what he had to do provided reassurance. He had murdered the only man within the organisation he might have been able to confide in.

And that was a good thing—*the person you confided in holds the keys to your downfall.*

The technology spread the bullets' impact, preventing Connor from going into shock—and thus saved his life.

That and his assailants having to skirt around the corner of the stairs in order to finish him off. They must have fired at his door-framed silhouette and now could not get a clear bead on him in the dark. He pulled and released the cocking lever to chamber the top round, the fresh magazine already seated.

The sound identified his position to the pair. A fraction of a second faster, his rounds tore into their centres of mass.

Fear-of-death adrenaline forced him upright. Firing another burst through the doorway, he bounded down the stairs.

The smell of freshly shot people always lingered afterwards—the burnt flesh, iron and propellant; he had heard it said if they pumped the smell of battles in war films into the cinema they would bomb at the box office.

He decided against throwing a smoke grenade to cover his exit from the building; people often fired into smoke. Instead, he threw another fragmentation grenade—the chances of a civilian's presence now minuscule.

He exited on the 'B' of the 'Bang', to see the grenade had shredded two potential ambushers. His mind screenshotted the image of the pair lying with their heads touching—one with torn intestines and the other with one side of his face ripped off like Two-Face of Gotham.

He sprinted across the street under a hail of fire. After a moment, he realised there were at least two firing points: behind and to his left flank.

His brain rejected an attempt to run for the nearest side street nearly fifty metres away, as the rounds were impacting like deadly miniature meteorites all around him.

He dived behind the dumper truck. He ripped up the top flap of his pouch to get at his smoke grenade.

His head snapped onto the movement to the right of him, and it dawned on him he had just killed himself.

He counted seven Black Axe running towards him with AK variants.

He had had it demonstrated to him during various penetration demonstrations—'pen dems'—just how little protection a standard car would afford a person from 7.62mm calibre rounds.

Although the dumper truck's undercarriage would withstand them, he had trapped himself, and with the numbers against him a simple tri-pincer would be the end of him.

Little point in throwing the smoke now, Connor again flicked the selector to Auto—ammunition conservation was no longer necessary with death imminent.

He felt a serenity plume within him.

He drew a bead on one of the armed militia. A fraction of a second before he squeezed the trigger, the man flew back, as if on a giant elastic band, his chest exploding. Then another target…and another.

He did not question who provided his lifeline. He moved back to the rear edge of the dumper truck.

He had ascertained it must be a sniper picking off his would-be killers. For that reason, he refrained from launching the smoke grenade—*best to let the sniper thin them out a bit before escaping.*

As the G36c could be fired from either the left or right shoulder, The Chameleon Project agent switched it to his left to make the best use of the cover the truck provided.

He crouched and whipped the G36 around the corner to take up targets on the opposite side of the street—there were none.

The truck's chassis still reverberated with the rounds hitting it, and Connor's instinct told him the firing position lay on the second floor, through the gap in the corner. From there The Black Axe attackers would be safe from the sniper's firing position down the alleyway, but they had a clear view of him.

He tore open a pair of pouch tops and grabbed a fragmentation and smoke grenade. He considered throwing it blind but instantly dismissed it—he would only get one chance.

The Chameleon Project agent would have one smoke and no fragmentation grenades left after this.

He cracked off the smoke and threw it down in the direction of the sniper's firing position.

Skipping back, he caught sight of the four of them, bunched together, firing into the smoke.

So engrossed in their supposed target, Connor was able to remain out in the relative open, watching the travel of the grenade.

It arced high before dipping just off their heads. The detonation exploded them out like a firework of pulp, bone, blood and entrails.

Connor's belly laugh erupted at the sight.

Get a grip of yourself. You're not out of the woods.

He reloaded with a fresh magazine—*snurgled* back to the front of the truck before peering out over the top of his rifle scope.

No one showed themselves.

Fuck it, he thought, bursting out from behind his cover, zigzagging the first ten metres before heading for the side street.

His back felt cold with vulnerability as he waited for the shots that never came.

If he could get to his bike, he might survive.

Carlo looked over the scope of his FR F2 sniper rifle with a burning admiration barely cooled by drops of disdain.

He'd had a great view from his vantage point on the top of the carcass of the disused hotel.

Whatever possessed the Englishman to think he could assault such a large congregation of armed

Black Axe soldiers by himself, only he would know. There was no doubt in Carlo's mind this foreigner would have died if he had not been there.

But Carlo had been there, and the man had survived.

It was clear from watching his weapons-handling, his tactical—if not strategic—decisions, his accuracy under fire, this Englishman was not just an ordinary criminal or soldier.

He had almost done too well; in eliminating that many foot soldiers, The Black Axe might hesitate to launch a counterattack against the Camorra.

It was almost a shame Carlo and this Englishman were on the same team.

He broke down and packed away the FR F2 into a carrying case, and jogged down the building's outside stairs.

The 'Ndrangheta would ensure The Black Axe looked to Naples for retribution. And with that, another key manoeuvre by this fresh Albanian boss will have been averted.

20

Luke lay on the firm hotel bed, having just put his phone down. Since being brought in to the 'inner circle' his phone time was not greatly increased but the type of usage had now changed. The amount of time messaging girls, watching YouTube videos and other video clips had mostly given way to liaising with the managers of the various businesses he'd been assigned to run.

Tom was under the shower in the en-suite.

Luke stared into the blackness of the switched off TV screen, and remembered a few years ago thinking he would not like anywhere near the responsibility his cousin Tom had; he thought the incessant decision-making would be draining.

However, even though he found it to be true, there was something…centring about being needed.

That said, he still felt a feathering anxiety when comparing himself to his two elder cousins. Tom—rock solid, stoic, pragmatic, always thinking—had held the family's reputation together back in the days when their Uncle Derek's ego and insecurities were intent on running it down. Now at the helm, Tom had been the driving force in growing and solidifying the business; diversifying and streamlining their contacts up and down the Isles, smoothing over tensions and creating systems. Tom could be ruthless and Luke knew he had killed more than a couple of people, one which he had helped bury. He had had the nickname of 'Tommy' a few years ago, not due to an extension of his name, but because his stature and ferocity resembled the *Goodfellas* character.

He respected Tom about as much as a man could respect another, but Connor had always held his awe.

Connor—enigmatic, razor-sharp intelligent, superb fighter, seemingly unshakeable confidence—had been Luke's idol as a child, who followed him to the boxing gym despite them living miles apart. Connor had a side to him that made scary people scared of him.

Now he had been brought closer to the two, Luke felt his inadequacies more acutely.

I'll just have to keep working hard.

He thought of his brother and a guilt swelled inside at how the cruel hand had been dealt to Dan and not himself.

Tom walked out of the shower with a crisp white towel wrapped around his waist. On his thickset but 'marbled'—as Tom called it—physique, read his ribs tattoo of *dictum meum pactum*, which Luke learnt was Latin for 'My word is my bond'.

His elder cousin checked his phone for a few long moments before saying, "Right, got some intelligence. Time for us both to formulate a plan."

Bruce watched tweed-jacketed Douglas Erickson peruse the *Cultural Highlights* section of the bookstore before sliding out a hardback. He waited until the young lady had moved away, leaving the white-haired Canadian on his own.

Bruce thought Erickson seemed remarkably at ease given he claimed to have been kidnapped and taken to an island to be tortured.

The girl moved away, and Bruce approached, running through his responses to guessed reactions from the man of almost exactly the same age.

Approaching from the side, he said, "Excuse me, Mr Erickson."

When the man's mouth fell open, Bruce quickly said, "I am in no way here to hurt you. Nor am I a journalist."

Erickson found his voice. "Who are you?"

"If it is true there is an apparatus kidnapping and torturing people into subservience, then I am a man who might be able to stop it, and bring some semblance of justice to those involved."

The architect slotted back the book, and walked away.

He slowed and stopped, remaining still for a few moments.

He turned back. "So you want to interview me?"

Bruce said, "There's a coffee shop upstairs."

Ciara's eyes drew in the scene of the massacre behind the police cordon. The flock of hooded crows flitted and squawked in and around decaying buildings. In a town as lawless as Castel Volturno, it had taken this much death and destruction to necessitate the presence of the *Arma dei Carabinieri*, a military-corps with police duties.

So far, there was evidence of over twenty dead, even though some of the bodies had been spirited away. With the Carabinieri present in force, many national journalists had appeared; usually they would not have dared tread these streets. The protection of the soldierlike cops and the pull of covering such a story proved compelling.

Ciara shook her head with a mixture of admiration and confusion. She surmised Connor must have been ambushed—she doubted he would have taken on even a quarter of the number of men she had heard whispered about, unless forced to. That he was able to fight his way out of it was a testament to his skill and nerve under fire. Ciara had not come from a military background and knew she would have died had it been her.

Still, even knowing—through witnessing and Bruce's telling her—of Connor's combat ability, both armed and unarmed, the number of people he had managed to kill on his own was shocking. Bruce had told her it had been a one-man mission, and he would not have time to designate other Chameleon Project agents to aid Connor.

Even from this distance, she could see the blood, body parts and empty casings scattered all around.

In ordinary circumstances, she and the other journalists would stay a day or two to question the locals and gather more of a picture. However, the Carabinieri would only remain as long as necessary—until the end of the day, she anticipated—and there would be no journalist capable of breaking the wall of silence the civilians of the area would greet them with should they dare try.

Ciara used her phone to take pictures of the scene, ensuring she caught the man who looked to be in charge, before slinking back through the scrum of journalists.

She whirled around and saw Adrianna Cruz leant on the bonnet of a white Fiat Panda. Ciara knew Cruz's wealth far exceeded what the car indicated—an expensive car would not be a good idea here.

Already, Ciara could see the Italian's—mixed with Albanian—beauty had not been exaggerated by the pictures she had seen. Her black hair had a gorgeous sheen and feathered her shoulders. The sunglasses reminded Ciara of a pair she had seen Audrey Hepburn wearing.

The cream dots on her black shirt matched the collar and skirt.

Ciara held her hand out as she came within range. "Ms Cruz, your reputation precedes you."

The soft hand had a surprisingly strong grip—though the force paled compared to what Ciara's could exert.

"Yours too—after much digging. And Mr McQuillan speaks very highly of you."

"As he does of you."

"I hope so," said Adrianna. She seemed to stiffen after saying it. Ciara understood—*she likes him.*

Adrianna's voice cut off her thoughts. "Quite the mess."

Ciara nodded. "Not unlike some of the war zones I have covered. Quite a thing to see in Italy."

"I have it on good authority The Black Axe leader, Okemiorukaye Akintimehin, might have been present here last night. His body has not been found, which makes sense as he has less desire to get his hands dirty in light of his rising status. But him being alive means war is a guarantee."

"Not for the first time," Ciara replied.

"There has been a massacre here before, true. The Casalesi clan murdered seven immigrants in the escalating war between the Camorra and African drug gangs—but it was nothing like this."

"So, we're saying that is the likely scenario—a reigniting of tensions between the two organisations."

Ciara knew Adrianna would feel as much of a pinch at hearing these words as she did saying them. They were both serious journalists who attempted to enter into any investigative situation with an open mind. This time, both would report the police suspected it to be a Camorra raid—which was true; but leave out what Arianna must have supposed and what Ciara knew—it was a false flag operation designed to plunge the Camorra into a bloody, vicious and expensive war with The Black Axe.

"The police suspect as much. The last time this occurred there were violent protests amongst the immigrant community here. The crackdown that followed might deter a repetition."

Ciara could detect guilt in the statement and said, "A lot of atrocities are committed in their belief of 'the greater good'. That's not to say one doesn't exist."

Adrianna looked at her. "How do you know whose greater good is correct or not? Some people's idea of it can convince a nation. That's not to say it's right."

"Maybe you're right. No one can anticipate how the butterfly effect will play out. But as far as I am aware, no civilians died in this. The Black Axe deals in drugs, kidnappings, fraud and human trafficking. Now many of them are gone, and the backlash will be directed at another organisation who deal in drugs, kidnappings, fraud and human trafficking. Let's hope the good outweighs the bad."

Adrianna said, "For both our consciences."

"Would you prefer inaction?"

Adrianna smirked. "I do not think that is either of our characters."

"So," began Ciara, "do the police have any evidence on the contrary to the narrative?"

"Not at the moment, however, the ROS team has taken over, and the lead investigator is a Raphael Del Piero—a very talented man."

"What are you thinking?"

Adrianna sighed. "He might not question the narrative that it was a Camorra ambush. The ROS want the government funding this will bring to fight the Camorra harder. So, if it was not a Camorra ambush, then whoever was behind it does not have to worry—perhaps."

21

Bruce sipped his black coffee, and held his tongue. Finally, Erickson, sat opposite at the circular wood table decorated in coffee stains, spoke, "What do you want to know?"

"Start from the beginning."

"You're Scottish," said Erickson.

"Aye, that I am, Douglas."

"My ancestry is Scottish."

Bruce didn't bother to tell him he already knew. Indeed he had deliberately raised the inflection of his voice to his native Glaswegian.

"Have you traced back to which part?"

"Stornoway."

"I should imagine the men from Stornoway back in those times to be particularly hardy."

Erickson slowly nodded. After a moment he said, "You know I cannot remember anything about being taken. One night I went to bed early as I had a flight to Germany for a work trip the following day. The next I wake on a hospital-type bed with tubes in me, in a white room with one side made of glass. Like a hamster in a pet store."

"Can you describe it?"

"Not much to describe. A cell really. Toilet in the corner. They'd take me out to another room with the same layout except it had a shower. Every time they did, they would blindfold me but it was an immediate left and thirty-three steps in a straight line and on the left. The therapy room was an immediate right fifteen steps and then to the left. The torture chamber was right across from it."

Bruce could not detect the markers of deceit in Erickson's body language or voice.

"What happened in the therapy room?"

Bruce watched Erickson's chest expand and then fall. "He was very old but very sharp. An American. Wispy white hair, and thick glasses. Never knew his name. I have never been more afraid of a man—his face and voice always remained the same, but I understood he enjoyed what he put me through."

Erickson went on to describe hypnotherapy, white noise, verbal abuse, psychoactive drugs and finally, with significantly more angst in his voice, the oxygen deprivation.

Bruce let the architect talk, though he already knew he'd be missing an important meeting, sensing it might help the Canadian to heal.

When the monologue began to slow, Bruce said, "I would have thought the experience would have turned you into a recluse."

The Scotsman saw the mouth quiver before the lips pressed together.

"I won't let them control me now I am out," said Erickson. "Besides, it's at night when I…I get…"

Bruce held up his hand indicating that Erickson didn't have to say *scared.*

"Why didn't the mind control work on you?"

"I had read a few books years ago about the subject—I tend to get obsessed about things for short amounts of time. So I understood submission would be my ticket out. There are subtle cues of breaking that the subject has to exhibit, I could not just simply fake sudden obedience because he would have known it to be false."

"I see," said Bruce, impressed. "What about the guards? Can you describe them?"

"They were more like soldiers. Spoke English but had different accents. Had armour and assault rifles. Had these chest harnesses with pouches on."

Bruce knew he was referring to the assault vests some soldiers preferred.

"Did you hear anything? Or see anything specific that can help me identify who was behind it?"

Erickson shook his head slowly, before tilting it. "The day they put me under again to transfer me out, they seemed a little more…animated. One of them mentioned the arrival of a 'Mr Milan'."

"Mr Milan?"

After a few moments, Bruce said, "Could I contact you again, or would you not welcome that?"

"You can contact me."

"Thank you," said Bruce, before taking out a card. "If you can think of anything. Or if you notice anything or in any way feel unsafe, then contact me on this."

Erickson looked at the card before looking up with gratitude shining from his eyes.

As Salvatore walked through the sun-drenched, forested hills of Calabria, he felt the low sounds of wildlife soothe him.

These vast stretches of majestic mountains crowned by stony crests, rushing waterfalls spilling into shingle valleys, and tranquil lagoons bordered by golden sands, had always been a friend to the 'Ndrangheta.

The Aspromonte National Park had been a particularly kind mother to the Calabrian Mafia. Back in the seventies and eighties, one of their original income sources was to kidnap the rich's loved ones. Salvatore remembered the words of his mentors—*"The rich, not wealthy. The wealthy have the money to pay and then hurt us; the rich just have the money to pay."*

When asked what the difference was, his mentor replied, "*Don't worry about that. You have to learn how to see the wealthy. But seeing the rich is easy.*"

It had taken Salvatore a few years to understand what that meant.

The police were not as much in their pockets back then, but finding kidnap victims and various contraband in an area of almost six hundred and fifty square kilometres, with the elaborate bunker system the 'Ndrangheta had created was like finding the end of eternity.

Finally, he came to the mound, pleased to see no signs it was man-made. His fingers traced over the scrub before finding the edge of green plastic.

He lifted it to find the black steel durbar lid. His thumb skimmed over the barely noticeable latch to reveal a rotary code lock. Marrying up the correct digits lifted the top. He made his way down the ladder, closing the top behind him.

The challenge came up. "Flash."

Salvatore replied, "Thunder."

His feet touched a floor surfaced with stainless steel. The same material covered the walls and ceiling. The smell of ammonia feathered the air—blood could stain almost any metal, and the chemical was valuable in removing it.

Grated gutters bordered the edges for rapid drainage, with a high-powered black hose lying in the corner like a coiled mamba. It had the dual purpose of washing away any DNA and for horrendous whippings. Salvatore himself had felt its bite as a youth.

However, that was mild in comparison to what Giorgio looked like he had endured. The policeman sat facing away from him on a steel chair bolted to the floor. Though it had armrests, which secured the corrupt civil servant's wrists with Italian police issue handcuffs, it had no spine support. This was a purposeful design to give free access to the back. Score marks of deep purple and red criss-crossed its entirety like a work of macabre art.

His breathing sounded like what sobs would sound like without the energy.

Three of his stony-faced men stood around him. With a wave of his fingers they moved away, allowing Salvatore to stand in front of him.

Giorgio's front mirrored his back. Tears had streaked his face, and urine stained his underwear—the only garment he was wearing.

It appeared a great effort was required to raise his head to look at Salvatore through wet eyes. When he finally did, he simply said, "Why?"

"I told you, Giorgio, the intelligence you provide should be of the highest order if your rate is to be doubled."

"I…it will be…it takes time."

Salvatore lifted his chin at one of his men who brought over the 'black mamba' and gave it to him. He stood back as to avoid any blood on his tailored shirt.

"No…please…no…AARRRGGGHHH."

Salvatore stopped at three lashes. "Giorgio, please do not lie to me again. You have had conversations. One of your most enlightening lines being 'I have the information he wants. I will just make him bleed a little. He has all the money in the world.'"

Giorgio began to shiver against a non-existent cold at his words.

Salvatore Mancuso continued, "I can see your reasoning, but yours is the reasoning of a police officer, whereas mine is the reasoning of a businessman. Do you know why most criminals make poor legitimate businessmen?"

Giorgio opened his mouth as if to answer before closing it again with a shake of his head.

Salvatore continued, "Because they do not concern themselves with terms like profit margins, or indeed understand the difference between net and gross profit. If you are selling contraband at a price many times a higher than the price you obtained it for, that concern would seem like an unnecessary headache—they think too short-term, Giorgio, but not me. I take the utmost interest in everything I spend and the value I get back."

Giorgio croaked, "If you kill me, they will come for you."

Salvatore's fingers smoothed the hair on the flinching head. "Do not be naïve. You are my employee. In most corporate enterprises, disciplinary procedures escalate given the severity of the misdeed or how many have occurred. This is level one—there is no need to go to level two."

"H…how…?"

"Your face has not been marked, Giorgio, though I would suggest you don't go swimming in a public pool for a few weeks."

The barest of sniggers escaped from his men.

"I am…am a policeman. You can't—"

"You're a corrupt policeman. A fact that will be known to everyone you wish it to be hidden from should you ever move against us. If you think I have not collected and stored substantial evidence, you live in a dream world. You are in my pocket, Giorgio. Do not ever forget that." Salvatore sat on his haunches and said, "Now, tell me everything you know."

Giorgio gave the nod of a broken man and began to talk.

"His contact met me in Bari two days ago."

"Do not be coy in here, Giorgio. I assure you any names spoken here will remain here."

"Tefik Mesi's emissary to me."

"And what did he say?"

Through laboured breathing, Giorgio answered, "He gave me the exact location of the airfield in Tirana that Andrei Faja inherited for distribution of his clan's cannabis."

"And why would Mesi impart that to you?"

Salvatore already knew the answer but waited for confirmation anyway.

"Because, if Faja wins this war with you, he will be seen as the man who brought the Italians to their knees. He fears Faja will then make moves to become an emperor."

"And so he wants me to destroy the airfield. To weaken Faja's position."

Giorgio nodded. "If the airfield is destroyed, Tefik can seek a ceasefire, as it is only Faja's clan that benefit from it. If Faja continues, Tefik will release more intelligence that will all but guarantee your victory. However, he does not wish to go down that road. He says he wants Faja alive—says he has great potential but needs to be kept in his place. And so he has offered you a deal."

"What is it?"

"Agree to destroy the airfield and then come to the table to agree a ceasefire with Faja. And he will give you what you most want—the identity and location of the woman who murdered your sister. And as dangerous as she is, he knows you know of men who are more than capable of hunting her down."

Carlo gripped the back of her neck, pinning her to his bed. Though he couldn't see her face, he was reminded of how pretty the spiky-haired blonde was, looking at her glasses perched on the chrome bedside cabinet. He remembered how they framed her gorgeous brown eyes.

Her arsehole sent a thousand pinpricks of pleasure coursing through his cock, but he knew this would not compare to the finale. The first time he had sex with someone like Bianca had been a fantastic appeal to his sense of freedom.

He enjoyed her song of alternating sweet cries and pillow-muffled moans. A trickle of sweat tickled his brow. He was getting close. He slowed.

"Turn over," he said, slapping her ass but remaining inside her.

With the nimbleness of a ballet dancer, she rose and spun slowly, her leg gracefully clearing his head to reveal her own cock—rock-hard and hairless.

Carlo stilled himself knowing any movement would set him off.

"Don't move. Don't make a sound," he commanded her. He looked up until the threat of his orgasm withdrew. Then he began to pound her with abandon.

His hand hovered over her cock, more out of courtesy—it neither turned him on nor repulsed him—but Bianca waved it away.

"I don't need it," she rasped.

The edge of masculinity in her voice sent his cum rocketing into her tight ass, as he felt the wet of her own orgasm splatter his abdomen.

As the throes subsided, he began to laugh, before withdrawing and telling her, "Very good. Get dressed and leave."

Not long after Bianca had left, he wandered over and sat on the balcony of his high-rise apartment—five stories up—overlooking the Colosseum.

Sipping his coffee, he lamented on whether he would have liked being a gladiator. On the one hand, it would have been a constant satisfaction to his addiction to combat-induced adrenaline. On the other, a permanent shackle on his love of liberty. He had been fascinated by the stories of famous gladiators, especially that of Marcus Attilius, a freeman who willingly chose to be a gladiator, and scored more than one victory as an underdog.

One gladiator he could not understand was Flamma—'Flame'—a Syrian slave who earnt and refused the *Rudis* more than once, a wooden sword symbolising the granting of his freedom.

To Carlo, freedom meant the freedom to explore what life had to offer—like she-males. Carlo still loved women but if there was anything 'different' on offer, he'd try it; from experimenting with drugs, travelling, and learning different skills, but most of all, conducting combat missions.

And he knew he was a whore; if Salvatore had not approached him first, he might have ended up in any one of the world's hotspots as a gun for hire.

He remembered where this love of adrenaline came from.

His father had never shown him any affection—Carlo's childhood love of comics, dancing and experiments with his mother's make-up had disgusted his father. And when taken up to the Calabrian hills to a gun range—as a lackey—the eleven-year-old Carlo, away from his mother's protective coddling, felt that disdain even more acutely under his father's vicious mocking of his future lack of manhood.

However, Carlo showed an interest by watching intently for days. Finally, his father allowed him shots on his customised Remington 700— a 'gift from a friend in America'— and despite more taunts, he had instructed Carlo on his firing technique too.

A few weeks passed, and as his proficiency grew, the ridiculing receded until all that was left was a cold nonchalance towards him. But he remembered one particular statement— *"Being good on the range is still a world away from shooting a deer. Which is a world away from shooting an animal that wants to harm you. Which is a world away from shooting a human being who is trying to shoot you back."*

Hunting roe deer in the snow-glinting Tuscan–Emilian Apennines mountain chain had indeed been a world away from the Calabrian ranges, especially as Carlo was made to carry much of the equipment, including the rifle, up the steep ascents. He refused to show weakness, much less cry, so as not to lose face.

Finally, just as he came to breaking point on the second day, his father turned to him and said, *"I will go up ahead and scout over the ridge. I believe them to be there. I cannot afford for you to come up with all the equipment as you might alert them. I will raise my thumb if they are there. You will set down the equipment and bring the rifle only. Do you understand?"*

Carlo had watched his father crunch up the hillside fifty metres away.

The wind died and he heard it behind him—a rustle of vegetation, then the skipping paws and hunger growls of an Italian grey wolf.

The predator bore down on him at full flight as Carlo's body exploded in cold energy. He moved in a fit of survival, cutting dead all other non-essential actions, including registering the scream of his father.

Now facing the wolf in an adopted kneeling position, he expelled his breath, and in the natural pause before inhalation—squeezed the trigger.

Part of the wolf's chest exploded, sending the animal sideways with a death mew. It lay, the condensation of its breath pluming from its tongue, before freezing still.

Only then did Carlo hear his father's shouting. The boy turned to see his run slow to a walk, his face flickering through a kaleidoscope of expressions—concern, shock, understanding and then a bursting pride.

"Mother Mary," his bellow echoing. *"You downed that wolf dead with one shot."*

Carlo became faintly aware of this nod of affirmation, as the older man continued, *"Not just a wolf but a wolf running towards you looking for a kill. And you killed it."*

The rifle was snatched away before Carlo found himself in the warm shock of his father's embrace.

As they walked back—equipment distributed evenly—Carlo did so with a diaphragm full of the appreciation of the beauty of life. He realised much later it wasn't his father's love—from then on never held back—that kept him addicted to the danger.

It had been the power he felt in the defiance of death.

He wondered if the man in Castel Volturno had felt the same. Maybe one day he should ask him.

22

Connor began to shiver under the freezing cold Rome hotel shower.

Years ago, he had researched the benefits of cold thermogenesis, and implemented cold showers into his daily routine. Connor thought the notion of 'twenty-one days to form a habit' was not true as, even now, he sometimes had to repeat those benefits to himself before stepping in.

Increase white blood cells to improve the immune system. Decrease in inflammation. Increase blood and nitric oxide to the brain. Increases cell longevity. Activates brown fat to torch the white fat. Stop being a pussy, you can get through seven minutes of anything and you'll feel great.

He had finished a callisthenics session, which had included pistol squats, handstand presses, door frame pull-ups, and the use of his jiu-jitsu belt to simulate an isometric deadlift.

He stopped the shower and vigorously dried himself. Having dressed, he sat at his laptop with a black coffee to begin his daily study. The hanging light resembled a bird in a cage, with the different settings changing the light's colour and brightness.

He heard the premeditated knock at the door.

He got up and as per his *SOPs*—stood back and crouched, arm outstretched.

"Who is it?"

"Your secret admirer," said a well-clipped voice feathered with Liverpudlian. Connor smiled—he insisted that be her 'I am not under duress' response to his challenge.

Ciara came in carrying her usual aura of confidence. Her silvery-blonde hair had grown out from its previously severe short-cut into a bob creeping down her neck, though swept well away from the eyes.

She wore a black vest top stretched over her breasts, displaying her arms' dense muscularity. Her green eyes shone from a face highlighted by only the barest of make-up—which she rarely wore unless the occasion required it.

"Fuck me, where's Ludmilla Drago gone?"

She shook her head with a frown. "Who's Ludmilla Drago?"

"A bird in *Rocky IV* played by Brigitte Nielson—she was very sexy. But you look great with the new hair."

"Was? She dead now?"

"No, she must be nearly sixty."

"Older women can't be sexy?"

"Well, I wouldn't kick Dame Helen Mirren out of bed, so I apologise for my ageism."

She looked at him. "White coffee without sugar would be lovely, thank you."

Within a few minutes they were sat across from one another drinking their coffees. Connor had placed the laptop away.

Ciara asked, "What's that T-shirt you're wearing? I haven't heard of 'Blur' before—the band maybe but not a clothing brand."

"A tattoo artist out of Bristol. He does these as a sideline, I think."

"What does that mean on the back? 'Sons of Achnacarry'."

"The design is based on the commando memorial not far from Spean Bridge in Scotland. The old-school World War II commando recruits would get off the train after a fourteen-hour journey, load their kit bags onto waiting trucks and then speed march it the seven miles to the training centre—which was Achnacarry Castle—in full kit with weapon, which weighed around sixteen kilos. Back then those boots probably smashed more shins than your favourite Thai boxer Buakaw. Anyone not completing it within an hour were fucked off back to their original unit. A bit of history for you there. The Sons of Achnacarry bit is a play on the *Sons of Anarchy* television show."

"I forgot, you ride a motorcycle now."

"Indeed," he said. "So, what have you got to tell me?"

"Initial guess is they will blame the Camorra, as planned," she said, flooding his system with relief. "I do not know how you survived that. Looked like a warzone."

"Yeh, I was lucky," he replied, without going into the specifics of the mystery sniper.

The silence hung in the air before she broke it with, "Can I ask you a question?"

"Yeah."

"Why do you do this?"

Knowing what she was referring to, he answered, "Why wouldn't I want to rid the world of evil people?"

"Well, many men might say that, but none actually do it."

"Bruce gave me the opportunity and apparatus to do so. That should be obvious to a brainbox like yourself."

She shook her head. "You've killed people before. And not just back in the marines."

Her statement—not question—surprised him.

"So?"

"So, why?"

"I don't know what to say to you. Why do you think?"

He regretted it as soon as he said it.

"I think something happened to you or you've seen something you shouldn't have as a child. And that's manifested itself over time—"

"Any amateur psychologist could say that about anyone unusual. It's like the vague statements of astrologers to con superstitious housewives."

He kept his voice as even as he could. He'd watched two debaters on YouTube recently and noted although one had the stronger logical argument, the other had given the appearance of winning because he kept calm.

Ciara said, "Well, we've known one another a while now. And we've been through some perilous times. Although you're guarded, you never really have a problem talking about your dad's side of your family. However, you never talk about—"

"What is this all about?"

"I am just curious. It's the journalist in me."

"I am your colleague, not some interviewee."

"I know that. I was just—"

"And you're not my fucking therapist, either. Not every man has to trawl through their childhood to become 'fixed' so they can fit neatly into society."

He became aware he was ranting but could not stop. "If I were hurting the good and innocent then maybe I'd consider it. But I like who I am. And I like what I do. So, stop asking, because I never ask you how you came to be who you are, because I like you just the way you are."

He took a breath, and its slow release calmed him. A glisten appeared on her lower eyelid, and she stood.

She walked towards him and he shunted his chair back, unsure of her intentions. She leant down and kissed him hard.

The two men looked down on the city of Reggio Calabria. The simmering sun had slipped below the sea's horizon, leaving behind the city's artificial lights to highlight the ocean's dark blue.

Salvatore looked across the stone table at his preferred soldier. Carlo sipped the wine from Salvatore's own vineyards, as he stared out to sea.

"It was just him on his own, Salvatore, I saw it for myself."

Carlo remained the only newly made man he allowed to refer to him by his first name. Salvatore had known the former legionnaire back when Carlo was a hellraising adolescent on the same streets they now had a view of.

His reputation for fighting preceded him as a teenager. Carlo had come under another *'ndrine*—family clan—to Salvatore, but the exploits of the mercurial youth had reached his ears back in those days, almost fifteen years ago.

"Just one man?" he said. "When I heard reports of the body count I assumed it was a team."

Carlo shook his head. "One man."

There were rumours the teenage Carlo would disappear without warning, only to return with an inordinate amount of money that he would hand over to his *capo bastone*—head crook—Baldovino Rocca.

Salvatore despised Rocca; the man was both a glorified pimp and a whore. He would say anything to appease anyone and stood for nothing. Carlo was a rising star—his rising star—until one day the reason for his hiatuses came to light.

A policeman from Rome, in the 'Ndrangheta's pocket, talked of a series of high-line armed robberies that had mystified them in the territories of the Camorra and Apulian mafia organisations. It was not long before someone worked out these robberies were occurring in sync with Carlo's absences. Shocking too was the fact that Carlo kicked almost the entire takings from these heists up to Rocca. That was when Salvatore knew Carlo loved the adrenaline more than anything else.

Rocca—snake that he was—caved and sent two of his men to punish the seventeen-year-old. Both returned disarmed and severely beaten, and Carlo disappeared, escaping reprisals.

Salvatore spoke, "I told Alessio to send him there as someone expendable. Maybe to ruffle some feathers, and which we could use to our advantage. He was never meant to return. And he was never meant to be so…successful."

Carlo nodded. "Can I ask what he wants?"

Salvatore usually kept his own counsel. However, he knew a soldier—as in a military soldier—like Carlo, would perform with more initiative knowing the strategic goal. The man was not just an underling—his talents for mayhem and destruction far exceeded anyone else's. Salvatore discovered a long time ago certain lines had to be drawn in the sand when commanding men and certain other aspects could be compromised on. And he knew Carlo needed to feel respected—because, despite 'being made', the man did not respect any rules or codes—just the addiction of combat.

"I've researched him. He seems to be a fixer of some sorts. He has formed links with Leonid Honchar, a very powerful man within the Odessa Mafia—as they like to call themselves—and Raymond Van Der Saar. His customer base seems a little hazy, but is a member of the Ryder family, despite his surname being Reed. This family is based out of one the north of England's larger cities. The family is now beginning to shed its coat of being a mid-level outfit, and this Connor Reed is looking to tap into our money laundering expertise."

Carlo smiled. "I do not doubt the audacity of the man to come from his little fiefdom to us, after what I witnessed."

Salvatore said with a tease, "You sound like a fan, Carlo."

"I admire any man who can develop that level of skill in gun fighting and have the nerve to execute it in a live situation," replied Carlo. "But he would have died had it not been for my presence. He allowed himself to get boxed in—the man could be reckless."

Salvatore gave a short laugh. "He is not the only one that accusation could be levelled at, Carlo."

"That is true. Now I have you here, I wanted to ask you about Baldovino Rocca."

"What about him?"

"His death."

"He had a heart attack. It is of public record."

Carlo looked at him. "He had a heart attack not long after I had visited my sister and mother, telling them I could not return because of his vendetta towards me. Three nights later he dies after a meeting with you."

Salvatore shrugged. "Someone had to be the last to see him alive. Just happened to be me."

"I also find it strange our friends in Foggia just blindly accepted the police's assessment of what happened in that bar that day."

Salvatore leant over and briefly touched his arm. "Carlo, we both know what this is. You are my most trusted…investment when it comes to physical combat with our enemies. A man who looks after his dragon finds his dragon looks after him. It is not only your ability that sets you apart from the rest of my men, it is your love for the work, Carlo—the work that I provide for you. You like the money to be sure, but it is war that you need in your life. It is a mutually beneficial partnership I want to protect."

Carlo did not speak for a few moments before saying, "I appreciate your honesty, Salvatore."

"Speaking of which, as you are aware, despite our best efforts, the Albanians are beating us in this ground war—your ambush of their lead soldier has helped stem the tide. But they have the benefit of knowing our points of contact and logistics network. Our revenue is down and our friends over the Atlantic are getting concerned."

"What can I do?"

"As you must know, not all within our families and extended families are happy with this conflict we have found ourselves in with our Albanian cousins. I will attend a meeting—I believe the outcome of which will be a demand I cease the war and make peace. And at this moment in time, I will have to obey."

"What must I do?"

"I have a mission for you, Carlo. Extremely dangerous but it may help to redress the balance."

"When and where?"

"Whenever you can make it happen. The airfield our friends in Tirana have. I would like to see it destroyed."

Carlo whistled with a smile. "I take it my plea did not convince our released hostage."

"He is now dead. Stabbed in the throat and dumped in a ditch with his tongue cut out."

"I see," said Carlo. "So, that would be an admission of guilt by the new boss."

Salvatore said, "A policeman in my pocket confirmed my suspicions. I will be extending an invitation to a certain young lady for an interview regarding the incident."

Ciara threw her arms around Connor as he stood. One arm wrapped around her waist and his other hand slid onto the back of her neck.

This felt different from the previous occasions. His hand moved from her waist to grasp her ass, as he ground her against his hardening cock.

They began stripping one another with abandon. She had always liked the combination of dense muscularity, light chest hair and his torso's beautiful tattoos.

When they were both fully naked she grasped his cock and growled, "Don't be thinking just because you might have thought you'd seen a tear in my eye that you're going to be making love to me."

"Wouldn't dream of it."

"Well…that's a lie."

They began to kiss harder before he switched his attention to her tits.

He gripped her asscheeks before penguin-walking her over to the bed and throwing her on to it.

He pinned her strong legs back and ate her voraciously. She smiled—he never quite hit the spot.

"Come here," she moaned. "Let's not pretend it's your thing."

She laughed at his laugh as he clambered up. She could taste herself on him, and felt a flutter in her stomach as his hardness brushed against her pussy.

"Put it in," she begged.

His hand gripped her throat. "Shut the fuck up, Ciara."

She writhed under the teasing tip as her hands gripped his wrist. She gasped as he began to ease into her. He released his grip on her throat and kissed her hard, sliding into her to the hilt.

A guttural moan escaped her as her pussy tightened around him.

"Come on," she snarled. "Give it to me."

His arms swam in behind her legs and, pinning her to the bed, he began to hammer into her. Even through her throes of pleasure, she could feel her wetness between them.

Every other time they had had sex, she had taken charge. This time, she surrendered to him.

They kissed again as she remained folded.

He slid out of her, leaving her feeling bereft. His patting hand co-coerced her onto her hands and knees. He appeared at her side and she greedily took him in her mouth.

His fingers gripped her hair—but not nearly as hard as on their previous occasions. She could taste him at the back of her throat as her hand cupped his asscheek, drawing him deeper.

His fingers delved into her before bringing her clit to singing life.

Bastard—she thought—*he does know where it is.*

He freed himself and mounted her. Rapture coursed through her as he entered her.

One of his hands spread her to his gaze as the other gripped her hair—harder this time—with his command of, "Look at me."

She did so—then narrowed her eyes and licked her lips.

This seemed to send him wild. Both hands on her hips now, he powered into her with a fury.

Her orgasm rushed to surprise her as she cried out and soaked the bed.

His roar followed, as she felt him unleash hard inside her.

After a few rigid moments, he mirrored her by collapsing face down beside her.

She murmured, "Thought you said we weren't doing this again after last time?"

He sighed. "Well, I could tell you made an effort with growing your hair out and putting on some make-up. I didn't want to break your positive feedback loop of effort equals rewards."

She smiled into the pillow. "Such an arsehole."

His phone interrupted his replying laugh.

23

Andrei stood with the impressive Tefik Mesi without any feeling of inferiority. And he could tell by Tefik's demeanour, the King of the Kyres could sense it too.

They stood amidst the party for the groom, dressed in their country's traditional dress, which included almost identical beige kilt-like fustanellas. Albanian weddings were a week-long affair encompassing the entire village. The northern hills of Albania still maintained centuries-old customs.

Tradition and family were two of the bedrocks of the Mafia Shqiptare, and Andrei had a lack of both.

"This here is our strength, Andrei. Our unity through blood."

"Of course."

"You know, your father would be proud of what you have become, Andrei. He was a man of true honour. But you have something he lacked."

"What is that?" said Andrei, bracing himself.

"Forgive me for saying this, sometimes your father's…hard-headedness clouded his judgement—his judgement of the long-term consequences."

"Can you name examples?"

"You know your father and I knew one another when we were very young. We did a lot of business together. On one of our business trips to Italy, we may have gotten over-confident. There was a shootout and your father allowed me to escape."

They didn't speak for a few moments.

"Why was allowing you to escape a lack of judgement?"

Tefik looked at him. "I used to think it was that he could have taken over the Tirana clan and he'd be the one who was the most influential."

"As opposed to you?" Andrei said quietly.

The nod was subtle. "Yes. However, look at how things have transpired under the eyes of God. His son is now the rising star, and I am duty-bound to watch over you."

Andrei could not detect a lack of sincerity.

"Perhaps it is just a coincidence."

"You are not a pious man, Andrei, and perhaps you feel that is a strength. But it is not. Faith rivets a man to the ground. It does not allow success to inflate his ego or dampen his resolve."

Andrei's eyes moved around the wedding party as he digested the words. "You speak with the authority of experience, and I will listen."

"Good. Then learn from an older man. One of the arts of negotiation is to be open when your hand is at its strongest."

"If one is looking for negotiation."

Tefik said, "Andrei, you have made your point. You have strengthened our hand. You must see a lengthy war with the Calabrese is not desirable."

"The total dismantlement of their organisation cannot be a short process. We must resolve to—"

"Andrei. You must give up this anger-fuelled fantasy. I know you loved Oso very much and you were right to act against the perpetrators of his murder. But this is a war that cannot be won, by either side."

"We did not start this, Kyre Tefik."

"I understand, Andrei. But the Calabrese are a global organisation and hold influence in places even we cannot yet reach. You have increased our revenue, but they will wait us out without our immediate and necessary reinvestment opportunities. They do not need their own soldiers—eventually, they will use their influence to convince other agencies to move against us."

Andrei turned to Tefik. "Are you telling me to ceasefire, my Kyre?"

Tefik met his eyes. "I am asking you to consider negotiations. I can guarantee neutral ground where you can meet Mancuso."

Andrei kept the unease, tumble-drying in his stomach, off his face.

"I am beholden to your wishes, Kyre Tefik."

Carlo looked at the airfield through the green tint of his night-vision binoculars. For the past two nights, he and his team had been observing, logging and recording everything pertinent to the Albanian paramilitary operation below.

The Calabrian had mixed feelings regarding the mercenaries Salvatore had recruited for him to command.

On the one hand, he knew it was necessary; the 'Ndrangheta had plenty of street gunmen and a handful of upper-tier assassins, but lacked true soldiers capable of planning and executing paramilitary operations.

On the other, their professionalism increased the odds in his favour and increased his safety—it lessened the thrill for him.

However, they were deep in enemy territory within the forest-covered hills of northern Albania.

The former legionnaire had anticipated the journey to cross the Adriatic to be fraught with danger from the collaboration between the Albanian Coastguard and the EU's Frontex border patrols prowling the sea in search of drug smugglers. Alas, the deep influence of 'Ndrangheta came into play, the said patrols gave Carlo and the mercenaries safe passage and documentation stating they were on a training secondment with the Albanian military. That the documentation was merely glanced at, as were the military-grade explosives and detonators they had in their possession, spoke of the power of the organisation he worked for—or maybe the man he worked for.

All the equipment the assembled group had now was of high quality, from their weapons, clothing, optics, down to their communication equipment.

The men with him were South African, and in his experience, the country seemed to produce—in general—superb soldiers, if lacking—with a few exceptions—a good sense of humour. South African men generally had a familiarity with the outdoors; when that outdoors held the dangers of a plethora of animals that could kill you, it developed one's tracking skills and fitness.

He had not asked the leader, Francois, his or his team's background; he had trusted Salvatore to have done his utmost to ensure his criteria for professionalism would be met. In turn, the only thing Francois had asked him that was personal was his first name.

Over the two nights and days, they recorded everything from routines to full descriptions of the personnel, including estimates of rank structure, equipment, weaponry and airfield layout.

The former soldier had been a little surprised at the seemingly porous nature of the security perimeter; openings in the fence line and gaps between sentry changeovers. He knew marijuana alone pulled in nearly three and half billion euros per year. Numerous airfields dotted the northern hills and the Adriatic coast but this was their mothership.

Carlo thumbed the pressel switch of his radio and said in English—the group's shared language, "One Bravo, close in on my position."

When Francois came, Carlo would share his plan with him and its timing—*these amateurs have never been taught to stand-to.*

The wind buffeted Connor's jacket as he rode the Moto Guzzi down the east coast of Italy. The traffic had died down at this late evening hour, allowing him to enjoy the view of the reflections of the rising moon and dying sun in the sea.

His senses sharpened as he neared the town of Foggia. Alessio had called him post-sex session with Ciara to inform him he was to meet a man— *"…who will decide your fate with our organisation."* Connor mused on the wording—*decide your fate*—not discuss a proposal. Of course, he had always known if he refused the mission, or certainly if he had pulled out of it after accepting, then his life could become forfeit. Whoever this guy was, he wanted to see him face to face despite his performance against The Black Axe. If he revealed himself and decided he didn't like Connor, then The Chameleon Project agent might die there and then. His not knowing why the 'Ndrangheta would choose to meet him in territory of the Società foggiana compounded this thought. After concluding the possibilities were numerous, he banished it from his mind.

He countered this negativity—*it's not like you're not going to meet him. It's an opportunity—this guy must have access to the upper tier, and it's the whole point of you being here. To provide intelligence so operations can be fought against them.*

He faded off the highway into the narrower, more volatile roads of the city.

The motorcycle's cylindrical SatNav eventually indicated he had reached his destination.

He parked the bike and stood next to one of the enormous pillars overlooking the *Fontana del Sele*—a lit-up fountain in the centre of a circular water feature which formed a traffic roundabout.

Buildings four to five floors high curved around to his right. He guessed he was being observed from there. He reckoned they would give it five to ten minutes to check for anything suspicious before coming for him.

As his eyes flickered about the scene, he began to think of his family, before realising he missed them—he couldn't remember doing so before. When he was younger, he did not spend as much time with his cousins as they did with one another. Between him living in the north of Leeds with his mum, and his dad's trepidation of him becoming embroiled in the 'family business' meant he did not see them as often.

However, when he did see them, especially when on leave from the marines, they treated him like a returning prince. Tom in particular always made way for him, and Connor thought this was because neither had brothers like the rest. And Luke had idolised him from a young age to the point of following him to the boxing gym, despite not being a particularly hard lad at the time.

Everyone on that side of the family had to be continuously reminded to call him Reed as opposed to Ryder.

He realised now why he had distanced himself when he went to work for Bruce—it was to avoid this feeling of fear for them.

It had exasperated Tom in the beginning—*"We're the biggest gangsters in Leeds. Loads of people want a piece of us—on both sides of the law. I don't know what you think you're protecting us from exactly that we aren't having to be wary of anyway. Unless it's aliens?"*

Connor acknowledged to himself the logic; a bullet was a bullet irrespective of the nationality of the gangster who fired it, or the crime boss who ordered it to be fired.

Feelings of closeness to his family had strengthened since Grace left his life, after he spurned her ultimatum to keep his sadistic streak against evil on a leash.

In moments of quiet—mercifully rare—he could slide into a melancholic nostalgia he would have to fight to get out of.

Fuck her—he thought—*if she can't accept all of you, then let her find a doctor who likes puppies and being outraged.*

A black van pulled up, and five men alighted from it—well built, unsmiling, black leather jackets with a bulge on one side. He guessed the bulges were as a result of the OWB method of concealed carry—weapon in a holster OUTSIDE-the-WAISTBAND on a BELT; one of the easiest to spot because the holster and gun on the outside of the belt created unnatural bulk in the area of the gun butt and the barrel end of the holster. It could often be seen if the person carrying had to lift his arms or bend over. Connor had his in the IWB style on his preferred firing side, his right hip. Having it inside the waistband, secured by straps on his belt, concealed most of the weapon, kept it close to him, and avoided the problems of carrying it inside his pants with no holster. Because he wore jeans with stretch fabric—to make running and fighting easier—it eliminated any discomfort from carrying it that way.

One stepped forward, the smallest but without any hint of 'small man syndrome' and said in excellent but accented English, "Mr Reed, please excuse, you must come with us."

He nodded. "What's happening with my bike?"

"The gentleman on my left can ride your bike to your destination—he will observe the speed limit. I am sure you are aware of why we must take you there ourselves."

"Because it'll be hard to ride the bike with a blindfold on."

Three of the men sniggered, and the man smiled. "Yes, Mr Reed. The location has to be kept secret."

Connor took it as a good sign as Alessio had asked on the call what his mode of transport would be. If he hadn't and if the guy addressing him now had been nonchalant regarding what would happen to the bike, then Connor would not have expected to see it again.

"I have a dagger up my left sleeve and a handgun on my right hip. Just letting you know so there are no surprises when you search me."

The man frowned. "Why did you bring these?"

"I am not sure," he replied, raising his hands in front of his face, putting a shake into them and looking at each hand in turn with an expression of exaggerated awe. "Since I could kill you all with these alone."

With that, he adopted a parodying Kung-Fu stance and let out Bruce Lee-like pre-fight cry.

The men's surprised expressions changed to smiles matching his own.

The leader nodded, fighting his own grin. "Let's go, Mr Reed."

24

Dan's brain slid in and out of consciousness like the waves lapping a beach. He had visited every night. In the beginning, the nurse had woken him with a gentle touch on his shoulder to indicate he should go home—more often than not he had refused.

His frustration with the lack of progress in her condition and gratefulness it had not deteriorated fought with one another.

He had felt a bitterness rise within him. His family were all criminals—most of them violent—and none of their partners had suffered this fate.

Dan reminded himself—*Uncle Greg, Michael and Derek are all dead. Uncle Ryan and Curtis came close. You've done the right thing staying out of it. Don't ever wish ill on your family who love you and you love back.*

His choice of career had caused him to leave Leeds, but it was Angela who made London feel like home.

They had met in a Polish class a few years back. Dan knew the West Slav people's work ethic would make them more prominent financial players in the future and he wanted to position himself as the man to come to. Angela had been a public defender at the time and often helped the local minority communities.

They had both arrived late to the first class, much to the teacher's chagrin, and as a result paired up together—and had been an item ever since.

He opened his eyes again and felt enraged seeing her inert face with the tubes feeding into her. His anger stemmed from his powerlessness to right this.

And even if Angela survived, the perpetrators would have achieved their objective by delaying the trial, or by having Angela's work passed over to a less committed and competent barrister.

You could strike back. Your family is one of the most dangerous in the UK. And they want to help. They— stop…that isn't the way.

He drifted back into the recliner before sleep gently guided him back into his dreams.

The loud, continuous beep shot his eyes and adrenal glands open.

The door crashed open and he felt himself bundled out of the room in a blur of turquoise, white and blue uniforms, and garbled instructions.

Fear ricocheted around his diaphragm like an agonising ping-pong ball, as he pressed his forehead to the window glass.

The minutes stretched out like the initial entry and stomach slice of a *seppuku* ceremony. His mouth fell open in anguish as the team stopped moving their hands and stood straight.

The world froze and he did not need anyone to tell him the love of his life had departed this world.

And if there had have been a *kaishakunin* on hand to deliver his decapitation—he would have welcomed it.

Connor was woken by light and sound of the door opening. On entering the black van he had been informed the journey would take more than a few hours. He decided to get whatever sleep he could, to be as tactically on top of his game as he could be on arrival, rather than attempting to ascertain his eventual destination through estimates of distance travelled and memorising every change of direction.

They had taken his phone along with his weapons on entering the van. If they managed to 'hack' into the security parameters set by Jaime—a minute chance, he reckoned—anything nefarious had been encrypted anyway.

He narrowed his eyes to let them adjust before taking in the scene around him. The white, cobbled road behind him had climbed up a great sunlit hill decorated with scrub, green trees and rocky cliffs.

In front of him stood a sandstone-walled fortification hosted by a twin-turreted castle-like entrance.

The men stood around him before the leader beckoned him to follow. After banging on them, the doors creaked open. The ground inside the fort matched the outside for a hundred metres until the cobbles faded into smooth stone paving and buildings.

As they ascended the steps, Connor admired the view of the adjacent hills topped with early morning clouds and a flat, calm sea.

A man stood tall against its backdrop. The shiny black hair was parted at the side, crowning a well-lined and strong face that saw its last shave two days ago. His all-beige attire, jacket, trousers and shoes, were offset by a white shirt and seemed perfectly contoured to his frame.

The leader gestured for Connor to go forward alone. As he did so, the smell of Italian cooking cruised into his nostrils.

The man held out his hand and Connor shook it—firmly, but not in an attempt to intimidate.

"Welcome, Mr Reed," the man said with only a hint of an accent. "My name is Salvatore Mancuso."

So, this Salvatore Mancuso, thought Connor. The intelligence report worked up by Bruce and Jaime included grainy pictures, which seemed strange in an age where everyone had a camera phone and every city was teeming with security cameras.

"Good to meet you," replied Connor. "You have good dress sense."

Mancuso said, "Style is a way to say who you are without having to speak."

"Thank you for that quote."

"Do not thank me, thank fashion designer Rachel Zoe Rosenzweig," replied the underworld chief. "I suspect you are hungry, Mr Reed."

Connor nodded. "Without being disrespectful, Mr Mancuso, I won't be eating if you aren't too."

Mancuso smiled. "If there is one thing we in Calabria like, it is to eat. You sit down with me."

With that, he called out, "Siamo pronti per mangiare."—*We are ready to eat.*

Three pretty, dark-haired young women appeared, carrying silver trays.

Connor smiled as his frittata Florentine was slid in front of him.

"I thought it was strange when he began asking me about my favourite Italian meals."

"We like to kill you with kindness." Mancuso smiled. "Which is why I chose our meeting to be early. The south Italian sun can be unkind to people north of the Mediterranean."

"You needn't have worried. I have *yomped* with ECM Blue in the kind of heat that would make Prince Andrew sweat."

"What do you mean?"

"I am used to the heat, that's all."

They ate in silence for a while before Mancuso asked, "Do you know where you are?"

Connor considered lying before saying, "Calabria."

"That is right. The land of my family," said Mancuso. "How is your family, Mr Reed?"

Connor felt some of the sentiment in his heart sink a little.

"As a collective, they are good."

"The details get blurred by the time they get to my ears but I recognise your family is rising within our world."

Connor looked at the powerful mafioso. "Our rise has been sharp in the last eighteen months due to a…change of management. As I said to our friend in Rome, we are now suffering from the opposite problem to most businesses—we have too much cash flow and not enough reinvestment opportunities. That is why I am here."

Mancuso dabbed his mouth when he had finished his meal. "Mr Reed, we come to an agreement today, so that part of your business you will not have to concern yourself about. But I want to know why you have taken the risk to come to Italy to propose this?"

Connor took a moment to realise what he was about to say was not a lie. "I want, one day, for my family to be so high in the stratosphere that they are not touched. Now, I understand this process may take years or even decades, which is why I want to start now."

The two men stared at one another, before Mancuso spoke. "My organisation—do you know where our name comes from?"

"The Greek word *andragathía*, roughly translates to heroism and manly virtue."

Mancuso smiled broadly. "That is correct. Here, the word '*ndranghitiari*' comes from the Greek verb '*andragathízesthai*', which means 'to engage in a defiant and valiant attitude'. A man who works for me told me you showed much of this in your actions against The Black Axe."

"Your man must have told you if it hadn't been for his team I would have been dead."

"It was only my man there," said the crime lord. "And since Alessio says you are familiar with the histories of ancient Rome and Greece, you will know Caesar and Alexander the Great found themselves in situations of certain death on many occasions, only to survive. It does not matter under what guise the angel is sent, only that God, or the gods, send the guardian."

"I am sure there's a subtext in there I am missing."

"Then I will be clear. You care for your family—and that is the one virtue that must reign above anything else. Our wider family expands across the globe and is oceans deep. But we have our enemies, the same as any successful family. We are currently at war with our cousins over the Adriatic. We could use a man such as yourself—a warrior, a leader, a businessman," said Mancuso, before sipping his coffee. "If you remain loyal to me, then any time you and your family are in danger, I will send an angel—in whatever disguise they might come in."

Connor sipped his coffee, weighing the proposition. "If those are your terms, then I accept."

"Good," said Mancuso.

As the waitresses came to clear the table, Connor's eyes flicked towards the curviest of the three, as she leant in to collect his plate.

When they had left, Mancuso asked, "What type of woman are you attracted to? How they appear?"

"Although I am not prejudiced," said Connor, "if you twisted my arm, I'd say I was partial to gingers—redheads—and curves—think Christina Hendricks."

Mancuso frowned, took out his phone and tapped it. "She is very nice."

"Quite."

"I have an assignment for you," said the Italian, putting the phone away.

"OK."

"There is a woman I would most like to meet."

"Redhead with curves?"

Mancuso shook his head. "Blonde with an athlete's body. My men are going to detain her shortly. They will bring her down to Puglia."

"Why is that?" asked Connor, feeling a swirl of unease.

"Because I believe she was the flame that began this war. And I am to meet my enemy. I want to see his reaction—to see if he knew."

Connor's heart began to sound in his ears. "What do you want me to do?"

"I want you to accompany me. I will be stepping into enemy territory and need a man who knows how to fight as you do."

"You need a bodyguard?"

"It is a dangerous situation. It is brokered by a man I trust, but it will be an opportunity for my enemy to strike. And this woman is a wolf in sheepskin—an assassin who makes people believe she is a journalist."

Connor kept his face passive when he asked, "What's her name?"

"Miss Ciara Robson."

Dread began to freeze him from the inside out—he had no means to warn her.

Luke stared at the street overlooking the bowling and snooker hall.

"This Mehmet Onel, is it definitely him?" he asked Tom in the passenger's seat next to him.

"Louis thinks it is. I've put some feelers out to see if anyone agrees with him."

"You know much about him?

"Not much outside of he's a nasty up-an'-comer," answered Tom. "Remember years ago, when you had the coppers shoot the bloke in Tottenham and the riots kicked off?"

Luke's forehead tightened before he remembered. "Oh, yeh. When the rioters were using their Blackberries to organise them'sens?"

"Yeh." Tom nodded. "Apparently, these streets of Turkish-owned businesses didn't get touched."

"How come?"

"Cos they were all out with their kebab cleavers. If I saw that, I'd just think, 'Nah, I'd rather fuck up a Woolworths'."

"Closed down, haven't they?"

"Yeah, all that lost revenue in stolen Pick 'n' Mix."

Luke smirked. "Connor would probably know the real reason without having to google it. Smart guy, isn't he?"

"Yeh, he is," Tom replied. "When you were driving around, listening to your Garage house, he was listening to how to invest, or doing a language course, or ancient history and that."

"Can I ask you something? What the fuck does he do when he's away? I mean, I just thought it was scouting for business, but I've never heard you ask 'owt when he's come back."

There were a few moments of silence before Tom said, "He used to keep away from us as a family when he first left the marines. It was only because of some aggro down Birmingham way our professional lives crossed. Anyway, he told me if he's going to be closer to the family, as in work-wise, then when he goes away I'm never to ask him where, or for how long, and I'm not to call him for any reason."

Luke kept his eyes on the entrance and asked, "Tom, you should have seen him when he dealt with those two Hellsbainz gangsters in the woods that time. It was like he'd done it a thousand times, and 'is face barely changed when he lopped off that one's head. What I'm saying is, and I know it sounds weird, but do you think he's some kind of assassin?"

"It doesn't sound weird at all. I've thought the same."

Before he could stop himself, Luke blurted out, "What's it like to kill someone?" He quickly added, "Sorry, Tom. Just came out. You don't have to—"

"No, no. It's OK. Luckily, we've scanned for bugs. I think about it—quite a lot. Everyone I've killed has been a threat to our family. Or in self-defence. And they've all been grafters too. But you think, 'Well, that bloke had a family too', or, 'That bloke might have turned out all right'. Then, I think, 'His family might do better without him' and 'Well, he might have gone on to become an even bigger cunt'. We just don't know. One thing I'll tell you is that it follows you around—you never know when it's going to come back to haunt you."

"What do you mean?"

"The last time I ended someone by myself was that guy, remember? Now, I don't know how my relationships with the people who helped me cover it up and bury the body will turn out. One day, Cara might get herself in trouble with the law, and we might be broken up, or whatever—she could easily roll over, a woman scorned and all that."

"But she'd be dobbing herself in?"

"I am sure they could get around that in exchange for my scalp. And that's with you until you die. Plenty of families get torn apart and secrets come out. What I am trying to say, something I've realised only recently, is if you ever find yourself in that position—and you have the choice—then choose to do it on your own, including getting rid of the body."

Luke thought for a moment. "Unless you both have an equal amount on one another. Connor said the reason Russia and America didn't kick off is they both have loads of nukes."

"There is always that."

Tom's phone rang, and when he answered it, although garbled, Luke recognised it was his Uncle Ryan's—Tom's dad—voice.

Tom's voice punctuated the garbles. "Fuck…all right…he still at the hospital? Yeah, he's with me. I'll tell him…all right, bye."

When Luke looked at him expectantly, Tom said, "Angela passed away, mate. Dan's in a state. Let's go over."

Luke stared at one of the streetlights for a few moments before saying, "How the fuck is that fair?"

"What do you mean?"

"I mean," said Luke, his grip tightening on the steering wheel, "our Dan is the only straight-goer in the men in our family, and it's his girlfriend that gets stabbed to death."

He had expected calming words from his elder cousin, but instead, Tom said, "Sometimes you have to right the wrongs yourself."

The three Turks, including Mehmet Onel, walked out of the bowling and snooker hall laughing amongst themselves.

Luke held himself to ask, "Any CCTV cameras around here?"

"No," came the reply. "The car's clean anyway."

Tom checks everything.

He gunned the engine, steeling himself to what he had to do.

He felt Tom's hand on his forearm before saying, "Nah. Let's go see your brother. These will keep and we need to plan for the fallout. We're not in the business of rolling the dice."

25

Ciara stood on the balcony, admiring the glinting forestry of the Etruscan countryside. The three-floored farmhouse lay fifty kilometres to the north of Rome.

When travelling abroad, the standard practice was to accept whatever hotel a newspaper editor might be willing to put her up in, or to purchase a room herself, before booking into another under a false name with a credit card that made tracing the funds difficult.

She sipped her coffee and tried to enjoy the scene before her.

This farmhouse was isolated, which was one of the reasons she chose it. Another was a two-week kendo seminar was being run in nearby Viterbo by one of the world's most renowned *Kendōkas.* She had not long arrived back after completing the arduous final day and the endorphins still had not left her.

She had kept up with her Thai, grappling and resistance training, knowing they were more 'necessary', but she had fallen in love with the Japanese art of swordsmanship. As the breeze floated over her, she realised this was the most content she had felt in a long while.

Bruce McQuillan's revelation that he wanted her as his successor had been initially daunting but she had now embraced the idea. She could not stay in the field for ever. Indeed, the score marks from the knife wielded by Eralda Mancuso were a constant reminder of how close she had come to death—and very few people are more useful dead than alive.

She felt a wave of disappointment in realising that being his future boss, she would have to stop sleeping with Connor now—in fact, she should not have done so the last time. However, something he said struck a chord in her—and she had never seen him that animated before.

She caught a glint of something in the treeline and snapped down on her inclination to look closer, instead stepping back into the room.

A recently adopted SOP required her to place miniature security cameras around any viable approach and access points to wherever she was staying.

She grabbed her iPad and, after a few a taps, brought to life the various screens. Her adrenaline rocketed as she deduced she was surrounded by armed police. This meant she could not simply shoot her way out, even if she had been inclined to do so.

Her brain quickly unjumbled the pictures of thuggish armed men and the man in the policeman's uniform.

The fact they were armed indicated they knew she was not just a journalist. She did not have time to dwell on how they knew.

She rapidly slung anything important and mission sensitive into her operational grab bag and made for the side bedroom.

Her pre-designated escape route had been through the loft. After the owners gave her a tour, before leaving to go back to their residential home, she had cleared a path through it, removing the sunroof panel and fixing a coiled rope at the top.

However, being surrounded, taking that option had to be abandoned. She picked up the iPad again and assessed.

An idea came to her—her heart chopped through her as she placed its chances at around fifty-fifty.

Giorgio could feel the stickiness of the soothing cream under his police uniform's shirt—the raw whipping welts would not heal anytime soon.

Ordinarily, had Mancuso asked him to lead his men in the kidnapping of a foreign national, he would have exploited the situation to its maximum gain.

This time, he had accepted it without question, despite his trepidation—this could be the woman who had annihilated half of Oso's security team.

Giorgio knew Mancuso had taken the unusual step of hiring mercenaries in his fight against the Albanians. However, these guys looked to be his usual 'Ndrangheta street soldiers, and not those with a great depth of military experience.

Giorgio was to chime the bell to get the woman outside; appearing at the door alone and in uniform being enough to disarm her mentally into opening the door. From there it would be down to Mancuso's men to take her.

He knew the crime lord saw him as collateral now—he'd be the closest when the gangsters made their move for her.

He could not understand why he had not sent his mercenaries, given her supposed reputation—*unless they are somewhere else.*

Despite its global reach and massive wealth, Giorgio knew blood ties were one of the bedrocks of the mafia; thus, Mancuso would have been wary of buying too many mercenaries, for fear of alienating the members of the organisation. That, and the increased chance of infiltration by an intelligence or law enforcement agency.

He squeezed his hands into fists to stop them from shaking as he approached the door.

Reaching for the doorbell, a noise similar to a spray can being used came from his left. A few seconds later, smoke billowed from the side of the house, accompanied by the snaps of gunfire.

Ciara stepped back from the side door and closed it. She studied the iPad and felt relief; her distraction of a smoke grenade, followed by specialised firecrackers, had succeeded in pulling the pair watching the back of the house off their position to join the presumed firefight.

Bounding up the stairs, she funnelled her way through the loft, before sliding out into daylight on the roof. Leopard-crawling to keep her profile low, she reached the rope and cast it down.

Checking her pistol and the security of her Ops-bag, she pulled on her leather gloves. She began her descent, her nerves pricking her heart, knowing she would be utterly defenceless until she hit the ground.

She swung her leg around the rope, laying it over her foot. This would enable her to use her other foot to stamp on it if she needed to brake.

Down she slid.

Landing, she looked left and right, then sprinted for the forest.

The treeline embraced her like a mother would a child chased by a wolf. Her car was parked—

purposely—over four hundred metres away, on the opposite side of the woods. She dodged through the trees as the sounds of a firefight began to fade with distance. She thought—*this is going to devastate my Airbnb rating.*

She smiled—*what a ridiculous thought.*

Dan stared at the framed watercolour of the pub he was in. He had slept at his mum and dad's rented flat the night Angela died.

The next day, with sorrow almost choking him, he heaved himself out of bed and, despite his mother's protestations—mercifully curtailed somewhat by his dad—took a taxi alone to his and Angela's own house.

He fought his initial hatred for the Middle Eastern driver, knowing to go down that road would not be good for anyone.

On pulling up outside their home, he found himself rooted to the seat, unable to get out of the taxi. Instead, he handed the driver a couple of notes and told him the address of a pub he had always wanted to visit.

He knew what the five stages of grief were. And he was aware he had skipped the denial phase.

Perhaps this had been because the scene of her dying could not have been made clearer to him—indeed, he knew before he had even been told. He was in shock but not denial.

The anger seemed to envelop him like a second being—as if his 'normal' self had been relegated to the sidelines, only to appear when dealing with the medical team, the female members of his family, and ordering his drink.

The pub's quietness was good in that he could be left alone, but bad in that he and his beer had time to think. It only took a handful of minutes before moisture peeled around his bottom eyelids.

As he closed his eyes and took a deep breath, he felt a hand on his shoulder.

He opened them to look up at Tom. His brother Luke stood on the other side.

Tom looked across at Luke and said, "What do you want?"

"Same as our Dan."

Tom left for the bar, and his younger brother sat beside him.

Without warning, the dam broke and the tears gushed from his eyes. He was vaguely aware of how awkward it must be for his younger brother to see him like this, but he could not help it. Instead, he held his head in his hands to hide his face.

After a few moments, he felt Tom's hand clasp his neck and Luke's arm snake around his back. Strength seemed to seep from them into him, and his weeping subsided.

He nodded to indicate he was all right, and their hands withdrew.

Nothing was said for a few moments and then Dan spoke. "We used to drive past this place on the way to visiting her parents. Always, always said we'd stop in. Always, always, I said, 'Next time'."

Luke looked around. "If it's any consolation, she didn't miss much. I'll be wiping my feet on the way out."

For some reason, Dan found this old joke to be hilarious, and all three began laughing like drains.

When the tide of their mirth swept back out, his feeling of sorrow returned.

Then he said, "You know, the reason I didn't tell you who the target was in the case she was working on was because—"

"We know who the target is, Dan," said Tom.

"Wha…what? I mean how? Why did you find out?"

"Come on," said Tom, with an edge of derision. "You didn't think we weren't going to at least make enquires after one of our family's women had been stabbed. And we know people in the know, even down here."

Dan took a few deep breaths and met his brother's eyes.

"We haven't done anything yet, out of respect for what you said. But it's always there—whenever, or however you want it. And don't worry about getting us into trouble. We're in the game of trouble, remember that."

After a few moments, he asked, "What has Connor said?"

Tom shook his head. "Connor is away and unreachable at the moment, but I can tell you what he would say."

"What?"

It was Luke who answered. "Dan, when Connor finds out Angela has been stabbed to death, he won't just kill the killer, he'll kidnap whoever ordered it and torture the evil cunt. Now, Tom and I are bit more…ahem…'let's get it over and done with' but we won't make any moves unless you OK it."

Dan stared at the painting again and had a flashback to Angela pointing to the pub saying, *"Let's go in there."*

He said, "So, you're saying even if I tell you two to leave it, Connor will make his own moves, anyway."

Tom nodded. "With stuff like this, he wouldn't even listen to me. There's a side to him you might have heard about but Luke and I have seen. He loves catching evil people and making them suffer. Finds their screaming hilarious. At least with me, I'll make sure it's quick."

Dan felt his anger claw at him. "I don't want it to be quick. I want them to suffer."

He saw his cousin and brother glance at one another.

Tom said, "We can make that happen too."

26

Though he had not been told, Connor knew by the distance and direction travelled that the island he was being dropped off at was Sazan—the Adriatic island perched just off Albania's south-eastern coast.

No one on the patrol boat spoke to him. He had simply handed a document to one of the crew and been ushered into a dripping side room that held all his kit. Not a single item had been missed off.

Mancuso had allowed him to 'zero' the C14 Timberwolf Medium-Range Sniper Weapon System in the hills of Calabria before his departure. The Canadian sniper rifle was a staple of *"our friends in Toronto"*. Connor knew Toronto to the 'Ndrangheta was like New York to the Cosa Nostra.

In addition to the rifle, there was a drag bag—a daysack designed to carry a sniper rifle—rations, *ghillie suit*, optics and a highly advanced comms set. He had also been given his pistol and commando dagger back, but not his phone.

Connor had thoroughly studied Italy and Albania's geography, both prior and during his mission, and knew Sazan to be Albania's largest island—around three miles long and one mile wide.

He had been given the GPS co-ordinates of the meeting between Salvatore Mancuso and the Albanians. And again, though he had not been told, he knew Mancuso's opposite number would be Andrei Faja.

Salvatore had told him the meeting was to negotiate peace—*a Pax Mafiosa*—and stressed that

Connor's role was to provide overwatch on the proceedings.

The black twin peaks, each over three hundred metres high, of Sazan were silhouetted against the dark blue of the pre-dawn sky and dragged the boat closer.

Eventually, they arrived at a point on the south-eastern end of the island, and he alighted from the boat to be confronted by densely leafed forest.

He felt a weight come off him; now he was on his own.

Using his GPS, he began to pick his way through the trees. The half-kilometre hike took him twenty minutes, including periodic listening stops and navigation checks.

As the sun broke over the island, Connor was already shunning the thought of how stiflingly hot it would be in the ghillie suit. Luckily, he wouldn't have to snurgle into position with it on. He remembered from his Royal Marine snipers' course that the stalking was more difficult than the shooting. Those left on the course by that stage had to stalk their way from distance to close position without being seen by the Directing Staff, who had a rough idea of where they were coming from.

All you have to do here is set up and lay in a hot suit for a couple of hours.

He came to the edge of the forest overlooking the small fort with the courtyard they were due to meet in. His position had a full view of it and the surrounding area and he saw no need to switch location.

After another listening pause, he set his kit down, touched his pistol as a reflex, and took the reel of fishing line out of his drag bag.

He created a roughly ten-metre perimeter by looping the line from tree to tree at just below shin level.

He checked his watch. The meeting was not for another three hours.

Stop being a girl and get in the suit.

Carlo felt a spiritual awareness as he ghost-walked to the first sentry; all his senses heightened to an animal-like pitch.

The matte-black blade absorbed the moonlight. Ordinarily, he would have used a suppressed pistol and fired into the base of the skull. However, after several days' observing the guards, Carlo knew none of them had their safety catches off, and more than a few did not even bother to 'make ready' their weapons by cocking them. Also, in the stillness of the night, he convinced himself the clacking might have aroused other sentries in a way a skilful blade into the voice box would not.

He knew, deep down, he had chosen this method as it was more of a rush.

The smell of the Albanian's cigarette smoke crept into Carlo's nostrils.

He deserves to die for smoking on sentry.

He bolted down his excitement as he got within two arm's-lengths of his victim. The sentry stilled himself as if he sensed something.

Carlo took a final bound, smacked his gloved hand over the mouth, and rammed the blade's point back through the throat, while sawing it side to side.

The muffled death mews could barely be heard, and the former legionnaire gently lowered the corpse down.

He knelt and waited. It had been impossible for his team to synchronise the murder of the Albanian security team precisely, but he waited two minutes.

Carlo had divided his team in two, with one on the ground and the other providing overwatch.

No gunfire or alarm raised could only mean his team had been successful. In the pre-action brief, he had instructed them to maintain radio silence until the end, unless there was an emergency.

He looked at the row of Piper planes with amusement and began placing the explosive charges.

When he had finished, he waited another two minutes before whispering into the comms microphone.

"All call signs. All call signs. Are you set?"

When he received the affirmative from each, he instructed them, "Withdraw."

He reversed back into the forest and met with the rest of the team five minutes later.

"Any problems?"

No one spoke and so he said, "OK. To your positions."

When they were in place, Carlo pushed the pressel of his radio set. "Bravo team. Open fire."

Set at a 90-degree angle to Alpha team's right, on the far right-hand side, a thirty-second cacophony of machine-gun and assault rifle fire rained on the barracks located at the opposite end.

A few moments later, the Albanians' expected counterattack came. Carlo knew Bravo team were already manoeuvring back into the woods as the heavy machine guns from the towers rained fury on their previous position.

Carlo thumbed the pressel. "Alpha team, link up with Bravo team. I will meet you at the extraction point."

He had half-expected a protest—this was not the original plan. However, the acknowledgement came back.

After two minutes, the Albanian security team had fanned out across the side of the airfield and began to move in a semblance of 'cover and manoeuvre'. It occurred to Carlo their seeming disarray was down to a supreme confidence they would never be attacked; raided by law enforcement maybe, but not attacked.

He waited until the bulk of the force was just past the airfield centre before detonating the charges.

The planes exploded in fountains of white fire. The burning petrol turned the Albanians into writhing, screaming caricatures of agony.

Carlo took no satisfaction from the chorus—indeed, it had almost been too easy. The smart thing to do now was to escape and rejoin his team before the remnants of the security detail regrouped.

The drag of combat overpowered him.

He took out his pistol and stalked through the forest towards the barracks.

On reaching the other side and peering through the trees, he saw three of them grouped together.

Drilled into any good infantry soldier is the need to keep distance from one another. Reaching into his webbing pouch, he primed the fragmentation grenade and two seconds after pulling the pin, bowled it within their midst.

The explosion cut their shouts of alarm dead. Carlo was already sprinting hard back into the depths of the wood. After a few moments, heavy machine-gun fire pounded the area from where he'd thrown the grenade.

The exhilaration helped his legs fight against the uphill terrain and scrub, his mind fought the urge to turn back and re-engage the fight.

He remembered a saying a British legionnaire told him not long after joining—*"There are bold soldiers, and there are old soldiers. There are no bold, old soldiers."*

He picked up the tracks his teams must have made making their way back to the vehicle departure point. As was the habit ingrained into him, he contoured them rather than treading in their footsteps. Insurgents placed IEDs on funnelled routes and, though it was improbable these Albanians would have, old habits die hard.

After ten minutes of hard running, he slowed, knowing the teams would have formed a perimeter and would issue a challenge.

But no one did.

He snaked through the trees until he saw them—or at least some of them.

The bodies were strewn like a devil's painting. The vehicles were gone.

Carlo did not step out to investigate—there might be eyes on the scene.

His mind spun before settling; he would have to make his way back to Italy alone.

It will be an adventure.

As he disappeared back into the forest—despite his heightened awareness—he couldn't remove the thorn of thought—*why didn't they ambush the teams before they destroyed the airfield?*

He stopped.

If they are waiting for me to appear, I won't disappoint them.

He began to skirt around the killing zone, using the trees and vegetation for cover, making a judgement on speed versus stealth.

He spotted him in the undergrowth—one of the team he came in with, his legs shot to pieces. Carlo made a scan of the surrounding area before taking the risk.

The man flinched, his eyes terror-wide, but he relaxed at the sight of Carlo holding up a calming hand.

The Italian knelt beside the rasping man and said in English, "I am going to get out your medical kit."

He had been taught in early Legion training to use the victim's medical kit and not your own. You never know when you might need it.

"No. You won't get me out now. My legs are broken and I am bleeding out."

Ignoring him, Carlo grasped one of the webbing straps to reveal the pouch the kit was housed in. As he ripped it open, the man caught his wrist in a strong grip.

"Listen, you don't have time. Leave the kit with me and I'll treat myself. The best thing you can do for me is to promise me to kill that bastard."

"Who?"

"Who? Mr Milan."

"What are you talking about? Mr Milan?"

"That's our name for him," rasped the fallen mercenary. "He is behind this, can't you see?"

"Why would he have his own men ambushed?"

"We aren't 'his' men. He paid us obscene money." The man laughed. "And this was to keep us quiet."

"About what?"

"There's a notepad in my top pocket. Second page in are the GPS co-ordinates. If you find a way there then you'll know what and why."

"You've been to this place?"

"We used to guard it. He wanted to keep it separate from your…organisation. He uses mercenaries like us. He wants to be the king of the world—which is why he ignored your high council's decree and hired us using his own money."

"How do you know this? And how would he have the personal funds to hire his own army?"

"We haven't got time. Go on," urged the man. "I will cover you."

Carlo took the notebook. His snapped towards the sound of men's voices in the near distance.

He said, "Don't let them take you alive."

The man withdrew a grenade. "I won't."

Luke had only been sitting on the cold pavement for a couple of hours but already he felt empathy for the homeless.

The clothes had been bought from a charity shop, as had the blanket he now clutched. The half-empty can faintly emitted the lager fumes, reminding him of his former love of *'the sesh'*. Those days were over and the other half of the can's contents had been poured down the drain.

He couldn't remember the last time he had just sat, without the distraction of his phone or the television. His mind wandered.

He remembered a conversation he'd had with Connor after his cousin took off his jacket in winter and gave it to a shivering homeless person.

"He'll just sell that for special brew, super strength and drugs. And yes, I've done my research—a charity did a poll and it showed about eighty per cent of them are crackheads and alkies."

"So what if he does?"

"Eh? I thought you and Tom made us go out of our way to sell our drugs in north Leeds and Harrogate to 'people who can afford rehab' cos you didn't want us being responsible for drugs in our communities. Hard drugs kill people."

"They do, and addicts will still do anything to get high or get pissed. If he sells that coat and scores, then that's a day or two he's not robbing his mum's handbag or your shed. I haven't got the time or temperament to volunteer, which I admit would be better than giving them money. Besides, he could be in the twenty per cent—might have just fallen on the hard times we are all closer to than we like to imagine. People come back from the abyss all the time."

Luke loved all his family, but especially Tom and Connor. Though they were only a few years older than him, he felt he had learnt more from them than his uncles, or even his own dad.

My own dad—he thought. Luke knew the rumours about Lee not being his biological father, and he had been sired by a man his mum had an affair with. At first, he never asked because he didn't want it to be true. Later, he never asked as he realised it did not matter.

The coffee cup in front of him had barely a pound in change in it; though it had only been two hours, he immediately doubted the rumours about professional beggars doing an eight-hour shift on the streets before driving home in a BMW.

Might be the location—he thought. A retail street in the Turkish quarter after commercial hours might not be a hotspot for beggars.

Sitting for this length of time drained his battery, and he wanted to get it over and done with.

He heard the drops patter in his coffee cup.

Fucking hurry up.

As if on cue, three men exited the furniture warehouse. He recognised Mehmet Onel, as the three stormed over. Luke tapped 'send' on the pre-typed WhatsApp message using the phone hidden beneath the blanket.

Luke got up with the lager can and began to feign a stumbling walk towards the brand-new black Range Rover, complete with tinted windows.

His heart thudded as the fear and fury danced within him.

He fell against it, spilling the rest over the bonnet.

The three crowded around him like piranhas, slapping his head and pulling him off the vehicle. He tripped over an outstretched foot onto his back.

"Fuck off where you crawled out from," sneered Onel, before giving Luke a sharp kick.

Although this had been fully expected—indeed part of the plan—Luke's hate sprang him to his feet.

A vague and muffled voice in the corner of his brain screamed he was fucking up the plan, but knowing what this savage was capable of sent him dizzy with the need to destroy him.

Hands grasped his clothes and fists began thudding punches in. He just managed to torque his hips away from the knee which would have crushed his balls.

The bare-knuckle boxer's fists fired short uppercuts and hooks which drew shock and pain on his assailants' faces. However, he was a few inches too close to generate the power for knockout blows.

The one on his left smashed a rugby tackle into his legs and he toppled under stamps and punches.

He heard the sound of a siren and soon a large vehicle speeding close.

"Let's go," shouted Onel.

Luke, still on the floor, snatched and held onto an ankle. He prayed it belonged to Onel, as two of the men ran off.

The frantic punches smashed into the back of his skull.

An engine screeched next to them.

"He is attacking me. You can see. I am trying to escape. You can—"

The Turk's words were cut dead and he fell beside Luke.

The floaty pain blurred his cousin's words.

"Luke, Luke…get up, get up."

He felt Tom's strong hands under his armpits, and Luke's feet began to reluctantly obey his commands. He stood on shaky legs.

Satisfaction roared through his veins as he watched an unconscious Onel being bundled into the van by Louis Allen.

27

Salvatore sat inside the old, refurbished CP231 patrol boat as it bounced over the waves at twenty knots. He would have preferred a smoother ride, but did not have the time for a leisurely boat journey across the Adriatic.

The island of Sazan appeared as a shimmer on the horizon as the sun crept up behind it. In the cabin with him were three of his bodyguards. In truth, they were more for show.

If Tefik Mesi said it was safe, then so be it.

Not that Mancuso had direct contact with the Mafia Shqiptare's boss of bosses. Their correspondence was done almost entirely through emissaries. Salvatore suspected Tefik feared cyber hacking of any electronic communication. Salvatore shared this concern, but he was also aware of the Chinese whispers effect of the passage of communications through multiple messengers.

Still, the system had worked well over the years and been mutually advantageous, helping them both to ascend to the top of their respective organisations.

The trick Salvatore had worked out, and he suspected Mesi had too, was even when it was apparent you held the most power within an organisation, it was best to deny it—to everyone. In organisations like the 'Ndrangheta and Mafia Shqiptare, which were full of ruthless and powerful men, the more power, wealth and status you outwardly displayed, the more of an attraction to others your position became, thus painting a target on your back.

This is what the Camorra failed to understand. One the one hand, the display of their lavish lifestyles did indeed help recruitment. However, it also encouraged almost continual internal warfare.

Despite this, Salvatore knew in the mafia, one's car, home, dress, all had to be better than the man immediately below in the hierarchy, or else there might be confusion as to who the higher rank was. However, he took care to keep the difference marginal—anything more created resentment.

The boat slowed before creeping between the high cliffs of Devil's Bay.

Not far from the shore, a white Jeep gleamed, with the driver, dressed in khaki, looking like a South African Safari guide.

With nothing being said, he and his three bodyguards got into the vehicle. Mancuso had braced himself for a manipulative play—perhaps a vehicle not spacious enough to accommodate his security team so one or two had to be left behind.

However, the short journey was made to the meeting place.

The white stone villa lay in a bowl-like depression of subtropical flora and fauna, isolated from the rest of the island.

The two Mafia Shqiptare Dons were sitting on one side of a marble table in wicker chairs.

Their positioning raised Mancuso's antenna—Tefik's role as arbitrator usually meant sitting in a neutral position. And where were the mirroring bodyguards?

Salvatore's instruction to the Englishman, Connor Reed, to provide overwatch had been born of professional caution. He was thankful for it now but became acutely aware Reed was but a single man.

The Jeep pulled up and Mancuso and his protection team alighted.

The Italian noticed Andrei rose from his chair to greet him fractionally sooner than Tefik.

Maybe he is trying to disguise any form of relationship between us.

Andrei sported a light blue jacket over a cream shirt. Though pressed, uniformly dark and undoubtedly expensive, the jeans he wore still had the intention—Mancuso knew—of irking the Italian.

Tefik's dark, tailored suit gave the discerning eye hints as to its expense—the finely woven wool, the lining—Bermberg rayon, the hand-stitched buttonholes, rounded corners and matching pattern.

Tefik shook his hand firmly and said in Italian, "I am aggrieved our first meeting has been under these circumstances."

"I agree," answered Mancuso in Albanian. "I am sorry my Albanian is only little. Your Italian is much better."

"I speak Italian fluently," answered Andrei. "We can converse in this."

Mancuso gave him a curt nod and they sat down.

"We appreciate your coming out this far to see us."

Mancuso responded, "I desire this to be resolved. One way or another."

He caught the subtle stiffening of Tefik's back while Andrei exuded calm.

It should be the opposite way around.

"We understand your anger," answered Andrei, smoothly. "If you indeed have been led to believe we were responsible for your sister's death."

Mancuso stared at Andrei.

"The person or persons responsible for the massacre of Oso Xhelli and his party has been conveniently laid at the feet of my organisation. The finger has been pointed at my sister, who herself died. Conveniently, there are no living eyewitnesses. And, Mr Faja, it has been you who has benefitted the most from that unfortunate event."

His adversary simply nodded. "It is true what you say. I have ascended to the position of Kyre with a speed not seen before. It is easy to see why you have drawn that conclusion. However, I cannot understand why you did not approach me for a meeting before you began this war. And why you did not keep this between you and my clan."

"What are you talking about?" said Mancuso, his eyes narrowing. "Are we still suggesting I sent my sister to murder your boss, and all his important people? To what end? To exert dominance? What stipulations have I since asked? Nothing. Mid- and lower-level strife is to be expected and I know this better than you, young one. I know it is folly to overreact."

Andrei nodded. "That aside. I had not declared war until the murder of Sali Rama and his men when arriving in an Italian port on board an Italian ferry."

"I did not have Mr Rama killed. That could have been any one of numerous suspects…either side of the Adriatic."

With Tefik's eyes fixed on him, along with his silence, Mancuso felt the supposed arbitration to be more of an interrogation.

"OK," said Andrei, seemingly in agreement. "Why did you choose to attack an airfield of ours knowing we had this meeting between us."

"Who told you that?"

Andrei raised his chin. "Your captured men told us that. Those that we let live, that is."

The 'Ndrangheta boss felt a whoosh of helium in his stomach. He kept his voice even and said, "A ceasefire is called when a ceasefire is agreed."

Tefik finally spoke. "Your rage flows from the death of a loved one. So you'll understand mine—since that was my clan's airfield and my son who died by burning to death."

Mancuso opened his mouth to speak. Like a finger flicking the top of a set of stacked dominos, it fell into place.

He looked into Andrei's eyes and saw confirmation. The younger man had engineered all this.

Mancuso spun his head and shouted an alert to his men, just in time to see one of their faces explode outwards like a disintegrating vase of bone, blood and brain.

Connor assessed not only the situation but his mission remit. The brief had been to keep a war going between the 'Ndrangheta and Mafia Shqiptare long enough not only to destroy any chance of reconciliation but to have them both continuously fight and weaken one another. However, Bruce had stressed of the two, he wanted the 'Ndrangheta to hurt more.

As Connor spotted the men stalking towards Mancuso and his team, he rapidly came to his conclusion—*If Mancuso dies, so does the war in essence. Besides, I need him alive to get me back to Italy.*

No aiming off would be necessary as he lined up the scope's crosshairs on the point man of the assault team.

Just before he closed his left eye, he caught it, the glint of another scope in an almost mirrored position to him on the opposite side of the meeting place.

He realigned and his eye dived back into his scope. Compressing all the necessary actions for an accurate shot into milliseconds, Connor's round smashed into his opposite number's face, slumping it against his rifle.

He rapidly switched back to the kill team—he was half a second late. The point man shot the left-hand man of Mancuso's security team.

Connor squeezed the trigger five times in rapid succession—bang, bang, bang, bang, bang—and the assassination squad of four were incapacitated.

He spun his sight back to the meeting point to be confronted by Mancuso and the second man at the meeting wrestling on the floor. The man had a knife and the top position, driving the blade towards the Italian's face, with Mancuso desperately pushing cupped hands against the wrist.

Andrei was nowhere to be seen, seemingly having torn off into the surrounding woods. Mancuso's security team were either dead or staying low.

Connor's crosshairs intersected the fierce determination on the man's face as the blade now moved within three inches of Mancuso's.

With Connor's trigger squeeze the man's head exploded like a macabre watermelon, and the headless corpse lay on a heaving Mancuso.

The former Royal Marine scanned for any other targets. Finally, the surviving two members of Mancuso's security team rose and hurried over to their boss, who had now pushed off his would-be killer's corpse and stood up.

Connor could see the Calabrese crime lord shrugging off his underlings' attempts to get him back to the Land Rover. Instead, he took out a phone, tapped it and held it to his ear, while looking in Connor's general direction.

Without taking his eyes away from his scope, Connor clicked the receiver button on the comms set.

"Yes?"

Mancuso's voice came on the line. "Where are you? I will come to get you."

"Stick with the original plan and head towards the boat. Be careful. If there is anything strange then call me. If not, then pick me up at the original drop-off point in thirty minutes. Capisce?"

"Capisco."

"Repeat what I have said back to me," ordered Connor.

There were a few moments of pause. "Stick with the original plan. Be careful approaching the patrol boat. If there is anything strange then call you. But if there is not, pick up at planned place."

"Esattamente."—*Exactly*.

The sunrays slipped through the curtain to stroke Ciara's face to wake her. It took a few seconds to realise she was at the home of Adriana Cruz.

On her escape from the house, she had immediately contacted Bruce on a secure line as she drove. Though his instructions had been clear and concise, she thought she heard a reticence in his voice when he instructed her to head to Cruz's house in Milan.

She understood.

Cruz was a civilian but because Ciara had informed him it was a police officer who came to the door—or someone dressed as one—then Bruce had decided to get her as far north of Rome as he could, before arranging her passage out of Italy.

Adriana had picked her up from an underground garage just outside Florence, and Jaime had somehow managed to temporarily disable the CCTV cameras in and round it.

From there they made the three-and-a-half-hour journey to Florence. The conversation between the two, though tense at first, became easier and Ciara found she liked the Italian-Albanian.

She got out of bed and began to go through a circuit of bodyweight exercises lasting for twenty minutes before showering in the en-suite.

After dressing in cotton trousers and a white T-shirt, she descended the polished wood stairs to the kitchen to see Adriana at her laptop with a cup of coffee beside her.

Ciara was struck by Adriana's elegance, even in her own home. The light green blouse flowed off one of her shoulders, set off against the blue of her jeans.

There was no hint of frizz in the jet-black hair diving into her shoulders.

She lifted her head and asked, "How would you like your coffee?"

"Do you have espresso?"

"I have every coffee you can think of."

Within a few minutes they were sat across from one another.

"Thanks for taking me in," said Ciara sincerely.

She waved her hand dismissively. "Si, figure."—*Forget it.*

Ciara nodded and asked, "What are you working on?"

"I have been gathering leads to discover if there is any truth to an underworld myth."

"What myth?"

"That a man controls an island where the valuable and vulnerable of this world are taken and held. There they are indoctrinated before being auctioned off to wealthy and evil men."

Ciara frowned. "As slaves?"

"Yes," answered Adriana. "However, not just as manual labourers or sex workers. There are reports of highly skilled men and women who have lost their way, being taken. A lot of this is merely dark internet rumour, but there have been one or two things that are concerning."

"Like what?"

"Three people. Two men and a woman. One Canadian, one Swedish and one Iranian. They escaped from their employment after being held in this facility."

"They overcame their indoctrination?"

"That is maybe the case. I am to meet a lady tonight in France. I will interview her."

"Which paper will publish this story?"

"Perhaps none."

"Then why are you pursuing it?"

The two women made eye contact before Adrianna said, "Because Bruce asked me to keep my eyes and ears open. Said it was a small chance."

Carlo had used a false identity to lay low in Sarandë, a resort on the Albanian Riviera. He had cached his weapon systems and military equipment before leaving the north of the country, but did not expect to ever see them again.

He did not think it prudent to escape via the port so soon after the airfield raid. And he also did not want to contact Salvatore in light of the mercenary's words.

For Carlo, working for Mancuso had never been for the money. It had always been for the adrenaline of combat.

The way Carlo saw it, drugs, gun-running and murder was practised by governments the same as any other mafia, and he had made his peace with that a long time ago.

He had known of Mancuso since childhood, as had his father. Carlo remembered one time his father saying of Mancuso:

"He is a practical man, not a lunatic crazed for recognition. But you can tell the ambition threatening to open him from the inside out."

Carlo had bought an android phone, and now lay on his hotel bed. Using a piece of software, he discovered the co-ordinates written in the mercenary's notebook to be a point out on the Ionian Sea. Using Google Maps, he frowned on seeing the blurred-out island.

So, I will have to steal a boat.

28

To Connor, anything in this world looked and felt better bathed in sunlight, and the Calabrian countryside was no different.

Still, he imagined it would be an impressive sight even in bad weather.

The comfort of the Maserati's passenger seat encased him as Mancuso drove it in its I.C.E (Increased Control and Efficiency) mode, as it growled down through the meandering hillside roads.

Mancuso spoke, "The power base within our family lies in these villages and small towns. It always has."

Connor answered, "I would have thought it was in Reggio Calabria, the city?"

"No. That might be where a lot of business transactions get done, but it is in the hills where the decisions get made."

"I see."

"Have you ever wondered why, even in the face of life in prison, the bosses in our and similar families choose to stay? They might hide, but they chose to stay."

"You mean, why don't they just fuck off to Florida with their millions and live a stress-free life of Viagra-fuelled romps, sunbathing and margaritas?"

"Yes."

"Because essentially they'd be a rich pensioner, bored without the friends and family they have grown with, and crucially without any power."

Mancuso nodded approvingly. "This is true. Family and power. With us, power is with the family.

Family is what makes you strong. This is why the lion is the king and the tiger is not."

Connor had a flashback to his grandad using the same analogy.

"So, what are you saying?"

"What I am saying is the larger and stronger your family is, the safer you are."

"Surely a family can be too big? Factions break away. Anthropologists claim humans aren't designed to have more than a hundred and fifty friends and acquaintances."

"Are there a hundred and fifty men in your family? I mean, in the family you work with?"

"No, there aren't."

"In a short time, you have solved a massive problem for us—seemingly against the odds. And you have also saved my life and the lives of my men. I would be glad to have you as part of my family."

"I was under the impression I already was as per our conversation when we first met."

"I mean officially."

Connor's forehead compressed. "I did not think that was possible. Thought you had to have your bloodline here."

"I do not say this family. I said my family. The old-fashioned way is just that—old-fashioned. I would rather have men of honour, men of professionalism, as part of my family than men who merely share a bloodline."

Holy fuck, thought Connor, *he wants to start his own multi-cultural mafia.*

The Englishman said, "I thought one of the reasons behind the bloodline was the families are easy to reach should someone choose to turn informant."

Mancuso smiled. "It is true that in the old days, if someone wanted to turn *Pentiti,* we could ask their family to convince them against such an act. However, we can reach the families of Eskimos now."

"I can see your logic."

"If you agree, you and your family will be the most powerful in the United Kingdom. And there will be no one who can touch you. Our expertise will be given to you. There will be no court in the land you will not be able to walk away from."

Connor felt a cloud of secure warmth wrap around him. He kept his face expressionless, and said, "This isn't wholly my decision. My family works on a quasi-democracy."

"Quasi? I do not know this word."

"It's means 'seemingly' or 'supposedly' or even 'partly', so I've probably misused the word as we are a democracy, but you know how these things work—certain people have more influence than others."

"I know precisely the truth of what you say," said Mancuso. "And you have the most influence?"

"One of two. My elder cousin leads the family. He would need to sign off on any arrangement."

"Is your cousin a forward-thinking man?"

"He is. However, he is a man who likes to have all his ducks in a row. He's cautious but ambitious—if that makes sense."

"Ducks in the row? Have everything in place before he takes action?"

"Exactly."

"That sounds like the correct balance. However, when men get older, they resist change."

"Are you referring to the man you are taking me to meet?"

Mancuso smiled. "Italo Mauro is a man I respect very much. He held our family strong through the civil wars of the nineteen seventies and eighties. It was because of him innovations were made."

"What innovations? Unless you can't tell me?"

"You have saved my life. I can tell you of things I would not tell others. Some things you will learn over time if you become part of my family."

Connor caught that he said 'my family' as opposed to 'our family'.

"What can you tell me now?"

"Italo knew for us to survive we needed to be able to communicate with the authorities—in safe places."

Connor murmured, "Masonic-type lodges?"

"Yes," answered Mancuso. "Reggio Calabria was undergoing growth in development—steelworks factories, railways, a steelwork centre and the port in Gioia Tauro. Italo took lessons from our Sicilian cousins' mistakes. You do not fight the authorities—you pay them."

"So, you're saying that innovative man has disappeared with age?"

"Yes, and the incident in Duisburg made him quieter. More cautious."

Connor knew the 'incident' Mancuso was referring to was of the six men shot dead outside an Italian restaurant in Duisburg, Germany over a decade ago in 2007.

"Why are you telling me all this?"

"Because you understand that what's good for people isn't always what they think is good for them."

"I understand."

As the vehicle crested the hillside, Mancuso pointed down and said, "It is there."

The two-tone stone wall curved around the estate and, had it not been for a vast swimming pool, Connor would have thought it belonged to a Japanese *daimyo* in feudal times.

Three similar-looking buildings lay inside, set in a semi-circle. The white and beige stonework blended into one another and drew the onlooker in like an optical illusion.

The centre building stood a couple of floors taller than its flanking counterparts. Various trees and statues placed together were ringed by beautiful flowerbeds.

As Mancuso drew close to the gates he said, "Italo speaks very little English, so I will translate."

The heavy wood and iron gates opened outwards. For a moment Connor feared they would hit the car, as they came within an inch of it.

The tree must be the marker.

As with anywhere new, where he would be in a static position, he began memorising the layout and the people. With the layout this would involve several observations regarding the materials the buildings, windows and doors were made of, the number of windows, doors and floors, the distances of key features in relation to one another, possible exits, and obstacles.

The way he would memorise multiple persons if given a brief window would be to disregard a complete *A-to-H* and instead pick out a key feature—big nose, or looks like Mr Bean, or straw hair—before filing whether or not they are armed, if he could identify their dominant hand, and an assessment on their strength and fitness by scrutinising their posture, body shape and jawline sharpness.

None of the men were obvious security. Although the gardener, valet and doorman did not overtly display weapons, Connor recognised the clothes' bulges to conceal handguns.

He knew the reason Italo did not need to live in a compound teeming with high-tech security and a small army was a testament to the many layers of covert security a stranger would have to pass through even to reach this point.

Deep in this rural land, with only one road in and out, the neighbours being fellow mafioso, reminded Connor of something his sergeant had told the troop with regards to carrying pistols, during his first tour of Afghanistan,

"Carry them if you want, but if you have to use 'em then something has gone wrong. It's one more weapon system you have to maintain and carry ammunition for. And I've seen more people shoot themselves and other people fucking around with these than anything else. It's up to you."

Connor guessed the old man figured that day and night security, for security's sake, was just a waste.

The tall, broad valet approached as he and Mancuso alighted from the car. He gave Connor a brief scan before receiving the keys from Mancuso.

The doorman and Mancuso spoke in Italian too rapid for Connor to follow, but he picked up on the consternation in Mancuso's voice.

Finally, Mancuso turned to him and said, "There is a matter I must urgently attend to. You will meet our…leader without me. There is an interpreter. A driver will drop you at my home shortly afterwards. I live only six kilometres away."

Connor kept the concern off his face and answered, "OK."

The doorman led Connor through the entrance of the central house.

The lobby put the Englishman more in mind of a museum than a home. The whiteness—white polished tiling, white stone walls and white sculptures.

As they rounded the corner, the hallway changed into patterns of beige, black and cream sprawling under the overhead lights. Woven chairs, detailed pottery and artwork were placed in between the various doors on either side.

The doorman stopped him at the final one and knocked gently.

A gravelled voice called out, "Entra."

Connor did so, and the smell of cigarette smoke hit him.

Alessio stood in beige trousers with an eggshell shirt next to a man seated behind a large oak desk.

Connor hoped that they both mistook his recognition for reverence.

The man was *Capocrimine*—the Boss of Crime—Italo Mauro. Except, Connor did not know until that moment he was.

Italo stood up, straight-backed, wearing a lilac shirt and jeans. The hairline was original, giving rise to snow-white hair, despite black eyebrows. The moustache was undecided which colour to take its cue off and remained a mix of black and white.

The lined face displayed a natural tan and the large Roman nose sat between his dark brown eyes.

He rested the cigarette on the lip of a thick, gold-tinted glass ash tray and approached.

"Mi aspettavo che assomigliasse più a Rambo ma più alto," said the *Capo dei capi* to Alessio.

Alessio laughed. "Questa è la versione della vita reale. Sono più conspicui."

Connor just about picked up something about being tall and Rambo. He thought Alessio might have said he was a real-life version.

So Alessio IS 'Ndrangheta, not just working for them, Connor realised.

Italo turned to him. "I speak only little English. It is nice to meet you, Signor Reed."

"Parlo solo un po' di Italiano,"—*I only speak a little Italian*—answered Connor.

Italo's face broke into a laugh before pointing to Alessio. "Welcome, translator."

They shared his laugh before taking seats around the desk.

Italo spoke in rapid-fire Italian again.

Alessio said to Connor, "Italo is asking if you smoke."

Connor shook his head. "The occasional cigar."

Italo immediately stubbed out his cigarette.

"No, it doesn't bother me," said Connor, waving a hand.

"Italo says you English are too polite. No one who does not smoke enjoys it around them."

"Ask Mr Mauro to guess what I did when I saw my girlfriend smoking."

Brief translation.

"He asks, 'What?'"

"Tell him I stopped and applied lubrication."

Alessio frowned before translating. On seeing the confusion on Italo's face, Connor held out his fist on an arm bent at ninety degrees, before enacting the universal sign to fuck.

Italo broke into uproarious laughter, and Connor and Alessio joined him, though not with the same vigour.

Italo spoke in stilted English, "You have girlfriend?"

Connor shook his head.

"Like men?"

He shook it again and said, "My world isn't a world I would like to bring a nice girl into."

After a lengthy exchange between the Italians, Alessio said, "Italo says a nice girl is not necessary but a 'right' girl is. You will need to have children to continue your bloodline. Great men come and go, but what lasts are dynasties. You understand?"

"Yes," answered Connor. A few weeks ago he had read about how the Mars family business was now four generations deep.

Italo spoke at length and Alessio said, "Sustainable power comes from moving quietly. Loud people and organisations do not last."

"I understand."

Italo smiled and spoke as Alessio translated.

"I told him you have an interest in Roman history. He's asking if you knew how Romulus and Remus were raised."

"By a shepherd."

"That is correct. They were simple men with a great ambition. He wants to know what yours is?"

Connor found the truth coming forth. "My family is down a path now. I can't change that and I am not sure I want to. What I do want is to make us stronger as an organisation. It is difficult to trust people who are not family—sometimes, it is difficult to trust those who are."

Once Alessio had translated this, Italo looked at him strangely before nodding and speaking.

"He agrees. Your family might be *per bene*, but blood is not always an indicator of trust. Do you know why the Roman Empire was able to expand and last for centuries and the Spartans did not?"

"Several reasons."

"Can you name one?"

Connor shrugged. "Well, aside from the fact it's debatable if the Spartans ever truly wanted an empire, I would say they ran out of their most important commodity—the Spartan soldier himself."

Alessio smiled broadly, as did Italo when Connor's answer had been translated.

The two Italians conferred.

Alessio said, "That is correct. The Romans offered citizenship to a foreigner—a *peregrinus*, in exchange for his military service."

"Well, in the auxiliary units, and they did not receive the said citizenship until they had completed twenty-five years of service."

Alessio asked, "Do you disagree with that?"

"Anything worthwhile must be earned. However, the foreigner might be best placed at the sharp end—might be better suited than any homegrown talent."

Alessio conferred with Italo again before turning to Connor, saying, "We are of complete agreement. The world is changing, and we must change with it.

Blood ties do not automatically translate to loyalty, and have little to do with competence."

Connor digested this and thought, *That is exactly what Mancuso said.*

He asked, "May I ask why Mr Mancuso isn't present with us?"

Alessio answered immediately, "We will keep our own counsel on that, Mr Reed."

"OK," replied Connor. "So, what has this meeting been about?"

He thought he knew but wanted clarification.

"You came to me looking for ways to clean your money. We have done our research. Your family is rising and when that happens, it draws attention. You may have already experienced this."

Connor looked at Alessio but said nothing. The financier continued, "Not only from others wanting what you have, but by law enforcement and the government."

"What are you offering?"

"You will never have to concern yourself with cleaning your money again. Our power within European law enforcement and judicial bodies is unrivalled. Though your operation is small, it extends from Ukraine right through Europe. You did this by yourself. Imagine if you had an ally such as us?"

"We already have a Dutch connection we liaise with."

Alessio frowned. "Because you have one friend you may not have others?"

"That is a good point, well presented," said Connor. "Although the Dutch are no longer entrenched in a war with the Albanians—you are."

Alessio smiled. "That is something we would like to bring to a close. Unnecessary bloodshed is not good for business."

It dawned on Connor.

"Mancuso is the one carrying this war on."

Alessio spoke quietly to Italo who simply nodded.

"We had hoped Salvatore's rage would quieten after a period of bloodletting. It has not."

"I was under the impression he went to Sazan to negotiate a truce?"

"A truce he was directed to negotiate," said Alessio. "And look at what happened."

"He didn't attempt to strike first—they did. I saw."

Alessio replied, "Salvatore is very determined on this matter. He might give the appearance he has accepted the decision, but he will ultimately find a way to achieve his objectives."

Connor digested this—*Mancuso orchestrated it?*

"If we are speaking frankly, what are his objectives? He can't believe he's going to be able to destroy that entire organisation?"

Alessio shook his head. "He does not. He wants Andrei Faja dead."

"So, you want me to assassinate Faja to end this?"

Italo shook his head despite Alessio not translating.

Alessio said, "No, we do not. The best ally is a stable ally. The man you killed was its most powerful member—a man best placed to provide this steadiness. We do not blame you for killing him. Indeed, you were completing the task asked of you."

"I see. Andrei Faja is now the man who might provide that stabilising force. And Salvatore will never accept it."

There were a few moments of silence.

Connor broke it with, "If my guess is correct, then what you have in mind does not seem an attractive proposition to me. My guess is you wish for an outsider to handle this to avoid a civil war. You want me because you know I am capable of it, and then you can use me as a scapegoat."

The two mafioso conferred.

Alessio said, "You are only partly correct. It is true we cannot ask any of our people—the risk he will be forewarned is too great. And it would create civil war. However, Mancuso will have told people you are simply a mercenary—one of the many he uses, and he thinks we are not aware of. If you were to disappear afterwards, we could make this matter evaporate."

Connor stared back with a neutral expression as his mind whirred. He did not know these men. If he were to refuse, they might not even let him out of the compound. He was not armed and did not know who else was around, as he had been brought straight there. Mancuso was a criminal—killing him would be no different than his assault on The Black Axe, a means to an end. He knew they would not accept a 'Can I think about it' answer. Besides, his mission here—at least the one he began on—was to help maintain a perpetual war between the two dark dragons either side of the Adriatic.

He looked at Italo.

"If you're going to insist on an answer now, then the answer is no. I am not involving myself in your inter-organisational politics. Your external enemies—as long as they are criminals like us—I would be open to. I am not in the habit of shaking a man's hand one day and shooting him the next, just because another stranger has told me to. However, you have my word I will not tell him what was proposed here today."

Connor's senses became heightened. He had already mentally rehearsed what he would do should the door behind him unexpectedly open: leap across the desk and snatch the old man in a rear naked chokehold, keep his back to the walls and leave with him.

The chances of it working would be minimal, but it was the best he could come up with.

The dagger of anticipation as his words were translated felt like a sword. He watched Italo's face intently, feeling the electric tension throughout his body.

Alessio turned and said, "Italo respects your position. We also value what you might bring to the table. Mancuso will ask what we have discussed. We have told him it was to propose the assassination of Andrei Faja."

Connor fought the relaxation the relief brought. That they were asking was a good sign—unless they had to, to lower his guard.

"Why wouldn't he have insisted on being present when you pitched this to me?"

"Because, one of his operations has gone wrong. Something that requires his immediate attention."

Connor nodded, and hoped it had something to do with Ciara. "I will tell him the line you gave me was to discuss the terms and conditions of my working with your organisation. Then I will tell him the real reason is to report back anything strange. That way, I gain his trust and he doesn't suspect your immediate angling to kill him. He is a stranger to me, so I do not see the need to get involved. However, I won't kill a man unless I deem him worthy of being killed."

More conference.

"How do we know you won't reveal the true nature of our discussion?"

Connor smiled. "We have already discussed the differences between dynasties and great men. I wouldn't throw my hand in with a man against you simply based on meeting him first."

"That is very…pragmatic of you."

"Thank you," Connor said. "What now?"

"Now you may go," said Alessio. "I have investment vehicles to run past you but we can do that another time."

Connor put on a mock frown. "What? No Italian supermodels frolicking in a pool, champagne, cigars and copious amounts of high-quality drugs? Very disappointed."

In the middle of Alessio's translation, Italo began to laugh.

Alessio said, "Italo says there is a saying his father once told him. 'Do not use your cock as a compass, it rarely leads you in the right direction'."

Connor smiled. "I'll take that on board."

"Just keep your eyes open to what is going on around you, Mr Reed."

As Connor nodded his acknowledgement, Alessio called out. When the door opened Connor quickly stood to face it.

The doorman appeared without any threat, but the Englishman conceded if they wanted him dead, then he would die.

As he was escorted back down the hall, he admired it more.

The sun warmed his face as he stepped outside.

29

Dan squinted with the removal of the blindfold. Tom, Luke and a tall, broad, handsome black man were leant against the large kitchen's counter, looking at him. The unit curved around them all, and on Tom's side sat a strange mix of cups, hot drinks-making station, saucers, masking tape, hammer and a drill.

The wooden clock with black, powder-coated metal hands and Roman numerals looked down on them all.

"Good trip, mate?" asked Tom.

"Was the blindfold necessary?" he asked.

"The less you know, the less you have to lie about," said Tom. "This is Louis Allen, a friend of ours."

Glad he's on our side, thought Dan.

"Thank you for this."

Louis stepped to him with an outstretched hand. "Can't say I am not a bit disappointed to see you here, bruv. Connor always bragged about how you were the only one to go straight."

His hand felt smooth but strong.

"I am still going straight. I haven't done anything yet."

The big man shook his head. "Cos it's just happened, your emotions might be getting in the way of that big brain of yours. If you leave here without telling 5-0 then you're an accessory. Don't kid yourself. You ain't seen him yet, so you can still walk away and plead ignorance if anything comes out."

The weight of the words hung in Dan's chest. He could walk away. Go back to his work, rebuild his life, maybe start a—the memory of the continuous beep rose to choke him.

"I'll always be emotional about it. Besides being my future, she was the salt of the earth. She suffered from Crohn's disease, had bad flare-ups because of the stress of what she did for a living. Doctors told her to slow down and her bosses offered to lighten her workload—she wouldn't have any of it. 'What am I going to do?' she'd say. 'Mope around the house knowing there're evil people who need to be taken off the streets?'"

Dan's eyes welled with tears but he continued, "Now, one year, five years and I'll still feel the same. The rat in there, and all the other rats like him, deserve to suffer."

Louis opened his palms. "All right. Can't say I disagree."

Dan looked at Tom. "Is it definitely him?"

"Ask Louis here."

Louis looked at him. "His is the only name that has come up on the grapevine. What gets said on the street and what gets repeated to the police are two different things. He hasn't been denying it to anyone—just gives a silly smile."

Dan felt the hate clench in his stomach.

"Does he speak English?"

When Louis nodded, Dan asked, "Where is he?"

"He's chained up in one of the containers outside."

"I want to go see him," said Dan, his legs trembling.

"I'll come with you, unless you prefer Luke," said Tom.

Dan shook his head. "Alone."

Luke spoke, "I don't think that's a bright idea, Dan."

"Why?"

"No offence, but he's an evil grafter who's stabbed a woman to death, and you're a civilian."

Even though he was Luke's elder brother, Dan realised he was his junior at this moment and circumstance. He replied, "But he's chained up, isn't he?"

The three men looked at one another before looking back with a collective nod.

"It's what he might say to you," said Tom, the concern in his voice.

"What could he say? Threaten me? With what? He's not getting out of here alive. And don't disrespect me by suggesting I could be manipulated by him. There are just some things I want to make him aware of."

"If you want to talk privately to him, Dan, then it's up to you. I'll just be outside the door."

"I'll come too," said Luke.

Dan saw Tom grab the roll of black masking tape and asked, "What's that for?"

"To tape his eyes, gives you an edge. His mouth is already taped."

"Don't," said Dan. "I want to see his expression."

As the three walked outdoors, Dan saw they were outside some kind of barn on the high ground of desolate rural hinterland. The still air cooled his skin.

As they crossed a patch of meadowland to the containers, Dan pointed to one and said, "It's that one, isn't it?"

"How did you guess that?" exclaimed Luke.

"Not sure."

His legs felt hollow as he approached the door.

Tom turned to him. "Wait here."

With that, he took out a knife and began to unlatch the crossbar locks. He stepped back and waited a few moments before walking in. After less than a minute he walked back out.

"He's secure."

"What if I want to hear what he's got to say for himself?"

Luke looked at Tom who said, "I wouldn't take the tape off his mouth. If you can't help yourself then immediately stand back, in case he bites. And be careful of him trying to *fleg* on you," said Tom.

"Yeh, fucking don't know what he's got," sneered Luke. "If you see 'im hocking back, slap him hard."

Tom nodded his agreement. "The cunt is secured down, so the only way he could gain any sort of control over you is through his mouth. Don't let him rile you. Get his attention and say what you have to say, and that's it. If anything untoward happens then giz a shout. Luke and I will be outside."

"Eeeyera, Tom, give Dan your knife in case."

Tom shook his head. "Nah, if he manages to do a David Blaine and slip the cuffs, then he's as liable to take the knife off him."

Talk of bites and knifes kept Dan's nerves on edge, but he steadied his voice to say, "I'll be OK."

His brother and cousin nodded, and he slipped inside the container.

Mehmet Onel, topless and without footwear, sat at the end of the twenty-foot steel box. Handcuffs secured his wrists, his arms stretched above him, a chain passing through an iron loop bolted through the wall. A similar iron ring, bolted to the floor, secured his ankle cuffs.

Dan might have felt a flicker of pity for him if it were not for the sneer on his face.

He thought he might have to push down the stirrings of empathy when he saw the man—especially chained up—but he didn't.

He sat on an upside-down milk bottle crate.

"You know, my dad, my uncles and cousins are all criminals," began Dan. "They rule the city where I am from—I mean, Leeds is almost four times smaller than London but it's big enough. Because of the family name, all of us got treated differently—good and bad. My younger brother always loved it, loved girls' attention—certain types of girls—and other naughty people. I didn't like it sometimes, how teachers, or any new person, looked at you when hearing your last name. But even then, it wasn't horrendous, because the family was known to have a certain set of ethics. Not something you would understand."

He saw the killer's eyes squint briefly.

"I love money—not in the way our Luke does. I mean, actual money, how it works, how you can multiply it and then get it to work for you twenty-four-seven. And I was great at maths and good at computers. Applied to a university down here, smashed my degree and got set on by one of the better firms."

Mehmet's eyes just stared blanky ahead and Dan continued, "Like I said, when I was growing up, the family wasn't hated or anything—people were more wary. My Uncle Greg ran it—firm but fair. Put a lot back into the community. Had contacts on the local council and police. From what I heard, he'd give other criminals an even chance before getting heavy with them. And do you know what? He got murdered—reasonable enough, you think, being in the game he was. Sickening thing is, I found out not long ago it was arranged by his own brother. I still can't compute it in my head—killing your own brother."

Dan became aware he was mostly talking to himself and refocused on Onel.

"I think when my uncle got murdered, I sort of pulled away from my family. Then I met Angela at a Polish class, and took her for a coffee afterwards. After one conversation, I knew I wanted to be with her—gorgeous, pretty, had her own money—I know that shouldn't be a factor but it is for me, it's not the fifties any more. And the more I got to know her, the more I fell in love with her. She worked tirelessly—I've never seen anyone work like that before. All to help other people. They relied on her, her kindness, her passion and her drive. I've seen their faces and how they are afterwards when they have received justice. You took all that away when you stabbed her."

When he saw the eyes crease in a smile, his heart swelled with rage. He reached out and tore the masking tape off. The eyes flashed anger before returning to their arrogant sneer.

Onel spoke in English with a mixed accent of London and Ankara.

"What? Was *Manz* sob story meant to make me cry? This is high above yer and her."

"What do you mean? How high?"

The Turk laughed. "Higher than I know. Our crew are just fish and you sitting there gassing yer family up, they are just minnows."

"Just tell me who's—"

"Shut the fuck up. She was warned—a few times. But she gave it all *airtime*. You telling me about what a Mother Teresa she's meant to have been—she wore a suit and drove a fancy whip. That's why, when the call to shank her up came, I was happy. When I saw her—you're right, she was *Peng*. Wish I picked a place where I could have had some alone time with the snooty—"

Dan's first punch knocked the words from the gangster's face. He kept on hammering; it was like a constant plume of anger between punches. He did not even register Tom and Luke rushing in.

As soon as Luke saw it was his brother doing the beating and not the other way around, he snatched Tom in a bear hug and pulled him back.

"What the fuck are you doing?" shouted Tom, as he peeled Luke's hands off him and faced him.

"My brother needs this."

Tom looked at him for a few moments until the understanding came to his eyes. "We need him alive, remember. And Dan doesn't need a murder on his conscience."

They turned to watch.

That his brother was not trained to fight was obvious—that the Turk was still conscious was sign enough. Whereas Luke would have simply grasped the hair and used uppercuts to the point of the jaw, Dan's wide arm punches were thrown like slaps with clenched fists in the general direction of the face.

Still, anguished cries sounded from both attacker and victim, and Luke had to remind himself that the shackled Onel had stabbed a woman to death.

Finally, the blows slowed—either through his brother's exhaustion or maybe the pain in his hands—and Tom nodded to Luke.

The two cousins gripped him by the arms and pulled him away.

"Enough now, Dan," said Tom.

Luke felt his brother sag against them. His words came out stuttering between breaths. "He said…said he fucking volunteered. They didn't make him, he volunteered—wasn't even sorry."

"Well, I think he now knows how you feel about the situation," said Tom. "But he still needs to answer questions, Dan. He might have done it, but he didn't order it."

They pulled him out of the container to the sound of the Turk's seal-like blood snorts.

30

As Mancuso stopped the car outside the towering gate, Connor asked, "What is this place?"

"This is my home," answered the mafia boss and the gate swung open. "You will stay here tonight."

Connor said, "You know, as much as I love Italy, I will have to return home one day.

"Yes, you will."

They entered the estate comprising a large, stonewalled manor and barn conversions. The outside, from the driveway to the walls, to the steps and lighting, had a rustic feel, as they bathed in the Calabrian sunshine.

Alighting from the car and walking into the marble and oak hallway, a porter came to greet them.

He and Mancuso spoke in rapid Italian.

"He will show you to your room. There are fresh clothes in your size in the wardrobe."

Connor frowned. "What if I don't like them?"

"You will. I know about these things."

Connor followed the porter up the spiral stairway. The porter opened the second door on the right along the lengthy wood-floored hall.

The room had an oriental feel to it, with the bed in the room's centre, resting on a dark wood platform raised six inches off the floor. The peacock-patterned throw lay over a cream duvet, on which sat blue cloud pillows.

The expansive windows gave way to views of vineyards and farmland stretching out to mountains in the distance.

He went into the walk-in wardrobe and after looking through the array of sharp-looking clothes, he murmured to himself, "This is his grand plan. To turn me into a fashion model."

He picked out a combination of dark blue trousers, light blue shirt with a light grey suit jacket and Oxford shoes.

After taking a quick, cold shower he found the clothes and shoes fitted him perfectly.

He walked out of the bedroom to find the porter waiting for him down the hall.

Connor continually made mental notes regarding the layout of the house, as he followed the porter out onto a large deck at the back of the building.

Mancuso sat on one of two chairs to the right of a stone table. A bottle of red wine without a label sat on top of it.

"Connor, do you like red wine?"

"Depends on how good it is," he answered, taking his seat.

Mancuso poured him a glass, and Connor swirled it before smelling it and saying, "I've seen people do this."

The Italian smiled. "Wine is tasted mostly with the nose. Swirling releases the aromas and also disappears some of the bad compounds."

They sipped in silence and Connor admired the distant mountain view.

"What was said in your meeting?"

"You know I can't tell you that. Can't break *Omerta*."

"That is good," said Mancuso, sipping his wine. "I know they requested you to kill me."

Connor felt the air cool. However, he said nothing and Mancuso continued, "And I know that you refused. You took a great risk."

"So, what was that? A test you all concocted?"

Mancuso shook his head. "No, they want me to die."

It took Connor a moment to think. "So, if they both want you dead, then you must have bugged the room."

"You know the value of intelligence."

"I don't understand. You're a family."

"They do not share my vision. These ways of ours were made in a time that was very much different to now."

"And what is your vision?"

"Tomorrow, I will show you part of my vision," Mancuso said, before looking at him. "You are correct, Mr Reed, a man should enjoy the fruits of hard and dangerous labour, or else he becomes resentful."

With that he shouted, "Le Signore."

Three women strolled out from around the corner. Connor sat in admiration, not only for their grace and beauty but because Mancuso had remembered his preference of a woman's figure.

"These ladies work in the city for me. They are here to make your time more comfortable. Redheads are not typical in my country."

Connor did not doubt Mancuso could obtain an escort of any hair colour or body type, but would only let people he knew into his home.

"Thank you," Connor replied sincerely. "You are spoiling me with three."

Confusion creased the older man's forehead and Connor realised he was meant to pick one, leaving the other two for Mancuso.

"If you want all three then they are yours. We have a long day tomorrow though."

"One is fine."

Connor, keenly aware a woman's self-esteem could be tied to her attractiveness, was about to ask the ladies to pick a number from one to three between themselves. However, one looked at him with greater intensity than the others. The black hair faded into a lighter brown at the tips, which flowed past her shoulders. The suggestiveness of her dark eyes and pursed lips juxtaposed her age, which Connor guessed to be around nineteen.

The see-through shawl, black bra and knickers showed off a pair of tits threatening to spill out, a narrow waist compared to the hips, and the *combat indicator* of a flat tummy without the lines of muscle definition.

Connor stood and stepped to within a foot of her. "Can you speak English?"

She stepped to within half a foot of him and said in heavily accented English, "Yes. You want deep conversation?"

"Not particularly. I just did not want to resort to repeating myself with sign language as I am ordering you about," he said with a wink, and the barest of a smile.

"That will not be a problem…sir," she answered with intense eye contact.

With that, she took him by the hand and led him back into the house.

The feeling Ciara had when Bruce arrived at Adrianna's house felt akin to a time when her dad had picked her up from school after an outburst when she was eleven.

She knew it likely the psychological profile she submitted to on entry to 'The Chameleon Project' would show her trait of murderous aggression was derived from a combination of her dad's early death and her mother's subsequent abusive relationship with another man.

Looking back now, Ciara could see there were seeds before that. The eleven-year-old Ciara had been so engrossed in conversation about the Olympics that she had not heard the teacher telling them to be quiet. She hadn't been aware of Mr Platt's displeasure until he had seized her arm to snap her attention back.

She had lashed out without thinking, being horrified to find she had cut his lip. Marched to the headmaster's office, she sat there wanting the world to swallow her whole.

Her dad arrived, and with a simple hand on her shoulder, she knew everything would be OK.

Bruce McQuillan's presence exuded the same type of reassurance. A presence she wanted to more than emulate in time.

He stepped into the kitchen, as Adrianna locked the door behind him, and Ciara stood from behind the kitchen island.

"I'll go and fetch my things."

Bruce shook his head. "That can wait."

She saw the look on his face and asked, "What is it?"

He looked briefly at Adrianna, then said to her, "Adrianna, you may as well hear this too."

They sat around the island table with the two women looking expectantly at the Scotsman.

He began, "Connor has gone dark. Haven't heard from him in over a week."

Ciara's heartbeat rose. "How do you know he's gone dark, and isn't dead?"

"We have a glimpse of surveillance footage of him at the port in Bari a few days ago. He may be dead now but I doubt it."

"Who is Connor?" asked Adrianna.

"He works for me."

"He's an agent?"

"Yes."

Ciara interrupted the exchange with, "Why do you doubt it?"

"Because he was with Salvatore Mancuso, and they were last seen heading towards Calabria."

"Why would he not make contact with you?"

"I think he's had his phone removed. I think Mancuso is attempting to woo him."

"For what? He's already shown them he's willing."

"Oh," announced Adrianna. "This Connor led the team against The Black Axe?"

Ciara admired the older journalist's powers of deduction. And her boss's unwillingness to correct her in stating Connor was acting alone. He simply nodded, before saying, "Our technical staff has been sifting through and pulling together information indicating that not only has Mancuso been hiring foreign mercenaries, but has been doing so without the knowledge of the wider 'Ndrangheta."

There were a few moments of silence before Ciara said, "If this is true, then surely Mancuso would have been able to win his war with the Albanians before now?"

"He's using them for some another purpose."

"Like what?" asked Ciara.

"I spoke to a Douglas Erickson, one of the alleged victims of an operation that sees people kidnapped and taken away to have their minds broken into subservience. I believed him."

"Dio mio,"—*My God*, exclaimed Adrianna. "So it is true?"

"It seems so," answered Bruce calmly. "We have identified the doctor to be an Andrew Roberts. Eighty-three years of age. Former employee of the CIA and DARPA. An internal government investigation uncovered he perpetrated some sickening acts on test subjects—not detainees but innocent US citizens in order to perfect his methods. He was quietly exiled to Argentina in the 1970s. From there he made his way to Europe."

"So he is behind it?" Ciara frowned.

"He's just an employee," said Bruce. "Erickson made mention of the nickname Mr Milan. This is thin, however, Salvatore Mancuso has attended Milan fashion week without fail for the past twenty-three years, and has shares in the millions in a few of the companies."

Silence fell on the kitchen.

Ciara broke it with, "So Connor could be on his way to that island now?"

Bruce nodded. "There's no telling what damage could be done if they break him. The information in his mind, and his skillset. Our tech guy is trawling for possible locations but it isn't promising at the moment."

"What shall we do, then?"

"I've moved a detachment down to the south to form a QRF. Wait for Connor's signal, if he sends one."

Ciara frowned. "Why wouldn't he?"

Bruce seemed like he was talking to himself when he said, "He might submit voluntarily."

"Never," she declared.

Bruce murmured, "How far would a man go to protect his family?"

Tom and Luke stood in front of the bleeding and bruised Mehmet Onel. Dan had long left.

Before either addressed him, the London-Turk said, "I know you're going to kill me. Because if you don't, my fam' will massacre yours. So don't expect me to talk after a slapping in'it."

The Ryders briefly looked at one another before Tom said, "That's the thing. We want it to take ages. The longer it takes, the more time it'll have to die down. You'll get replaced and the energy into finding out what's really happened to you will ease off. In the meantime, our disinformation can set to work. Make out it was someone else got rid of you because of the amount of heat you were bringing down. Maybe someone sent from the old country, eh."

Though Onel weakly replied, "They won't believe ya," when Luke saw the look in his eyes, he knew that Onel knew it was a plausible story.

Tom replied, "We both know they'll want to believe it. Palming it off means no aggro for whoever is going to slide into your *Sabahs*."

Luke turned his head to Tom. "What are Sabahs?"

"A type of Turkish shoe, apparently."

The London gangster croaked, "What now? You just going to leave me in here?"

"Nah, mate," answered Luke before shouting, "Go ahead. He's ready."

The Turk became wild-eyed, as he looked around the container. He barely noticed the drip of water on his head. His eyes narrowed with confusion and, after another minute, another drip landed. He shook his head.

Luke continued, "The thing about our family is, we have many talents among us. Our cousin, Connor, told us the Chinks used to—or maybe still do—torture their prisoners by putting them under a drip. Enough time passes, and the prisoner will give up his own mother to make it stop. Anyway, our other cousin, Charlie, designed and built one using a hose, valve and this tilting device—in fact, I can't be fucked going into it, but it works—can set it to regular or irregular intervals, which is what we are going to use. You'll be tearing your hair out to reach it. I wanted to torture you with a knife or a red-hot poker, but this is meant to be way, way worse."

Luke could see the Turk wasn't convinced of the potency of this form of torment. In truth, neither was he, but Connor had been adamant.

Tom looked at Luke before looking back at the Turk. "We'll let you think about it for a few days."

They both turned and walked away.

31

It had taken Carlo a few days and nights of scouting the marina to seize the opportunity. He found a couple of potential access points the first night and noted the security personnel had been cut to two. He had also identified the boat he wanted to steal.

He understood why boats were not commonly stolen despite the evident ease of doing so compared to cars. It was not worth the risk for an average thief, unfamiliar with nautical charts or marine navigation symbols, to take them out onto the ocean's billiard table before storing them at a pre-arranged location.

And for what motivation? Just to sell them for parts a person could easily buy online.

Luckily for Carlo, none of this applied to him. Post-Legion, during his stay in South America, he had paid a Uruguayan harbour master to teach him how to drive small- to mid-sized craft. And he only needed this boat for one journey.

The Cranchi Mediterranee 43 HT seemed superficially a little worse for wear, but he knew it to be seaworthy as it had been out the previous day. Not only that, but he had piloted the model before.

Clouds floated across the face of the moon and he watched the wandering sentry through the fence line. Carlo estimated the guard would return to the office in approximately twenty minutes to wake his colleague.

The former legionnaire checked his watch—02.57—*good enough.* He pulled the balaclava over his face.

Taking out the small tool wallet from his backpack, he took four minutes to remove the wheelie bin stack on the side of the fence line, climb under where it had frayed out, walk across to the panel fastened to the wooden cylinder, open it and disable the CCTV covering the marina.

He saw the office dim with the monitor screens going black, and kept his eyes on it as he skirted the dark edges. There didn't appear to be any movement.

He crept his head into the open door and couldn't help but smile. The man wasn't only asleep but leant far back into his chair, drool tremoring with the snores.

With nearly a quarter of a million illegally held firearms in a country of three million people, this security company had obtained a lawful dispensation for its personnel to carry them. His arms hung past the Berretta M9, begging for Carlo to relieve it from its holster.

He considered drawing it and pistol-whipping the man unconscious. However, pistol-whipping—though he had gotten adept at it—was not quite the failsafe Hollywood films would have a person believe; the risk of death, or simply hurting a man, causing him to cry out, was significant.

Carlo gripped his dagger.

His idea had been to let circumstances on the ground dictate his actions; however, he knew it would involve either securing and gagging the two guards or murdering them.

Securing them involved a lot of moving parts, and he found killing two amateurs—especially with one of them asleep—distasteful.

The idea came to him. He took out his phone and snapped a few pictures.

Then he roared in Italian—the tongue of the management, "Wake up!"

The guard's face burst into stunned fear, his hands scrabbling around for his gun.

"What were you asleep for?" shouted Carlo.

"I…I…" sputtered the man.

His colleague appeared at the door, breathing heavily with his gun in hand.

"Put that away now," ordered Carlo. "What is this? The night shift is where you both stay awake! Not where you take it in turns! What am I paying you for? This marina opened three months ago and already the discipline is gone to horse shit."

"Errr…sir…who…who—" spluttered the man at the door, mercifully in Italian.

"Who am I? You pair of rock apes do not even know the owner of this marina?"

The man who had been sleeping began, clearly attempting to inject some confidence in his voice, "Sir, we are new here and do not know—"

"You are new, and still think it's acceptable to sleep? My seven-year-old son knows you cannot guard shit when asleep. Wait. WHY IS THE MONITOR OFF?"

The man dived forward and began tapping the mouse and then the monitor.

"I…I am not sure, sir."

"The both of you listen. I am taking my yacht out—that is, if it has not been stolen. When I get back in a few hours that monitor better be back on. And if I catch either of you ever, and I mean ever, asleep on a night shift again, I will kill you. I do not mean I will shout at you, or take your jobs, I mean I will kill you. This marina has cost me enough money without you two disrespecting it. Understand?"

The pair sounded off in unison. "Yes, sir."

"Good," he said, glaring at the man he'd caught asleep. "Go get me the keys to Cranchi in bay thirty-six."

Connor stood on the deck of the CP 829 Giubileo as it approached the strangely artificial-looking island in the distance.

The first layer appeared like natural stacks of rock, but he could see how well they fitted into one another even from this far away.

Slabs of rectangular stone made up walls he estimated to be around twenty-five metres high.

He could not see an entrance so surmised it must be on the far side.

Mancuso joined him on deck.

"It is officially listed as a research station for biohazards and dangerous chemicals," said the Italian.

"I take it the entry point is on the other side?"

The older man shook his head. "You will see as we get closer."

"OK," said Connor, a little bemused. "So, what happens if someone does come out here to check?"

"No one has in eighteen months. The location is not near the usual shipping lanes. If anyone from the Italian government wants to come and check what goes on here, they may do so."

As the vessel got closer, a coldness began to grow within Connor.

"Watch this," said Mancuso, holding up to his mouth the strap wrapped around his wrist. "Show the entrance."

With that, part of the wall blurred before an entry point revealed itself as a dock within the structure.

Surprise assailed Connor, who eventually said, "I have seen cloaking before but nothing nearly that big."

Again the Arthur C Clarke quote came to Connor's mind—*'Any sufficiently advanced technology is indistinguishable from magic'*.

He could now see some of the armed guards within the compound, counting eight overlooking the dock from the high walls.

He noted how each man had the butt of their rifles wedge firmly within the crevice between their shoulder and pectoral. Connor had seen all sorts of ill-discipline with security teams, including the cradling of their weapon systems, which ate precious seconds to bring them to bear.

Not these guys.

They carried the HK416 assault rifles which Connor liked using. The gas-operated, short-stroke piston design fired a NATO standard 5.56mm round, and had a cyclical rate of 900 rounds per minute on automatic.

He observed the men kept to their designated arcs without being drawn towards himself or Mancuso as they docked.

Connor tightened the screw top of his metallic water flask and left it on the boat, before stepping off the vessel.

One of the mercenaries stepped out of an office forged from steel sheets and walked down the gangway to meet them. Connor winced on the inside when he heard the Midlands accent.

"Welcome, Mr Mancuso."

"Thank you, Mr Smith," replied Mancuso.

"I must search your companion here."

Mancuso said, "Not this one."

It surprised Connor there appeared to be a stand-off for a few seconds before the soldier relented with, "Of course, sir."

He handed Mancuso a fob, and the 'Ndrangheta crime lord led Connor down the gangway.

As they walked, it changed into a pavement and began to dip to a lower level, not unlike some railway stations in the UK.

They came to a large, steel door with a serrated centre, interlinked like giant's teeth. Mancuso used his fob, and it opened with a hiss similar to a steam iron.

"How big is this compound?" asked Connor, as they stepped onto the rebar-reinforced floor covering a vast area, littered with vertical cylindrical chutes attached from roof to floor.

"What are these?"

"Containers containing various biohazardous materials."

"Why?"

"One reason is so we can explain why this island is isolated."

"Aren't all islands isolated?"

"You are correct. I meant, these materials hide our true agenda."

"Seeing as you are now bound to show me, instead I'll ask whether it concerns you that you have men teeming with guns in and around these containers?"

Mancuso laughed. "These can withstand any small arms fire. An attacking force does not have to know that. And an attacking force can be trapped here under the threat of its release."

"Who told you this? The manufacturer?"

"Not directly. The person or people who reached out to make this all possible."

Connor slowed. "So, you are not the architect of all this?"

"You do not know what all this is, yet. But no."

"Then who?"

"I do not know. It is all done by secret messages and code. I would guess 'the old white men' we all are told about, who will pay a *Ginzo* like me so they might keep their hands clean," said Mancuso. "Such are the ladders of this world. Come, and I will show you."

Connor looked around and saw various entrances on all four sides. "You could fit an Amazon warehouse in here."

"The area is 432 metres by 547 metres."

"So, some of these doors lead off to other places."

"It is a labyrinth—it is designed to be."

"Why?"

"To prevent escapes."

"Who's escaping?"

"You will see," said Mancuso, walking them over to the far end. Connor saw him press the fob repeatedly but seemingly in a sequence like Morse code—*dot, dash, pause, dash, dot, dot, dot, pause, dash, dot, dash, dot. Fucking ABC.*

The corner flooring peeled back like a spiral. Looking through it, Connor could see they were at least three floors up.

The former marine looked back to see one of the sentries using his palm to open one of the entrances. It took him a couple of seconds to realise Mancuso would not have wanted his palm print associated with this place.

They descended before reaching a lower floor corridor.

"Come," said the crime lord. As they walked around a corner, the scene punched horror into Connor's chest.

32

Carlo had struck a balance between quickly putting distance between himself and the marina, and conserving fuel.

He knew, should the co-ordinates lead to nowhere or omitted access to whatever the place was, he wouldn't have enough fuel to reach land. Then it would be a case of sending out an SOS and being carted off to a police station.

He thought about what the dying mercenary told him.

Why would Mancuso hire foreign mercenaries without the approval of the wider 'Ndrangheta? Why would he want to alienate an organisation that had not only made him rich and powerful, but could have him killed for disobedience?

And why wouldn't the wider family permit him? Surely, once they had gone down the road of war against the Albanians, they would have seen the sense of farming out some of the taskings to professional soldiers. Within Mafia Shqiptare ranks were veterans of conflicts in southern Serbia and Macedonia in the late 1990s and early 2000s.

A block appeared in the distance as the yacht neared the co-ordinates. His heartbeat rose as he grabbed the binoculars.

He focused them—*it looks like a mini-Alcatraz.*

He couldn't see any entry point, and so hoped the island was not too large in diameter, as the fuel gauge read 'low'.

The yacht buoyed closer, and he took a wide arc around the structure in case of any small arms fire being brought to bear on him.

After the fifteen minutes it took to circumnavigate the entire piece of land, he thumped his hand down in frustration—there was no entry point.

He turned the yacht towards it and got within ten metres before starting to skirt around it.

A red light; the fuel gauge warning him he was running out of diesel. As he went past full circle, he lamented he would have rather come under gunfire than to be floating around in obscurity.

His forehead scrunched on seeing the entrance—he was convinced he had already fully circumnavigated the structure.

As he steered towards it, nerves shot electrical signals all around his body.

Armed men perched like giant bats on the high walls of the docks.

Connor kept his face neutral as they walked around the corridors of glass cells. Each contained humans of all ages, ethnicities and genders, in varying degrees of alertness and distress. The muffling of their sounds played sinisterly on his ears.

"What is this? A psychiatric ward?"

Mancuso laughed. "Maybe a type of psychiatric ward—louder sometimes. All these corridors are completely soundproof. Let me ask you, what is the most valuable thing Elon Musk, Warren Buffet and Bill Gates own?"

Connor shrugged. "Their brains?"

Mancuso nodded approvingly. "Very good, Connor. Everyone else says things like a private jet or luxury boat. But stripped of their worldly possessions, they would still earn their money back, in time, as long as they retained their physical health and mental sharpness."

"So, what is it you aim to achieve here? Physical health and mental sharpness?"

"You have been in the military, have you not?"

Connor nodded his affirmation at the rhetorical question.

Mancuso continued, "They put you through harsh training, forging you into what they want and then they send you on missions not of your choosing."

Connor felt a lurch in his stomach—this hadn't been the first man he had heard justify hideous acts.

"So, these people are volunteers?"

"They have been volunteered," Mancuso said without a hint of embarrassment.

"So, who are they?"

"They have a range of talents and professions. From engineers, scientists, architects, surgeons, all the way down to thieves, whores and forgers."

Connor asked, "So, after their training, how do their 'postings' get selected for them?"

"The highest bidder, I should imagine."

"You imagine?"

"Come," said Mancuso, ignoring Connor's implied question. "I have much to show you."

The agent didn't like the feeling of being led deeper into a lair. Every so often they would pass an armed guard.

Mancuso pressed his fob again in a pattern Connor memorised and another doorway appeared on the right. Connor followed him in, and with the metallic clanking of their feet, down another spiral staircase.

The older man seemed to have no concern with regards to turning his back on Connor.

Another door opened into a corridor similar to the one upstairs. The rooms were more extensive. Within them were various patients undergoing various procedures.

They stood outside one of the rooms where a remarkably attractive woman with jet-black hair stared at a steel marble attached to a chain. It was being swung in front of her eyes by a man whose white laboratory coat matched his sparse hair and thick-rimmed glasses. Connor guessed him to be over eighty—the collagen in a person's nose and ears broke down with age giving the impression they didn't stop growing; and this man's ears reminded Connor of sliced cabbages.

A smile crept on Connor's lips as he thought of a British comedy sketch involving a hypnotist. The smirk dissolved as he realised he was watching the enslavement of a person's mind.

"Who is the man performing the hypnotism?"

"That is Doctor Roberts. A former employee of both DARPA and the Project MKUltra."

Connor knew the Defence Advanced Research Projects Agency designed and manufactured technologies for the military. And was aware the MKUltra project to be a CIA mind control program sanctioned in the early fifties and officially discontinued by 1973.

"What enticed him to come here? Money?"

Mancuso shook his head. "He would have accepted much less than what he receives to carry out his life's work on mind control. The US has become more…politically correct in these recent years."

"Does he have a staff?"

"It is just he who deals with this side of the operation."

"I see," said Connor. "And what will be her mission?"

"She is one of the world's better translators—an exceptionally talented linguist. She will help to keep important men happy."

"I see," said Connor. "And she needs to go through this 'training' to achieve that?"

Mancuso shook his head. "She needs to go through this training so she remains loyal."

"You mean, so she doesn't run away or tell tales?"

Mancuso paused for a moment. "Yes."

"So, a bit of a holiday. A bit of hypnotism, a bit of therapy, and voila, people's skills for auction; people who will love doing whatever they are chosen to do, for whoever has chosen them to do it. Everyone is a winner."

Connor kept any inflexion of sarcasm out of his voice.

"I am glad you see the logic," Mancuso said. "Unfortunately, some of the methods used have to be a little more…insistent than hypnosis. I will show you."

They rounded the corner, and Connor counted four guards pacing up and down the far end.

As they looked through the glass, the pain and horror etched on the man's face echoed in Connor's stomach.

A man of around fifty, dressed in an orange jumpsuit, clawed at the padded walls, gasping for air as the veins banged out of both neck and temple.

After a few moments, he slumped with relief.

Mancuso murmured, "The room is designed to monitor not only the oxygen level within the room, but the oxygen saturation within the trainee's body—a sensitive technology that accurately measures in tiny detail the exhalations of the trainee. The program is set at intervals to deprive the individual of oxygen without killing them."

The Italian tapped on the glass, and continued, "The science behind it was explained to me—any lesson associated with pain becomes deeper rooted in the individual's mind. Disobedience can be completely disappeared through such methods. There is no risk of the individual dying and no need to monitor them. Just place them in here for a certain time until they are more…responsive to some of the softer methods. Doctor Roberts could explain in more detail."

The Brit kept the revulsion off his face even though he knew not even Mancuso could lack the self-awareness that he would find this abhorrent—*Because he doesn't care. Maybe he thinks his offer for me and my family is too good to refuse.*

Connor went through the motions of assessing his options, even though he knew it was futile.

Unarmed, alone, trapped in a subterranean base in the middle of the sea, outnumbered many times over by professional mercenaries with minds etched with an unerring loyalty to Mancuso, he could not envision a way out.

Still, he knew he was going to try. The 'Ndrangheta crime lord—if he could be called that now—had brought him down here to subvert him to being his unwaveringly loyal attack dog. Not only did he not relish the process—especially this monstrosity of an oxygen deprivation chamber—but the thought of no longer controlling his mind terrified him the most.

I'd rather die than be a bitch for some satanic chopstick.

"What about them?" said Connor, indicating towards the armed men at the far end of the corridor.

"The same. They were brought here, and now they are used to their full potential."

"Working for you?"

"Well, these work for me. However, they are soldiers with the aptitude for guarding installations. What I need are soldiers with the skill and daring to perform missions for me worldwide."

Here it comes, thought Connor.

"These guards. Have they undergone this treatment?"

To his surprise, Mancuso shook his head. "All the mercenaries here are just that—mercenaries. Money is what got them to work here. Insurance against their families is what keeps their mouths shut."

"I see. Why have you brought me here if I am not going to be working here?"

"What I need," Mancuso began, "is for you to lead the…recruitment."

"You want me to kidnap people and bring them here," said Connor rhetorically.

"Yes. I will pay you millions. And your family will be forever protected. You will—"

A breathless guard cut short the sentence as he came to a running stop beside Mancuso, and began to quietly but rapidly address him.

"A man has arrived by yacht. We have detained him. He claims to work for you."

"What did he say his name was?"

"Carlo Andaloro."

Mancuso took a moment. "Bring him here with a security detail of four. Ensure he has no weapons, and be careful."

"Yes, sir," said the foot soldier, before jogging off.

Mancuso looked at Connor. "No sense in saying the same speech twice."

33

Carlo knew, as the three guards formed a circle around him, any hope Salvatore still considered him an ally was gone.

These guys had a professional, if robotic, air about them. He decided to play *Signor Obbedienza* in what he knew to be a slim hope of relaxing them.

As he followed them down into the metallic labyrinth, he wondered what this place was—*a psychiatric unit guarded by mercenaries?*

The lead guard used his palm on what looked to be black ceramic panels to access the doors.

As they led him further down, his nerves sang. Carlo loved to flirt with death but only in the sense it amplified the feeling of being alive. He would take on the most dangerous missions to immerse himself in the sensations, but much of that thrill came in the escape.

However, he now found himself in a situation where he was purely at his employer's mercy.

Another door opened and Carlo took a moment to process the scene that hit him.

The soldier whom he had saved in Castel Volturno stood with Mancuso. Carlo observed the sandy-blond-haired man seemed uncomfortable—nothing obvious, just subtle signs in his body language.

Mancuso faced him and quietly said in Italian, "Carlo. I thought you were dead. I am glad you are here."

"You thought I was dead because you arranged for me to be," Carlo said flatly.

"You know that is not true, Carlo. I have big plans for you. Your escape demonstrates your value to me. You are a wild card, this is true. But now I have seen what they can do here, this might not be a problem any more."

Carlo's stomach lurched as he registered the words. Wanting to lengthen the conversation, he jutted his chin towards the blond and asked, "So, is he my replacement?"

Mancuso smirked. "My organisation will be too large and too strong to limit the talent."

"Your organisation? Ours has no one leader?"

"That is the problem with our organisation—decisions cannot be made without the consent of old men stuck in the past."

Carlo's forehead knotted. "We are one of the richest companies in the world? The system is not broken."

"We are still beset by forces more powerful than ourselves. I will change that."

"I will not help you."

Mancuso smiled. "You don't have a choice."

The crime lord then switched to English and said to his soldiers, "Take him away and secure him."

Connor cursed his lack of Italian and instead focused on the two men's body language as they conversed.

The armed guards seemed wary of the man with olive skin and shorn hair.

It took the Englishman a few moments to realise that, despite their low tones, they were arguing.

Mancuso switched to English. "Take him away and secure him."

Connor's body reacted before his brain knew what it was doing.

His left arm snatched Mancuso around his face, clasping his jaw before whipping out the plastic blade hidden in his collar.

Holding it to Mancuso's throat, he pressed just enough to draw blood. "Put down your weapons or I will slit his throat right now. I'd rather die in a hail of bullets than be subject to whatever goes on down here."

As they hesitated, he pressed the blade a touch harder and Mancuso gave a subtle nod.

They slowly complied.

"You," Connor said to the man who had been brought down. "Can you speak English?"

"Yes."

"Your name is Carlo, yes?"

"Yes"

"My name is Connor. Do you want to leave like I want to leave?"

"Yes."

"Then pick up a rifle."

When Carlo did so, Connor said, "Do you have any issue helping me kill everyone in this place who holds a weapon?"

Carlo shook his head. "Carpophorus is no longer here, so I will kill these beasts myself."

Connor nodded. "That was one of my favourite gladiator stories too."

The Italian smiled before saying, "I think you should start with that dishonourable motherfucker you have there."

"You two have thrown away your lives," sneered Mancuso. "And with it a chance to become leaders in the most feared organisation in the world. You will now—"

Carlo's rifle-butt strike cut off the rest of the sentence, slumping Mancuso back into Connor, who kept him upright.

As Carlo brought the rifle to bear on Mancuso, Connor shouted, "No! I need to interview him. And I know just where to hold him."

"OK," said Carlo, before turning on the mercenaries and stepping back. Connor dropped Mancuso before picking up a rifle and inspecting the chamber.

The mafia soldier then said, "I would have expected their response time to be quicker."

Connor thought back to his metallic flask. "I blocked the signals to their surveillance and radio communications. Might have bought us some time."

He saw the Italian open his mouth, then close it before asking, "What about these men?"

"They agreed to do this for money," the former marine answered, before opening fire into the mercenaries. The former legionnaire joined him in shooting them into blood, bone and flesh-spurting corpses. The detainees and Doctor Roberts watched in awe from behind the glass screens.

Doctor Roberts's face fluttered into fear as Connor pressed the access button. The woman recoiled back into her chair with an expression of terrified uncertainty.

Connor bared his teeth. "Doctor, let's see if these methods work on their architect."

The old man's hoarse screams cut through the air as Connor snatched him by his ears and dragged him out. The agent opened the oxygen restriction chamber, releasing its previous occupant who flew out like a bird released from a cage.

Connor threw the doctor in and the zapped the door closed muffling the shrieks.

They stopped when Connor switched the machine on.

34

The security detail commander frowned at the blurring of the security footage. This had happened before, but previously this had only been for a few seconds at a time and this was now reaching the thirty-second mark.

He looked on as one of his men hunched over the monitor's box before turning to him and saying, "I've cleaned the connectors, and they seem fine. I'll get the diagnostics kit."

The commander nodded as he felt something in his stomach. He grabbed the communications unit and attempted to raise the leader of the fire team that had taken this Carlo Andaloro down to Mancuso, "Foxtrot One, Foxtrot One, come in, over."

Static answered.

He immediately switched the mode to 'all call signs' only to be met by the same static.

He spun around and said to the two soldiers in the security observation room with him, "I don't like this. Communication and security feeds are down at the same time, just as two strangers have arrived. Split up and issue a Bravo protocol to everyone."

The two men nodded and bolted out of the door.

The two general protocols that got drilled regularly was Alpha—external hostiles attempting to gain entry, and Bravo—detainees trying to escape. A thought occurred to the team commander: there wasn't a protocol specific to two professional soldiers attempting to escape. Although their military background had not been confirmed, the commander had been around enough dangerous men to know the pair were not suits.

Still, if he had to guess, he would think this was something Mancuso had concocted to test the security detail's reaction, speed and efficiency—to maybe show this off to the pair. And the commander had a determination not to let his boss down.

Within a few minutes, the fire teams had formed at the various entry points. The commander secured his chest rig, ensuring the pouches were fastened correctly and checked his rifle.

He walked down the gangway and bellowed in their common language of English, "All commanders on me."

It took half a minute to form a semi-circle in front of him.

"Communications are down and so is the live feed. We don't know why, but we must ensure the boss's safety and the security of this facility. Now, the man he brought, and the man brought down to him, look like soldiers to me. That the boss asked for the yachtsman to be escorted by the armed guard should tell us he's potentially dangerous. We'll have to go through our areas of clearance without communications, except verbally when you reach *AOE*. Understand?"

They nodded.

"There's only the pair of them, unarmed and without body armour. They shouldn't be too difficult to overcome."

Despite the adrenaline coursing around his system, Connor couldn't help smiling, as he watched Mancuso crane his neck to hold it above the invisible water he now found himself in. He wished he had all day to watch.

The Calabrian's access fob now lay in the Yorkshireman's possession.

The previous occupant lay outside the oxygen restriction room, gulping huge lungfuls of air, relief and gratitude shining from his eyes.

Pools of claret spread out from the executed security team. Connor remembered how fascinated he was watching the blood spread the first time he had shot someone in the head.

He and Carlo donned the body armour from two of the corpses. They stuffed as many magazines and grenades on their person as were viable to carry.

The Italian looked at him. "You will take the lead for now."

"You have confidence in a man you've never met?"

"I watched you in Castel Volturno."

After a moment, Connor said, "It was you who saved me?"

Carlo simply shrugged and said, "Give me your blade. That one opened the doors using his hand on the scanner."

"We don't have time to get through the bone with it," said Connor. "Unload a magazine into the elbow and we'll twist it off. We can negate ricochets by resting the arm on one of the bodies."

Connor grabbed the wrist of one dead man and held the arm straight over the torso of another as Carlo fired four bursts before the arm came off with Connor's crunching twist. Using a bootlace stripped from one of the corpses, Carlo tied a loop and attached it to the arm's wrist.

Connor's smile at the surreal scene of Carlo having a severed arm swinging from his shoulder was matched by the Italian's.

"Good to go?" asked Connor rhetorically, feeling a strange calm, despite knowing they were going to die.

Carlo nodded, still smiling.

They checked their weapon systems and pouches before making their way up the corridor, Connor on the left and Carlo on the right.

An image of a dragon with its jaws open flashed into Connor's mind as he saw the steel door. The two men squeezed themselves flat to the walls. With the scanner on Carlo's side, the lifeless arm came up and pressed against the plate, as Connor dropped into the kneeling position for firing.

The door steamed open to reveal a group of four manoeuvring towards the door. The sudden revelation of the pair seemed to instil a second of shock into the quartet.

Connor's and Carlo's rapid, precision fire, scythed them down with only a couple of mercifully high death-twitch shots fired back.

They covered and manoeuvred forward, keeping six inches away from the walls to guard against ricochets.

As they approached a second corner, Connor heard the clang before it appeared. His brain flashed a scene from a childhood family party.

Notwithstanding his years of experience, Carlo found his muscles tense in anticipation of being shredded by a HE grenade.

Time slowed as all his senses amplified to fever pitch, as he observed the Englishman kicking the grenade back around the corner.

Even in his current state, he mirrored his battle partner's action of jamming his fingers in his ears and opening his mouth.

The sound and reverberation of the blast brought his senses back online. He snatched his weapon system back into a firing position. He patrolled up to the corner level with Connor.

"I'll go long. You go short," said Connor.

Carlo nodded his affirmation, and the Englishman blasted around to the far wall, and he turned the corner.

The enemy soldiers lay like a horrific red paint-splattered frozen dance troupe, the smell of iron pungent in the air.

"They all have the same weapon systems. Let's take it in turns replenishing our ammunition," said Connor.

They did so in turn.

The sound of multiple boots chopped through them.

"Here. It's a spiral staircase that leads to the upper floors. If we stay down here to fight, this fire team might know the correct delay on a grenade."

Carlo nodded. Connor took out the fob and using the Morse code he had observed earlier, opened an access portal. They both went through.

"Wait," whispered the former Royal Marine, as he hovered by the access point and rifled into his grenade pouch.

The former legionnaire covered his arcs, facing up the stairs.

When the voice issuing commands and the sound of footsteps were almost on top of the pair, Carlo heard the clang of a thrown grenade and the hiss of the shutters seaming shut.

The giggles of the Englishman rode over the muffled bang and screams.

Carlo smiled—*I knew he had to be crazy.*

35

The team commander's fear focused his resolve. As his fire team stepped around the third group of dead bodies, he could see now he had been over-confident.

Half the security detail lay slain.

He snapped his arm up, and the section of eight halted behind him, four faced the rear and three mirrored his position with their rifles facing forward.

The team commander broke off and walked back to his second in command.

He whispered, "They have gone to the upper floors—using this access door is the only way they would have been able to throw that grenade and escape its detonation zone. We need to split up. They can hear us coming as a team. It isn't soundproofed above here. If a pair engages they'll draw the rest of us to the fight."

His second in command nodded, and they split to brief their respective fire teams. They could not synchronise their entries as their communications were down and wrist watches had stopped.

Once everyone knew what their entry points were, they dispersed.

The team commander knew that a battle pair or two might be sacrificed, but this was the way to guarantee victory.

He didn't know where Mancuso was, or if he was still alive.

Fucking hope he is, the commander thought, *best money I've ever been paid, or ever will.*

Connor averted his focus from the pleading eyes of the detainees trapped behind the glass cages. Hope fluttered in his stomach that he might survive to free them. The teams they had encountered had not shown a supreme level of professional ability—the lack of cover and manoeuvre, and the premature release of the grenade being telling. He suspected the security team's remit had been to contain the prisoners and maybe hold off an underwhelming external attack.

He heard the sound of multiple entrances opening on this floor and the one above.

"Let's separate but keep within visual. That's our only hope now," hissed Connor.

Carlo nodded, ghost walking over to a cylindrical steel pillar, putting around ten metres between them. He wondered if they trusted the manufacturer's guarantee of small arms fire not piercing the containers. Not that it mattered to him, being dead anyway.

In spite of their obvious attempts at stealth, he could hear the soles of their boots whispering death.

One of the soldiers appeared and began walking towards him without noticing him.

Connor looked around for other targets—this would be it, as soon as he shot this one the weight of return fire would pin him and his death would follow soon after.

I'll see my dad and grandad again—unless I get sent somewhere different.

In his peripheral vision he caught Carlo's throwing motion.

The grenade went off mid-air at the far end.

The explosion threw the soldier forward onto his front next to Connor who pile-drove the rifle's barrel with all his might. He heard the vertebrae crack at the base of the soldier's skull. Connor dragged him around the corner, out of view.

Their pursuers cut their attempt at stealth as they hurled questions and orders at one another.

A voice sounded out, quietening the others. "Sweep the perimeter and then we will work in. Do not get distracted."

"I've lost Delta Two. He was clearing through the southwest corner."

He looked at Carlo, who gestured to exactly what Connor was thinking—grenades.

They both ripped a pair each, removed the transit clips, pulled the pins and, with a nod, each threw their pair in different directions.

Several of the enemy bellowed, "Grenades!"

Carlo pointed to the access point. On the fourth detonation, they eschewed the 'fire and manoeuvre' principle and bolted for it.

"Targets in the open. Southwest corner."

The pair dived for the refuge of the steel wall, as bullets rained their promise of death behind them.

Connor scrambled up, smacking the fob against the screen. As the access point opened, a detonation threw him out in the daylight of outside, the blast spinning him in the air. Burning fragmentation shards sliced him on his right side from calf to shoulder.

He felt his left shoulder pop under impact, lengthening his now dead arm by a few inches. With a great effort, he rolled onto his back. He switched the selector to auto, and despite the roaring agony of moving his left arm, he forced the butt into his right armpit.

Carlo lay motionless beside him. They had landed to the left of the access point and the Yorkshireman could not see back into the facility.

A strange whirring sound danced on his eardrums.

At any moment the enemy would scream out like rats and kill them both.

Take as many down to Hell with you as you can.

The point man appeared.

Except his rifle was angled towards the sky. He went down under Connor's burst.

Then red tracer-mixed fire screamed from above. He looked up—the whirring sound in his brain were helicopter rotors.

It floated down like a protective dragon breathing fire on the opening.

Soldiers rappelled from their black ropes. They moved with such speed, precision and cohesion that Connor knew the mercenaries inside were dead.

He craned his neck to watch them enter, before turning to Carlo and reaching for him.

A shadow swept over Carlo, and Connor squinted against the sun, trying to identify the figure with his eyes, before his ears did the job for him.

The Glaswegian voice soothed him. "You know, sometimes you can wait for cavalry before starting a battle."

Connor forced himself into a sitting position and shrugged his right shoulder. "No plan survives contact—especially the one you're unaware of."

"Looks like you almost didn't survive either," said Bruce, before nodding to his shoulder. "It's dislocated. Want me to do the honours?"

Connor nodded reluctantly.

Bruce knelt in front of him, took hold of his wrist and elbow before stretching it out and placing the hand on his shoulder.

"First time?" he asked.

"Yeh," said Connor, trying to relax. "Let's get it over with."

Bruce frowned. "What you flinching for? What do you think I am going to do?"

"Yank it *Lethal Weapon* style."

Bruce shook his head, and began massaging the biceps up. After a time, the muscles relaxed before the joint popped back in.

"Magic," said Bruce.

"Thanks," said Connor. "Shouldn't you be coordinating this instead of playing nurse?"

"You've taken the communications out. Nothing I can do until they have secured the place."

Bruce began to check over Carlo with his fingertips before rolling him into the recovery position.

"How are they going to get access through the doors?"

"Jaime has equipped them with a portal device that emits a pulse," said Bruce, putting his ear to Carlo's mouth with his hand on his chest.

"He's like a modern-day wizard, that kid."

"This one is breathing," said Bruce. "Who is he?"

"His name is Carlo. He isn't a part of this."

Bruce knelt next to Connor. "Please tell me you left the manager of this alive."

"There're two. The doctor behind the…science, and our mafioso friend," said Connor. "The pair of them aren't having a good time of it at the moment."

"All right."

"How long do you need with Mancuso?"

"Why?"

"Because I need something from him."

36

Mancuso's mouth stretched tight around his teeth in a reverse scream. His lungs clawed for oxygen that wasn't there. His desperation held his body rigid. He heard it—the oxygen steam in. And he collapsed in a sucking relief.

He clutched his chest and looked up into the teary eyes of the Englishman—they were of laughter.

He had answered every question the older and taller British man with the silver-tinted black hair had asked. He had broken every *Omerta* he knew in the three-hour interrogation, just to put an end to these cycles of being dipped into death. His indignation left after the first three cycles. He cracked his silence on the fourth. Stopped telling lies and half-truths on the seventh.

The man's words were, "You have my word. I will not subject you to this any more once I have everything I need. And I promise not to kill you."

The crime lord knew enough about liars to know he was telling the truth. The man indeed left only to be replaced by Connor Reed.

Reed did not ask him a single question. Instead, he watched Mancuso in seemingly genuine hysterics as the Grim Reaper snatched his lungs out of his mouth before throwing them back in.

Reed now fell to the floor in a fit of laughter at the sight of Mancuso crying.

Finally, Mancuso ran face first into the reinforced glass—not in an attempt to break through but to knock himself out.

Reed's laughter abated and he called through the glass, "All right, I have memorised enough now so I can masturbate to this scene later. If you want it to end, all you have to do is cry, 'Mercy'."

Though registering it meant death, Mancuso frantically drew his scrambled senses together to croak the phrase that would release him.

"Mercy."

He saw Connor nod. "After this one."

"No, No, Nnnnn…"

Through his slide into death, he saw the eyes of Reed change colour; red, blue, red, blue, then finally amber.

As the former marine withdrew a dagger, Mancuso became aware of being in a different dimension. A black hooded figure stood on a small wooden boat by the riverside. Mancuso knew it was Charon, ready to take him to the underworld but refusing to—Mancuso had no means to pay.

Tom, knife in hand, opened the container door to find Onel murmuring to himself. After a few moments, the Turk seemed to come back to reality and focus on him.

"Ready to talk?"

"A man jumped my men as I was coming out of one of my restaurants—"

"Which restaurant?"

"La'Kezvan."

"What happened?"

"Came out of the shadows. Tazered them both from behind. Pulled a gun on me. Led me over to my Merc. There was a case leant against it—half a mil—

said it was a gift. Said he would call to offer us work. A security question was sorted out—"

"Slow down. Did you get a name?"

"He didn't give one, did he."

"Describe him."

"He spoke English with an Italian accent. Stocky. Bald. Can't remember what he was wearing."

"He came in with a case of cash and you weren't suspicious."

"What the fuck was I gonna do? Say nah, fam, keep your half a mil you're giving me for free?"

"All right. Then what happened?"

"He pointed at the restaurant sign and said Manz be contacted by phone—and make sure it's safe by asking the restaurant's name. If he was right then it was OK. If not, to end the call and chuck the phone."

"Then what."

"Then I'd get a call from an unknown. Tis one of those computer voices. It tell me where to look, and then there would be a package—money in it. The note would tell me what to do, and that I'd get the other half when I'd done it."

"What jobs?"

"I burnt down an office. Shook this councillor wit' a death threat. Organised this robbery of this Jewish jewellery store—was given the codes and everything. Then we ran over a police officer. Swimming in money, fam. Then the fuck-off wedge for shanking the barrister."

Tom's face didn't show the cold fury he felt at the Turk's final words.

"What did you do with the notes?"

The Turk's forehead creased. "Burnt 'em, what the fuck do you think I did?"

"So, apart from your phone, there's nothing to go off?"

"I switch my phone on a regular. I slung the phone I got that last job in the Thames. Pufft."

"Then what good are you then?"

"Didn't you hear me, fam'? Got over two million stashed. I can lead you to it—give you a mil. We'll forget this ever happened."

"You know you're lucky my cousin isn't here."

"Which? The blond one or the one that hits like a 'ickle bitch?"

"Neither of them. He'd have liked to have met you. Luckily for you, our friend whose land this is wants you moved on, and—"

The container door opened again and Luke walked in.

"What's he said?"

"Spilled his guts."

"Well…not yet."

"A bit messy that. I was going to use this," said Tom, showing Luke a plastic drawstring bag. "But he has an offer for us."

Luke held out his hand. Tom frowned at him and shook his head. However, the insistence shone from his younger cousin's eyes. Tom thought for a moment and handed it over.

Luke stepped closer to the flinching Turk and said, "What's this offer then?"

"I have two mil in cash stashed. I'll give ya half. I've done told your manz here. No one has to know about all this and—"

The bag whipping over his head cut his words off. The face began to resemble a demented chimp. As his wide-open mouth sucked in the plastic in a desperate attempt to draw in oxygen, it reminded Tom of an album cover of The Prodigy.

After over two minutes, the muffled screams died and the head slumped.

As Luke went to remove the bag, Tom stopped him. "He's gone unconscious. He isn't dead yet. Give it another minute or so."

They watched the still body in silence.

"How you feeling?" asked Tom.

"A little strange. Like different but nothing too strong," said Luke quietly. "Am I going to see this cunt in nightmares?"

"Probably," said Tom. "You know you didn't have to do that. You don't need to be a killer to be a gangster."

"To be honest, I've been thinking about it since we snatched him. I'd have more nightmares thinking we'd let go a cunt who thinks it's all right to stab a woman. Let alone it was my brother's girlfriend."

"Yeah, but I was going to do it."

"I wanted you to know that I can and would kill if I needed to—best to get my first out the way on someone like this."

Tom nodded, seeing the logic. He stood and said, "We keep this to ourselves."

"We can tell Connor."

Tom shook his head. "Remember what I told you—only tell people if you need to. Besides, I've not heard from him in a while."

"Think something has happened to him?"

"Not sure, mate. Let's hope not," said Tom. "Come on. The clean-up is always the clanger after a party."

Raphael Del Piero struggled to make sense of the scene and his emotions.

Civilians were huddled together in a state of wide-eyed shock. They were rapidly transported away after being searched.

The tip as to the location of this concentration camp at sea had come to him by encrypted e-mail. He had read it several times before taking it to the higher-ups.

Raphael, despite his reputation, had found it difficult to get the wheels moving. However, when his exasperation reached breaking point, the ROS received a call from Chen Zhao, Interpol's president. Raphael was not sure exactly of the conversation's details, but found himself lead investigator on a flotilla of Italian law enforcement vessels alongside both ROS and biohazard teams.

After the victims had been processed, and the biohazard team had deemed the structure safe, Raphael took his team down through the levels of this disturbing island. All the access points were open and each floor presented another macabre revelation.

Dead soldiers strewed the top floors, with scorch marks decorating the steel walls, grenade fragments and empty casings littering the floors. The pungent smells of nitroglycerine, sawdust, graphite and iron permeated the air.

On the lower level were rooms made of reinforced glass. All were empty—except one.

A bizarre sight of a headless corpse—blood still fresh—with its left hand forming the thumbs up sign, and the right hand clutching its flaccid cock.

37

Ciara watched the sunrays piercing the trees as Bruce drove the seemingly endless road.

"This another safe house?"

"No," answered Bruce. "I am taking you to see a man integral to the Project—perhaps even more integral than me."

"Jaime," she said simply.

"That's the one. You're very privileged."

"Connor has seen him."

"That was more out of necessity than choice."

"What was the upshot of our favourite Yorkshireman's exploits?"

She caught a seriousness in McQuillan's eyes as they flicked to her that she hadn't seen before. Throughout her time of knowing him, his professionalism had been beyond repute. However, she had never seen him phased by any situation—even the most seemingly dire.

"Salvatore Mancuso was not the head of the snake."

"What's led you to that conclusion?"

"He told me."

"What makes you believe him?"

"It wasn't my first rodeo."

She nodded. "Who is behind it?"

"We don't know. Everything was done by e-mail and bank transfers. They were passed over to Jaime four days ago. I have inquired about his progress earlier this morning—it was the first time since I've known him, that he's expressed doubt regarding his ability to locate an individual or organisation. The e-mail leads nowhere and the transfers of massive sums have been bounced around so many phantom accounts that not even the software at his disposal can unpick it."

She stared forward. "Where do we go from here?"

"I am formulating a strategy—however, to have the facility to renovate an island, recruit mercenaries and run an international kidnapping operation requires money and influence of seismic proportions. Every time we reach out, we'll be risking ourselves to an unknown entity. We can trust Chen. He used his influence on the ROS after I contacted him. He wouldn't have done that if he was part of it."

"Good," Ciara agreed. "Doesn't it stand to reason they—whoever they are—already know who you are?"

"Aye. But if they believe that I believe the trail ends with Mancuso, then they might avert their gaze. We need to stay still for the time being."

Ciara had a restless feeling in her stomach. "What about the people held at the facility?"

"The Italians have taken responsibility for the rescue operation. The detainees have been quietly processed, extradited and compensated. We do not yet know the extent of the psychological damage. The strange thing is, most do not feel aggrieved, which is a testament to the effectiveness of the coercion."

"So, the Italians are not making a statement to the media?" Ciara said incredulously.

"Not if they can help it. Seems unlikely they can keep a lid on it, but I guess they will dress it up as attempting to protect the victims from the scrutiny of the world."

"So, Mancuso's reached out by himself to Onel and others like him without the knowledge of the other 'Ndrangheta Godfathers."

Bruce nodded. "I have pointed Kathryn in the right direction. It seems Mancuso had a talent for seeking out the gifted and disturbed."

"Speaking of which, how is Connor?"

"The fragmentation wounds he's sustained were mostly superficial. His shoulder will stop hurting in a few weeks."

"His state of mind?"

"I can't see a difference in him—though I don't profess to be a psychologist. He flat out refuses psychological debriefs, and I can't force him to undertake them."

"He's a very unusual person."

"One of the psychologists told me childhood trauma can develop creativity—the need to solve a problem by themselves, the desire to escape using your imagination cultivates ingenuity, apparently. You've seen the effects of that."

"You can say that again," murmured Ciara, thinking back to the Castel Volturno scene. "What was that smile for?"

Bruce looked at her. "Jaime is a big *Star Wars* fan. He described Connor as 'a Sith—no, Dark Jedi—who hunts Sith, with the charisma of Han Solo'. I thought it was quite an apt description of him."

"Where is he now?"

"Calabria, tying up loose ends."

Ciara asked, "Is he in danger?"

It took a moment for the Scotsman to answer. "In some form or another, Connor Reed might be in danger for the rest of life."

Alessio knew of Connor's presence hours before he arrived.

The sight of a lone rider on a Moto Guzzi V7 was flagged immediately. As it passed through the next hamlet, a photograph was taken and sent to him.

They had not heard from Mancuso since he left Calabria, and he suspected Connor Reed would tell them the truth of the situation.

Despite Reed being a known entity and alone, Alessio still posted the guards on alert; especially since Reed carried a bulging, black leather rucksack on his back.

Eventually, the Englishman arrived outside the estate. After cutting the engine, he stepped away from the bike, dumping the rucksack and alighting from the motorcycle.

Alessio smiled as he removed his jacket and T-shirt—seemingly with discomfort—before twirling around and exposing his ankles. Either Salvatore had told him where the cameras were—though he had never been told—or Connor Reed had guessed.

"Open the gate. Keep your weapons trained on him and don't get too close. I will come out."

Connor pulled his jacket back over his top as the gates opened. Alessio stood in the centre, flanked by two of his men. They kept their rifles pointed in Connor's direction but at a forty-five-degree angle to the floor.

"Mr Reed. I did not expect for you to return alone."

"I am not alone," replied Connor, gesturing to the rucksack. "My companion is inside. Should I open it or yourself?"

He saw the momentary indecision in Alessio's eyes before he stepped forward. The guards pointed their weapons straight at Connor. Alessio gingerly unzipped the bag.

The Italian stared for a few moments before zipping the rucksack back up. He turned to him and said, "Let's go inside. Italo would like to see you."

The investments manager gestured to one of the guards, who stepped forward with a device that looked like a hoodlum—a handheld scanner used to check for the presence of IEDs within doorways.

He caught the subtle nod the guard gave Alessio.

"Come in, Connor."

The Englishman followed the Italian back to the same room in which he had sat just a few days ago.

Alessio opened the door to reveal Italo, sat dressed in a dark suit.

Connor stood in the centre of the room as Alessio whispered in the elder man's ear.

The boss of bosses gestured to the bag. Connor reached in and gripped the knot of the transparent plastic bag containing Salvatore Mancuso's head. Despite several hours' drainage, a film of blood pooled on top of the knot as he held the head upright to the Godfather's gaze.

Italo spoke in rapid Italian and Alessio said, "Put it back in the bag and pass it to me. Take a seat."

When Connor did so, Alessio continued, "Mr Mauro would like to thank you. We are curious to know what made you take us up on our offer?"

"I think you had suspicions of Mr Mancuso's extra-curricular activities. The nature of which was abhorrent even to someone like me."

"It is good to have moral boundaries."

"I agree. Even if they are perverse."

"So. What can we do for you? Our infrastructure and expertise are open to you."

"I don't want anything. But I am grateful for the offer."

Alessio frowned. "You went through all this…just to turn down what you have earned?"

"I may request assistance in the future but I do not want a long-term partnership. One of the things I have learnt during my visit to your beautiful country is it is warm beneath the wing of a dragon until it turns on you."

Alessio spoke again to Italo in his native tongue.

He saw a smirk creep on the old man's face before he replied.

Alessio translated the old man's words. "Mr Mauro thinks he will be stealing your dragon quote."

"He is welcome to…I stole it from Leonardo DiCaprio in *Gangs of New York*."

Alessio smiled before saying, "We are disappointed you do not wish for a more… permanent alliance. Mr Mauro says you have earned the right for us to respect your decision. He says again, if you or your family need anything in the future, do not hesitate to contact me. We are currently in your debt as you have not only solved this…challenge," he tapped the rucksack with his foot, "but also helped with our cousins in Naples."

"There is one favour I wanted to ask."

"Of course."

"Carlo Andaloro. He saved my life and equally contributed to bringing down Mancuso—he didn't know of Mancuso's…side ventures. I would like very much for him to be pardoned for his association with Mancuso. As far as he was aware, he was operating as a soldier to the organisation."

After a back-and-forth exchange with Italo, finally Alessio said, "Do not be troubled. Carlo Andaloro has nothing to fear. You may go now."

Connor nodded, and hid his adrenaline—if they were going to kill him, the time would be now, as it would be easier to contain.

Alessio stood and walked with him through the mansion.

The gates opened, he shook hands with Alessio and turned for his bike, feeling a cold between his shoulder blades and the back of his neck and head.

38

Richèl Vergeer instinctively knew sleep would never come as easily again. She lay in bed, looking out of the green-framed window. The moonlight percolating through the tree branches outside had a calming and hypnotic effect on her.

Still in the safe house in Italy, they had told her she could leave whenever she wished, to continue her treatment in Brussels, or Holland. She had undergone several evaluations over the past few days, and although she knew she would return soon, had asked to stay for a while longer.

All the care staff were women, which she understood, but did not especially appreciate—she would have preferred men with guns.

She realised these thoughts were ridiculous, she could not be under armed guard forever. Besides, even though back on that day—the day she and the others were liberated—their heads had been covered, and they had been told not to look around as they had been escorted up the levels to freedom, she couldn't help but look and see all the dead bodies of the guards.

Perversely, this had a calming effect on her.

Her thoughts began to detach themselves from her conscious mind as she descended into sleep. The last image she had before sleep took her completely was of the dark-blond man reaching into the room like a black spirit to grab her tormentor by his ears, before throwing him into his self-designed own hell.

Is the dark-blond saviour even alive?

Andrei Faja stood before the high council, with fifteen expectant eyes on him. Tefik's younger brother, Esad, a man whose disposition seemed fortuitously calm, now sat in his deceased brother's seat as his successor.

It had been a precarious few days. Any suspicions of his involvement in Tefik's death seemed to have been lost in the flood of blood-lust against the 'Ndrangheta.

No one made a sound and Andrei could hear the faint caws of the black crows outside the castle.

He put the leather handbag on the grand circular table and unlatched the straps.

He noticed an almost imperceptible leaning back from his fellow Kyres.

He placed the severed, but now bloodless, head of Salvatore Mancuso on the table.

"This is our Calabrian cousins' olive branch for peace. They have told me of their understanding that they will need to atone and pay recompense for this…dishonour. I have told them that I will discuss our terms with you all and they will have our decision shortly."

He felt the relief in the room, for he had given them all what they craved—an honourable release from a potentially ruinous war in exchange for an upturn in their finances.

Though a sense of authority now buoyed his being, it was edged with the knowledge that the reason he now held this exalted position was largely down to Connor Reed. And Andrei had not heard from him for a long time.

Esad cleared his throat. "What do you suggest, Kyre Faja?"

EPILOGUE

Luke felt a warmth bloom in his torso. Sat in The Buxton Arms with most of the Ryder men, except for his dad who was manning the bar, and his cousins Connor and Dan, due shortly.

The Leeds United game had ended, and the pub's atmosphere floated on the buoyancy of victory.

"There's no way that lass has looked twice at you, Curtis," exclaimed his Uncle Ryan to his younger cousin.

Curtis had asserted that Jennifer Booth, a cheerleader for the city's Rugby League team, had propositioned him. His Uncle Ryan's reaction mirrored his thoughts.

"I went around to her house but her parents came back. And this and that happened but I'll get around to smashing her eventually," announced Curtis.

"What does 'this and that' mean? I think—" began Ryan before Tom interrupted him with, "Here they are," at the arrival of Connor and Dan.

Dan made his way over to the bar to hug Lee as Connor walked over to the group.

The group stood and they gave him the familial hugs, being careful of his left arm, once he drew their attention not to touch it.

As he sat down, Ryan announced, "Connor, our Curtis thinks he's been a cock's hair from bedding this *two-looker*. Look at the arse on her."

With that, Ryan showed him his phone.

Connor frowned. "Jennifer Booth. I've slept with her. Fuck me, that's a story and a half."

They all leant in. Before he could begin, Dan arrived with a pint for himself and a gin and tonic for Connor.

"Like that, is it?" said Ryan, standing to embrace Dan.

"My dad said you all had only just had a round in."

"Just winding you up. You've obviously been down south too long."

It made Luke smile to see everyone embrace his brother heartily.

"Sit down. Connor was going to tell a story about him banging a worldie."

Curtis crowed, "Must have been cos you did a good job that she wanted me then—knowing it must run in the family."

"Maybe," said Connor.

When he didn't embellish, Ryan prompted, "Don't keep us all in suspense. What's the story then? And if it's a good one, I'll keep blind to what you are drinking."

Connor smiled and took a sip of his G&T. "Well, I'd met her on a train on the way back from Scotland, believe it or not—gave her the patter, and we were messaging on and off for a while. Anyway, she said she was looking after her parents' house and her brother, as they were away. There're ten years between them—he was some sort of miracle child, you know when the woman is going through menopause and they get a bit slack with birth control, thinking they are safe."

"I've heard that before," said Ryan. "Curtis, you didn't mention her brother."

Curtis nodded. "Yeh, she has a younger brother."

Connor spoke, "Anyway, I gets there, and she's looking stunning—dolled-up—the eyes, the lips and the hair are all gorgeous. She has jeans and a white T-shirt and I can clearly see her black bra-encased tits through it. Gives me this lingering hug and I can smell her perfume—I am already getting hard and then—clomp, clomp, clomp—her brother comes banging down the stairs. This thirteen-year-old, or whatever he was at the time, is the size of a fucking man bigger than me—isn't he, Curtis?"

"Yeh, he's a unit like."

"Anyway, straight away, before she confirms it, I can see he's developmentally challenged—I forgot the official term she told me. So he lands in front of me and says, 'Oh herrohh, my name is Alex', and he grips my hand in this fucking vice-like grip and shakes it like Charlie Chaplin. I am trying not to show it's pissing me off cos she's looking at me—I just keep this daft grin on my face."

The family mirrored Luke's actions of leaning in and grinning.

"So," Connor continued, "he says, 'Watch this' and starts doing his version of the *Riverdance* which looks like a tap-dancing bear. But the soles of his trainers are flashing red every time he lands. Anyway, my face is starting to hurt cos of me keeping this smile on my face, but it turned into a genuine one because I start egging him on, getting him to do twirls and break-dancing moves."

Giggling rippled through the group.

"Eventually, she breaks it up and fucks him off up the stairs. She's thinking I am lovable for showing an interest. So we end up on the sofa watching *Groundhog Day*—"

"Great film that," said Ryan. "Could watch it again and again."

Luke realised it must have been a joke by the way Tom and Connor groan-laughed. He'd ask Connor later, who continued, "So after a time—waiting for her brother to go to sleep—we get to *necking off* and heavy petting, and eventually she whispers that we should go upstairs. I am mesmerised by her arse as she's leading me up, by the way." Connor, taking a sip of his drink, carried on, "She stops by his room and puts her ear to the door, then shoos me into her bedroom. We start stripping one another, and she's like, 'Oh my God, I've never seen one like that on a white guy'—joke, I made that bit up—and she's stunning, no signs of too much definition or rolls—just the right balance, and her arse…it's like fucking cartoonishly sexy with how big and round it is. Normally, I like to fuck in the missionary—being romantic and that—but I get her on all fours so I can watch it. Her pussy felt as addictive as popping bubble wrap—well, not that addictive, but still awesome. Now one—"

"I had my hands on it. It's awesome," interrupted Curtis.

"Let 'im tell the story," admonished Ryan. "Go ahead, Connor."

"All right, where was I?" said Connor. "Right, in my opinion, one of the sexiest parts of a woman is the creases between the upper thigh and hip, and I like to put my fingers in them for purchase in that position. Her wardrobe at the side of the bed doubles as a mirror, so I am checking it every so often, pulling

American Psycho and antler poses before going back to smashing her. In the corner of my eye, I noticed this flicker through the slit between the doors. Didn't think anything of it. Then she's getting louder, and I'm getting close—and this flashing is getting faster—then I cottoned on to what it was."

Laughter came in waves and Charlie asked, "What was it?"

"What do you think it was? It was her brother's trainers."

Amidst the cries of laughter, Curtis exclaimed, "Honestly?"

"No," said Connor through his own laughter. "I don't even know a Jennifer Booth, let alone if she has a brother. I just wanted to make up a story better than yours."

The laughter turned into roars, and Luke felt moisture creep in the corners of his eyes. Despite his red face Curtis said, "No, I was going along with the story to not spoil it."

The roars got louder at this, lasting over a minute.

Though Luke hated how Curtis's insecurities could manifest themselves, the situation sneaked into being uncomfortable, and so Luke was glad Dan interrupted the group's mirth with, "I'd like to say something."

He waited until the laughter died to a simmer. "Right, this business of yours is expanding and you need…investment advice. That's when it gets dangerous, because if the authorities get hold of that person they'll roll over on you. So, I'll take over this side of the business."

The sporadic titterings from Connor's story died.

Ryan began, "Don't be daft, Dan. You're doing well, and you don't—"

"I want to do it. Angela is gone now. There's nothing down there for me. Leeds is small enough that I can compete. You are all up here. Gran's getting older. I want to be here and I want to be part of this—this family isn't going to stop, and it would kill me if anyone of you ends up in a cell for something I could have prevented."

Tom spoke, "Dan, we'll be fine. We know good people and none of us are going anywhere."

Luke saw Connor place a hand on Tom's forearm.

Connor said, "He's right, Tom. We can't ever trust outsiders like we can trust one another."

His two older cousins looked at one another, and Luke saw something in their expressions.

Finally, Tom stated, "Welcome to the family business, Dan."

The End

GLOSSARY

A-to-H— A sequence used within the British military for logging and reporting the identities of individuals.

Actions-on— Predetermined procedures that are to be carried out if certain events were to occur during the mission.

Airtime— South London slang; to give someone or something 'airtime' is to ignore them or it.

ANPR— Automatic Number Plate Recognition. The registration numbers are fed to a database to highlight any vehicle of interest.

AOE— Area of Exploitation. The predetermined area the soldier or unit must not cross, usually to avoid friendly fire incidents.

Berimbolo— a grappling position that requires the guard player to spin upside down in an attempt to disrupt the balance of his opponent. This spin will cause the guard player to either get a sweep (reverse the position), or take control of his opponent's back.

Bird— British slang for a young woman or one's girlfriend.

Cob on— to be sulking.

Combat 18— a neo-Nazi terrorist organisation founded in the UK in 1992. Numerous arrests made between 1998 and 2000 dwindled its influence.

Combat Indicator— A sign of the enemy's intentions, for example the absence of locals in a usually busy marketplace could be a combat indicator of an enemy ambush.

Many military and former military personnel apply the term in everyday life, for example an *'If you can't love me at my worst, then you don't deserve me at my best'* social media post could be a combat indicator of high maintenance.

CPS— The Crown Prosecution Service, the main criminal prosecution agency in England and Wales.

De-service and re-service— the cleaning and repairing of military equipment after exercises or operations to ensure future serviceability.

Dicker— Originally a slang term given by the British military to describe civilian lookouts sympathetic to the IRA. Some use it to describe hostile lookouts of any operational area.

First floor— In British English the floor of a building at street level is called the ground floor with the next above being referred to as the first floor. In American English, however, the floor at street level is usually called the first floor.

Fleg— Northern England slang for 'to spit'.

Ghillie Suit— An all-body camouflage suit usually comprising of netting, strips of hessian, cloth or twine. Name derives from the Scots Gaelic word *Gille*, referring to a young man or older boy who works as an outdoor servant.

Ginzo— a derogatory term used in the United States to describe someone of Italian heritage.

Grafters— slang within the UK underground to describe fellow criminals.

Guard— a grappling position whereby the person with their back to the ground attempts to control the opponent with their legs.

IBJJF— The International Brazilian Jiu-jitsu Federation is a company that hosts several of the biggest Brazilian jiu-jitsu tournaments in the world.

Kaishakunin— an appointed individual beheads the one who has performed seppuku, Japanese ritual suicide, at the moment of agony.

Kimono— Roughly translated from Japanese as 'a thing to wear', is a term sometimes used in grappling circles to refer to the 'Gi'.

Het up— Northern English slang for upset or excited.

Manz— Oneself.

Mong— An offensive British term insinuating a person is so stupid they must have learning difficulties.

Necking off— Deep kissing.

Oppo— An affectionate term for a friend within the Corps—an opposite number.

Peng— slang for attractive.

Pentiti— an Italian term for a person who aids the judicial system with their investigations.

Sesh— British slang for a period of sustained social drinking or recreational drug taking.

Sneaky-beaky— Stealthy.

Snurgled— Walked or crawled to a position in a stealth-like manner.

SOPs— Standard Operating Procedures; that particular military unit's current standard procedures for certain taskings.

Spackas— a derogatory term to insult someone of perceived low intelligence. Derived from the word spastic.

Spin you a dit— Royal Navy and Marine term for 'Tell your story'.

Splinter Cell— a computer game emphasising stealth.

Squirter— A person, assumed to be an enemy, running away from a military attack.

Stand-to— In the belief that an enemy is more likely to attack a camp just before dawn, the soldiers are 'stood-to' beforehand in position ready for an attack.

SUSAT— the Sight Unit Small Arms, Trilux, or SUSAT, is a 4× telescopic sight, with tritium-powered illumination utilised at dusk or dawn

Two-looker— a person so good-looking you have to look twice.

Vellai im— Albanian for 'my brother', inclusionary form of reference amongst those within their criminal fraternities.

Yomped— Royal Marine term for a march with heavy equipment over difficult terrain

ABOUT THE AUTHOR

Quentin Black is a former Royal Marine Corporal with a decade of service in the Corps. This includes an operational tour of Afghanistan and an advisory mission in Iraq.

Black has competed in numerous boxing and Brazilian jiu-jitsu Gi and NoGi matches.

AUTHOR'S NOTE

Any reviews would be greatly appreciated.

If you would like a **FREE** E-book of The Bootneck and other discounts, or to contact me directly, you can through my website https://quentinblackauthor.com/ or the various social media platforms.

If you have spotted a mistake, I would like you to let me know so I can improve reader experience.

Subscribers will be given the heads-up on any new releases and periods of discount.

Other books by Quentin Black.

The Bootneck

Lessons In Blood

Ares' Thirst

Northern Wars

Printed in Great Britain
by Amazon

62840626R00227